The Third Daughter

FIONA FORSYTH

First published in 2022 by Sharpe Books.

To Siobhan and Ailsa

CONTENTS

Prologue – 22CE

I am so old I am becoming a legend - well, to half the population. I don't think it would occur to many men to think about me. I don't mind. I have considered very few men for the last sixty-four years. But all over Rome, women ask about me, "Is she really still alive? Even Livia is younger than her, isn't that right?"

I am alive and older than that viper Livia, or Julia Augusta to give her the full honour of her titles, thoroughly deserved in my opinion for putting up with that dreadful Augustus for so long. And no, I do not contradict myself there, I am perfectly capable of admiring a cold-blooded animal, as you will see when I tell you about my mother. For all my life I have watched women staying married to men who did not deserve them, while I lost my husband, whom I loved, far too early. Why did I never marry again? Well, why should I? It is a decision I have never regretted.

Nobody in Rome knows exactly how old I am, and I like to watch them try to work it out. My great-nieces and nephews ask me if I remember various historical events so that they can help me pin down the exact year but when you are an old woman it is very easy to convince people that you are confused. Don't assume from this that I dislike my young relations - I am pleased that they still visit me, and in return they are getting an account of the last hundred years or so of our recent history. I can relate tales from Julius Caesar's early career to our present Emperor. They may not trust my memory, but they ask me about it all the same - and of course I do remember most of it extremely well.

I am Junia, third daughter of Servilia and Decimus Junius Silanus. Nobody now has heard of him. It doesn't matter. I loved my father dearly, but in the great scheme of things, he did not matter.

My father was Consul of Rome in the year of the Battle of Pistoria, my mother was Julius Caesar's favourite mistress, and my husband was Caesar's assassin. Of course, what I should have done there is described myself in terms of the men in my life, as a good Roman lady should do Anyone who ever met my mother will understand why she gets onto that list. Maybe I have

1

been unfair in choosing her love affair with Caesar as her epithet, for my mother was remarkable, even in an age which has produced many formidable women. And I should have included my brother, Marcus Brutus, who also helped to kill Julius Caesar. I am related to some interesting people.

So now for the really interesting piece of information – I believe that I am Julius Caesar's daughter, the last of his children alive. By blood, I have far more right to rule Rome than our current Emperor, so thank goodness I am only a woman.

Chapter 1

So why am I writing all this down - for posterity? No of course not, this will never be published. The times are not right for a book by a cantankerous old lady who does not approve of anything that has happened for fifty years or more. I am doing this for myself, and because my new secretary, Tiro, is very good and needs a task to occupy his idle hours. He has instructions to send this story to one person, my friend Sulpicia, another remarkable woman, trustworthy, brave, and the person who knows me best in all the world. What she does with it is up to her.

I firmly believe that I have led an interesting life, and now that I am ninety years old it seems fitting to take stock. Like someone writing a will, I leave something for the future, but I am also indulging myself. We Romans aren't supposed to indulge ourselves, are we? We work hard, make money and keep our troops pouring into an ever-widening empire. We are always looking forward. But we also love our past and are forever rewriting it. This current regime under our leader Tiberius is an excellent example of that. Well, I shan't rewrite the past to serve a present ideal.

As I start telling this story, I must admit that it does cause me a slight pang, the thought that my sisters, who will figure prominently in this memoir, are both dead. Throughout my childhood and even into our lives as respectable married ladies, my sisters were the heart of my life, the people who were constant. Every time I turned around, one or other of them was there - irritating at the time and comforting now. I see them both as clearly as if they were sitting and listening as I dictate this. Junia is a little anxious at being the centre of attention and worried that I am going to attract the ire of the authorities, while Nilla is unconcerned by such things but absolutely focussed on how she will appear. At any moment she is going to ask me what she will be wearing in the story. And, no doubt, argue with me over it.

I was born in the consulship of Lucius Caecilius Metellus and Quintus Marcius Rex, men from two of the leading families of the age, though many families like that seem to have vanished now. This was how things were - the great families filled the great offices on an annual basis and that year was labelled with the names of the Consuls.

I was the daughter of Servilia and Decimus Junius Silanus, and they had been married for about six years by then. I had two elder sisters Junia and Junilla. Ridiculous names of course, but nobody ever knows what to call a gaggle of girls. The eldest receives her father's family name, and the second has to do with a silly pet name based on the same name, my second sister we always called Nilla. Of course, every third girl born to a family gets called "Tertia", but you may as well just call all of us "Not-a-boy" and have done. There was a gap of several years between me and Nilla and I imagine that my mother may well have had a miscarriage in between the two of us If so, I hope it was not the boy that she must have wanted. My father never gave any indication that he was disappointed in his three girls and my memories of him are all good. He smiled all the time to my mind, his eyes opening up a fan of lines at the corners that I found fascinating. He was quick to kiss and hug us, to lift me up to his level and talk as he carried me around. "Your sisters are too big, Tertulla, but you are just the right size." I concluded that being the youngest was worthwhile if it meant that I got carried when my sisters did not. And as you will have noticed, my father came up with a special nickname for me - Tertulla - and that stuck. I was his "Little Third". Of course, once one is grown such a name seems slightly odd, but my closest friends and family continued to use it. Still, how ridiculous sometimes, as a lady of more than sixty or seventy to suddenly find someone calling me "Little Third".

Names were taken far more seriously among the men of our class. We used them to know whether someone was the right sort of person or not. My mother knew everyone in Rome and one of her main contributions to our education was an elaborate knowledge of family trees. If we were not related to a person, she knew somebody who was.

My brother, Marcus Brutus was the son of my mother's first husband, about fifteen years older than me. I adored him when I was young, and it seemed to me that he was an excellent big brother, unfailingly kind to me. In fact, I can remember having a conversation with him about happiness when I was little more than six or seven, and there are few young men who would have the patience to hear out a little girl on this topic. He had looked surprised and amused and had told me that I was clearly cut out to be a philosopher. I wasn't entirely sure what philosophy was, but I knew that Brutus had studied philosophy himself to an elevated level, and so I was pleased at this compliment. For many of you, I realise, Brutus is the reason you are still reading, because you have heard of him – Brutus the assassin. Even now, it is considered unwise to talk of Brutus as anything else. People are aware that if they do not condemn the killers of Julius Caesar, they are criticising Caesar's heirs, and that of course will not do. Ridiculous, but I suppose I had better not seek to bring more trouble on my family. I have stayed true in one important matter though - my instructions for my funeral have made it clear that for once in my life, I wish to be known for my family. My brother will walk in my funeral processions alongside my other relatives and ancestors. My relations will just have to be embarrassed, but funerals are sacrosanct so they should weather any scandal. I have lost count of the families to whom I am related, but it will make a good show when I am gone. I have set aside the money and even consulted the manager of the leading company of actors who provide the people who wear the masks and process at funerals. A strange way to make your living but as good as any I suppose.

To return to my mother, I had assumed that she did not love me or my sisters, because she was not a demonstrative person. This was not fair, for she had many qualities to admire, as I hope to make clear. There is no point in wishing someone to be anything other than what they are.

My earliest memories are of sharing a bedroom with Nilla while Junia and Nanny slept in an adjoining room. A doorway had been knocked through the wall between the two so that we could have our own suite - the Juniatrium my father called it.

"In any Roman house, the atrium is the largest and most important room," he told me. "I can't give you that to play in so we shall make you your own atrium - your Juniatrium." Junia liked that because it sounded so grown-up. Nilla and I didn't care about being grown-up, but it was nice to be together and later on another room was added where Felix taught us, so the Juniatrium grew with us. These rooms, all our own, were at the back of the house across the enclosed garden from the kitchens and slaves' quarters, so we were always able to hear birdsong and people talking, and we could smell the earth and the flowers and the dinner. When it rained, Felix would let us stand in the covered walkway that ran around the garden, and the smell of wet earth and rain on dusty stone was marvellous. Really, we had everything three little girls could need - Felix and Nanny, our little suite of rooms, a garden courtyard for us to play in.

The next most important room in my childhood was that of my mother. Wherever she lived, my mother made sure that she had a room to herself It was not a sitting-room, in which a married lady may entertain her friends, nor a room for dressing and getting ready. Most of the women I knew had rooms like this, but my mother also had what would have been called a study if she had been a man. The gods know that my mother worked as hard as any man of her class. In the family house on the Palatine Hill, this was the room to which we were summoned to be told important news, such as our marriages, or the deaths of relatives. My mother would deliver a short and clear speech, while we stood and listened, and when she was sure we understood and knew what was expected of us, we would be dismissed. I treasured those visits for one reason, the painting.

As you entered the room, the furniture was along the sides – desk and chair at the window, bookcase and couch across the room. I am sure that these were of a high quality and elegant, just like my mother, but I never took much notice of them. The wall opposite the door was covered in a painting of a garden, and it was glorious. Against a pale green background, three trees in large wooden planters towered up the wall, and garlands thick with pinecones and ears of corn hung between them. The trees themselves bore large dark-green leaves, creamy flowers and golden pears, which my sisters said was impossible in real life, but I did not care. I would make sure I stood next to the wall, and study my favourite tree, the one in the middle. As I grew, I got to know every crack in the bark, count the petals on each bloom and imagine that birds were hidden in the branches. In spring and summer, the scents of herbs and flowers blossoming would come in through the study window, and I would stand by my painted tree and sniff, imagining that the flowers were about to be picked and the fruit gathered for our supper. Junia would nudge me if I were too loud, as my mother was not sympathetic to any indication that we were not paying her our full attention.

Once we had trooped back to the Juniatrium, I would ask my sisters about anything I hadn't understood, and we then would turn to Nanny and Felix for anything none of us had understood. And one day, Nilla asked an especially important question,

"Felix, today Mother said that we must be proud of being her daughters. But she didn't say anything about being our father's daughters. Is Mother - I don't know how to say this but - is she better in some way than Father?"

Junia, always the nice one of us all, looked stricken at the idea that we must now have a competition to decide between our parents. Nanny and Felix exchanged what I can only describe as a knowing glance but seemed unsurprised by the question. Certainly, Felix avoided the issue smoothly by concentrating solely on one parent.

"Your mother is from a very old and grand family," he said, with Nanny looking approvingly at him and nodding. "The Servilii have been leaders in Rome for hundreds of years - they go all the way back to the founding families and are patrician. You know what that means, don't you, Junia?"

"Patrician," said Junia promptly, "means that your family is descended from a small group of men who were especially honoured by Rome. The first patricians were the one hundred top men chosen by Romulus, the founder of Rome himself, to form his council. The last family to be made patrician were the Claudii, and that was over four hundred years ago. Everyone who isn't patrician is plebeian."

7

I wanted to ask what "plebeian" meant but Junia saw me and added hastily, "Plebeian just means someone who isn't patrician."

"Well done," said Felix, allowing Junia to bask a little. Felix praised often and hardly ever scolded, but that didn't mean we grew bored of his approval.

"So, we - our family - go all the way back to Rome's foundation," said Nilla, who loved to be important.

"It may well be that the Servilii were related to Romulus himself," said Felix diplomatically.

"And he was the son of the god Mars and the Vestal Virgin Ilia," said Junia.

Nilla was practically bursting at the thought of being related to a god, though I wanted to ask how a Vestal Virgin could have a baby when they weren't allowed to be married. I was sceptical even then - I must have been about seven. I decided however to go for another problem I had spotted in this story.

"But wasn't Romulus a frat- frater- ..."

"Fratricide," said Felix automatically, continuing, "A fratricide is a person who kills his own brother, as Romulus killed Remus. Well, another story has a different account of your origins and tells that the Servilii came from the ancient city of Alba Longa at the time of the third king of Rome." Nilla pouted, but only a little. After all, this was still old. And Romulus had indeed killed his brother Remus while they were arguing over founding Rome, so maybe wasn't the best ancestor in the history annals.

"What sort of things did our ancestors do?" I wanted to know. "Did any of them kill an enemy or a monster?" Nanny had been telling me stories of the heroes Perseus and Heracles at the time, and I imagined a noble-browed and heavily bearded great-great-grandfather clapping a helmet onto his curls as he left the house to slay a hydra or ravening lion.

"Your ancestor Servilius Ahala was a hero who defended Rome when an evil man named Spurius was trying to make himself ruler. Though it was illegal of course to kill someone, Servilius Ahala knew that Spurius threatened the safety of Rome. Despite the risk that he would himself be charged with murder, he unhesitatingly drew his dagger and stabbed Spurius. He then went into exile voluntarily."

Nilla frowned. "But isn't it all right to kill someone who is a threat?" she asked.

"If everyone agrees with you, then you are safe," pointed out Junia. "But you know what Rome is like."

We all nodded wisely. We knew what Rome was like - a heaving mass of competing men, all striving to have their voices heard and all claiming to be thinking only of the good of the Republic.

"There is no doubt that Servilius will have had enemies only too ready to accuse him," said Felix. "Great men are always envied by those who are not as great."

"Just like Tertulla envies me, because I'm prettier," said Nilla sweetly, and was promptly whisked off by Nanny for one of her Talks. Nanny's Talks inevitably involved a spat between me and Nilla. Junia was above Talks.

You will have noticed that our father's ancestry did not get examined and dissected in this conversation and Felix was right to take this course. My father was from a perfectly respectable lineage, but it did not compare with my mother's. My mother clothed herself in this glory, though by the time I was born, being patrician was of less importance to public life in Rome. It was hard to keep the line going when the pool of available and suitable partners grew smaller. Several patrician families had died out, others had not played a prominent role in Roman life for years. Tradition gave them some authority, but they were increasingly seen as irrelevant. More important, as ever in Rome, was wealth, for if a man had no money what was the point of being patrician? But my mother's family had not only kept in the political arena for hundreds of years, they had also made money, married wisely and produced numerous offspring. My mother's forebears had fought against Carthage in three wars, risen to the consulship many times, led Rome's armies, pleaded in her law courts - in other words they had done just what a top family is supposed to do. And of course, some of them had exhibited the worst features of my class which are greed and arrogance. My mother to give her credit was not guilty of these vices. She was everything a noblewoman should be, hard-working, charming, an excellent housekeeper and beautiful. She wrote and spoke Greek as well as Latin, and all her life read widely and supported the arts. She was never idle, and we saw little of her when we were young.

I was therefore aware at an early age that my family was important, and I also learned that though I was not a boy, I was an asset. My fate became crystal clear to me one evening, as we were dining as a family. This happened regularly, as part of our education according to my mother, but also because my father always said he enjoyed the time with all his girls.

"What about Tertulla?" my mother asked my father. We were starting to settle down as the slaves were bringing in the first course. The conversation had clearly started earlier in my father's study and, now they had come into the dining-room, they were just carrying on. My father at first looked startled - he hadn't realised that the conversation was not considered over. But he smiled quickly and said with barely a pause, "Oh I have plans for my Tertulla." And he winked at me.

"What sort of plans?" asked Nilla immediately.

My father laughed. "Families like ours are always planning for their girls. We never stop worrying about you."

"Why are you worried?" I wanted to know.

"Because Father has to decide our marriages," said Nilla smartly.

"I don't want to get married," I said and even as I said it was struck for the first time that this was not an option for me or my sisters. Whether I liked it or not, I would be married off to a man of my father's choosing and - what? Have a family of my own, and run a house on the Palatine, and arrange a marriage for my daughter.... My life stretched out in front of me, and it was all planned and unalterable. It was not that I did not approve of such a life, it was that I could not escape it. Suddenly I felt my eyes fill with tears.

"Tertulla, are you crying?" asked Nilla, not because she was concerned but because she wanted to ensure that our parents saw. I rubbed my eyes and glared at her, but she was not going to be quiet. I must have been irritating earlier that day and now she was going to enjoy upsetting me. She turned back to the table and said, "Tertulla is crying but of course she is very young. Maybe she isn't old enough to discuss these matters."

"If she isn't, then your father and I will deal with it," said my mother and immediately turned to Aratus to enquire as to the freshness of the eggs in the first course. Nilla slumped down on her chair. She should have known better, and when my mother turned back, she immediately said in a sharper voice, "Sit up straight, Junilla, and do your best to avoid teasing your sister at the table please." Nilla sat up straight, fixed her eyes on her plate and made sure that nobody could see her fury at being called "Junilla". I don't know why she hated it so much, but it was one of the few revenges I could exact upon her easily.

"When you say "planning", Father, are you going to offer any of us to be a Vestal Virgin?" said Junia, attempting a change in direction; it was a safe topic for her as most girls were given to the Vestals at about eight or nine. My father looked around and saw our faces - Junia secure, Nilla horrified, me scowling no doubt - and laughed.

"It is a huge honour to serve Vesta, and through her, Rome," my mother said. "But your father and I have not considered it. We do not consider that any of you are suited to the life. And anyway, the Vestals do not need any child applicants now."

"What sort of girl is suited to it?" I asked, thinking that I would rather be married than be a Vestal and wear those ugly clothes and be very bored.

"A girl who shows the least sign of obedience and piety and respect," said my father solemnly, then smiled. "I couldn't possibly spare any of you anyway. I would miss you too much."

"It is a very important role," said my mother to him, a little reproachfully. "And the Vestals are respected as no other woman is."

"I am not denying that, Servilia," said my father and the two of them turned towards each other, while we watched.

"A woman has few opportunities to do real work for the Republic," my mother began. My father gestured with his wine-cup, though carefully so as not to spill anything.

"I realise that you think so, Servilia, but you must admit that for most woman, the traditional role is what they want. Providing continuity and stability through faithful marriages and children - that is a very important role too."

"And one which every savage in the frozen North can perform just as easily as me."

"A savage from the North would not suit me as a wife, I can assure you," said my father and nudged her with his shoulder, until she gave in and smiled. "I like having a wife who can discuss everything with me, one who supports me wholeheartedly. You bring beauty and intelligence to everything you do, Servilia, and I appreciate that. And I am not the only Roman man who finds his wife the most valuable asset in his life. Don't underestimate us."

My mother said, "Then make sure you find men like that for our girls. I have a feeling that they take after me."

"Our girls will manage their men just as you manage me," said my father and my mother laughed.

I looked at them curiously. I liked seeing them so comfortable with each other, but my mother's point had struck home. I faced some difficult realities, being a girl and belonging to a family like mine. I would never plead a case in a law-court, or travel abroad, learning how we governed our provinces, as my brother did. I could not join the army, something which my brother did not seem too keen to do anyway, so maybe that was not such a bad thing. But I would never go to the market or a temple or a friend's house on my own, and I would have no choice about my marriage. My mother's words shone light on the limitations that lay ahead of me, though I grew to accept the things I could not change, as all women must. I had the advantages of money and the one thing which saves women like me - girls of my class often were, indeed still are, educated to a high standard. My mother was indeed intelligent, and she had been educated with her brothers, so when Brutus outgrew his tutor, Felix, she saw nothing wrong with simply reassigning Felix to be her daughters' tutor. Under my mother's direction, and with my father's approval, Felix started off our education.

I need a break from reminiscing about my childhood, so let me turn to my greatest friend, Sulpicia. I have mentioned her above, and she is my inspiration for this memoir, the leading literary woman of our age, and the person who told me to record my life. I first met Sulpicia about thirty years ago - although Horace and Tibullus were still alive, so it must have been more. But one thing I have discovered about my age is that people indulge me when I get numbers wrong. My secretary is creasing his brow dramatically and tells me that by his reckoning, I must have met Sulpicia forty-five years ago. I expect he is right. He too will get old and forget things.

I got to know Sulpicia through her uncle Corvinus. He was just a few years younger than myself, and his father had been Consul the year after my father. He had gathered a small coterie of poets around him - such things were more fashionable and popular then, before Ovid disgraced himself. I was on the periphery of this group as a friend of Corvinus, known to be interested and encouraging of the young people he collected, and so I soon met his niece.

Sulpicia was a very beautiful young woman, and as you have probably realised from what I have told you about her relations, she is well-connected. She was living in her uncle's house as his ward from the age of about fifteen, waiting for her rather dreary betrothed to come back from serving the empire. Early marriage was all the rage, copying the example of the Emperor's own family of course. She was a well-educated girl, clever, kind, and funny, and despite our age difference we immediately made friends. She was an only daughter and envied me my sisters, and so we talked about them more often than her own family.

"I love my brother of course," she rather sweetly informed me early on in our friendship, "but I have often wished for a sister. I need someone to tell everything to."

"What about friends?" I asked. "Don't you young people tell everything to one another?"

"To be truthful, Tertulla, I don't like my friends very much," Sulpicia said, with just a hint of a smile to make sure I got the joke.

She had a point. Like many girls of our class, her friends were carefully chosen and unless you were lucky and chimed with someone, your friendships could be boring and repetitious.

"Let me guess," I said. "Your mother and father allowed you to meet girls of your age from the families of their friends, and you were all supervised by your nannies as you met at each other's houses. You were allowed to play a little, or encouraged to sit and talk of suitable topics while sewing - how am I doing?"

"Oh Tertulla, isn't it dreary?" she demanded. "Even when we meet at a park or a large garden owned by someone's grandfather - a picnic should not be supervised, structured, boring! And all anyone could talk about at the last one was how not to get sunburned."

"Not getting sunburned is important, but I agree I was lucky to have my sisters," I said. "And to be the youngest."

"I just want someone to…." Her voice tailed away as she looked at me and blushed. "Oh, I am sorry Tertulla - I do have you, I know. You really are the nearest thing to a big sister I have."

I felt for her. "But it is not the same. I know."

Sulpicia and I met increasingly frequently as she got older. Her mother and father lived out of Rome for most of the time and she came over to my house on the Palatine often. Her uncle Corvinus was aware that she needed female company and I was suitable, being well-born, rich and clever. And childless…. Already interested in poetry, Sulpicia started to write herself as I suppose was only natural in the company she kept. We would discuss, not just her poetry, but several favourite topics such as how best to educate a Roman woman. By this we did not just mean a woman like us, rich enough not to need to worry about money. You will be unsurprised to hear that we both approved of the education in literature and philosophy we had ourselves enjoyed, and we wondered how we could extend that opportunity to more girls. Sulpicia, a remarkably forward-thinking woman, wanted to establish schools specifically for girls of the middle and lower classes, to ensure that more women could at least read and write a little.

"Your problem will be to persuade their fathers that such skills are desirable," I remarked.

"And if such an idea comes from me, a female love poet, no Roman father will be persuaded," she said. "It needs to come from a woman of unimpeachable virtue."

I did not think for a moment that she meant me. My virtue is, in fact, unimpeachable, but my connections are not.

Chapter 2

It seems a world away now to look back and see the scene on our schoolroom. Nanny is beside me watching me carefully carve out letters on the big wax tablet, the one that had been used by my sisters before me. Beneath the wax one could see the myriad pinpricks and scratches made when the pen point went in too far as laborious fingers dug it in. Next to me Nilla is carefully writing out longer sentences, copying them from a much-loved sheet of papyrus onto a slate, and Felix and Junia sit at the other table, reading poetry. Poetry was considered suitable for young ladies as long as it wasn't interesting, and I did not enjoy Latin poetry until I was old enough to be allowed to read the more modern poets such as Catullus. When we were children, Ennius' Annals was considered suitable and I don't know if you have ever read any Ennius, but I would not recommend him. I still remember the long serious lines of dull syllables that did not roll so much as stamp around the room. Despite Ennius, I took to reading more widely than my sisters, and Felix encouraged me. After a few years my Latin was so good that I was allowed to join Nilla in learning Greek.

I don't think she was particularly pleased that I had caught up with her, so she put a little more effort in, but not enough. She was happy to move on to other subjects. For once, I did not take pleasure in outstripping her, because I was occupied in the sheer enjoyment of Greek. Just learning the Greek alphabet is a delight for a child. The letters are rounded and smooth and the range of sounds is soft and musical. And the Greeks wrote such wonderful poetry - I defy anyone to get bored of Homer. Felix and Nilla and I read the Iliad and Odyssey while Junia was already considered old enough to learn how to manage a household. When Nilla moved up to this stage, I went on to the great playwrights – Euripides and Menander were my favourites, and finally, because Felix said I was ready for it, I read Plato. All children should read Plato. He liberates the mind.

The upshot of all this is that while you will be unsurprised to hear that I can weave and sew and organise a dinner-party and even check accounts when my steward submits them, I can also tell good literature from twaddle. It is a useful skill in today's world, when even poets and historians must serve the state.

Our domestic education began when my mother arranged for us to shadow senior members of the household so that we could see how each section worked. Sometimes we would sit with our mother as she discussed domestic matters with Aratus, the steward. He was her liaison with the entire staff, taking her orders and distributing them as necessary to the laundresses, the kitchen, the wardrobe mistress, gardeners and cleaners. We had to be trained in some distinctly feminine arts so Nanny showed us how to spin, weave and sew, not because we would have to do these things for ourselves but so that we could supervise the teams of women who did. Once we knew the basics, we would be taken to watch those groups of women at work. Sometimes, if they forgot we were there, as we sat in a corner and watched the fingers twisting the wool and the spindles bobbing up and down, they would begin to chatter and laugh and tell jokes. Even against the background of loom-weights clacking rhythmically on the frame against the wall, I could pick up interesting information from slaves. They seemed to know everything about our neighbours, and I was intrigued by how many of them appeared to be unhappy in love. I would sit next to Nanny, and my sisters, trying to take in everything.

"Now you watch what I'm doing here, Miss Nilla…" clack, clack, clack, clack

"And he said that's not a chicken…"

"Doesn't matter what he promises, you keep your knees together…" clack, clack, clack

"Spinning's the easy bit, Miss, you just look at what goes into the weaving…"

The room was full of small, precise movements, but as I watched I saw that there was no universal rhythm. Even though everyone was working towards one goal, each woman had her own way of moving as she span or wove. In my mind I put together the movements and constructed an elaborate dance in which wool, then thread, then cloth passed from one woman to another until a length of material hung on a pole, waiting to be examined and discussed, cut and shaped. Maybe all the women of our house were doing the same with me and my sisters, spinning us, shaping us, making us fit for purpose, but if so, I decided, I would choose my own cloth and my own cut. I was pleased with the extended metaphor and wondered why Homer had never used it.

"He does use the word "weave" to describe Odysseus and Athena concocting plans," said Felix. "And other poets see themselves as weavers of songs."

He made weaving sound much more glamorous and romantic than it really was. But this is how a Roman lady learns to be a Roman lady. The women around her are all in charge of making sure that she speaks correctly, acts correctly, thinks correctly - and runs her household well. When on a Roman tombstone you see the phrase "she made wool" it does not mean that this particular woman spent her days spinning wool. It means that she could manage her household. Of course, they put that on the tombstone whether you are competent. Somehow, through the ages, making wool has become for Rome the symbol of womanhood and the womanly virtues, thrift, modesty and chastity. And there is nothing wrong with any of those virtues. I have practised them all my life, through choice.

Chapter 3

I knew that my father was rich and important of course, but it is no exaggeration to tell you that in the world of the Republic the most important thing in any Roman man's life was reaching the consulship. Nowadays it is a reward for good behaviour and means little, but then being Consul was all that mattered. Even to us women, it mattered. It was the pinnacle of achievement for our husbands and fathers and brothers, and its glory shone on us too. Of course, events made sure that my husband and brother never reached the consulship, though both were on track for it. It is foolish to grieve over that one thing, but it seems a waste of their expertise and training.

Let me explain - the Senate of several hundred men were mostly elected - not recruited, mark you, but elected by the citizens - from the best families and a great deal of thought went into making a young man ready for his role. It helped if that young man were from one of the established high-ranking families. If not, then he had to show that he was worthy in some other way, maybe by being extremely talented in the field of military matters or in the law, then he might be allowed to join the Senate. A huge effort lay behind preserving this system. Firstly, there were certain basic requirements. A man had to prove a certain level of wealth, and once in the Senate there were very few legal ways of maintaining that wealth, because all sorts of business activities were banned for Senators. A prospective Senator had to make sure that his money was in land, farming, rents from properties. This was a deterrent to some equestrians. My mother's friend Atticus quickly made the decision that he preferred business to politics and so never became a Senator. I have often wondered if a relaxation of that particular rule might not have benefited the entire system. Allowing Senators a wide range of ways to make money might have saved them from feeling obliged to make it illegally, as even my own brother did. However - once the finances were in order, a prospective Senator would campaign for the office of

Quaestor, the most junior level of the Senate. Elections were held in the summer to give people a chance to come to Rome to vote, though as the empire grew, the idea that citizens could travel to Rome just to vote became ridiculous. In the end, the people of the city and the nearest towns controlled the elections. And at the end of all that, twenty men would be successful and enter the Senate. Twenty was considered a good number to replace those Senators who died, fell ill or were thrown out of the Senate for various reasons.

It was Junia who asked Felix about this number one day, spurred by our interest in the campaigning, for my father was aiming for the consulship.

"Felix, if twenty men enter the Senate each year but only two men can become Consul each year, what do the other eighteen do?"

Felix positively beamed at this excellent question and he and Junia went off into a long and enthusiastic conversation while Nilla and I stopped our more boring tasks and listened in for all we were worth. The upshot was that most people who entered the Senate then did nothing very much except turn up to meetings. I was astounded. Everyone we knew was Consul or aiming to be Consul - did that mean that some of them, people we knew, weren't going to make it? Did we know - may the gods forfend! - failures?

"It is simple numbers, Tertulla," said Felix gently. "Not everyone can become Consul." Then seeing the consternation in my eyes, he added quickly, "Of course some people are practically certain to become Consul, because they have the support of the most prestigious people."

Here Nilla asked one of the most intelligent questions I can remember her framing (and Nilla was no fluff-head, whatever she might want you to think), "Felix, who are the most important men in Rome? Who does our father need to get on his side to gain the Consulship?"

"Whom does your father need," said Felix. "We need the accusative form of the pronoun there, Nilla. As to your excellent question - well, what sort of man do you think should be influential?"

We all thought.

"A Consul has to be wise," said Junia slowly, "because he runs the Senate, and the Senate runs the whole city and sends out the men who will rule our provinces. So, he needs the support of men who - men who are experienced in politics and government."

"And the army," said Nilla.

"And have you heard of any man who is experienced like this?" asked Felix.

I must have been about five at that time and had heard of two individuals who, it seemed to me, fitted these criteria.

"Crassus and Pompey," I announced.

"Maybe Cicero," said Junia thoughtfully.

"Who?" I said, though the name was familiar.

"Oh Tertulla!" said Nilla in tones of superiority. "Don't you know who Cicero is?"

I bridled but a flash of memory gave me the opportunity to squash her by quoting my elders.

"He is an intelligent upstart," I said. "Mother said so."

"He is also the current Consul," said Felix with just a hint of reproach in his voice. "And he supports your father's candidacy."

I absorbed this and thought that maybe Marcus Cicero was not so bad. An upstart was a good thing. But it had not sounded like that as my mother pronounced it.

"Felix," I said, "What is an upstart?"

Felix did not answer this question but redirected us onto our father's campaign for the consulship.

In fact, I learned much later in my life that my father had not been made Consul on his first attempt and had needed the support of many influential people on his second attempt. And Marcus Cicero had been important in getting our father that precious consulship, but only because he did not want someone else to be elected. But you can see how the whole subject - Senatorial elections and who was going to win - was an endless source of conversation and argument among us. You cannot get excited about the senate nowadays. They specialise in keeping their heads down, and high office brings little glory.

I was only five when my father attained Rome's greatest honour. The household was buzzing with the excitement, and we held a great number of expensive parties. Not that we three daughters were allowed to attend, but we did occasionally see people arriving and looking very grand. What I noticed was the jewellery worn by the women, gold dripping from necks, ears, and arms. My mother, I saw, did not take this approach, often contenting herself with a silver bangle on each wrist and her favourite pearl drops in her ears. Felix, Nanny and my mother did their best to keep the Juniatrium as calm and quiet as possible, maintaining a daily routine which kept us grounded. They must have been successful, because I can remember little which I can say with confidence happened that year. I suppose that now and then we were able to go out to watch my father do things which only Consuls could do, but I imagine that Junia was the most likely to be taken, as Nilla and I would have been too young to be reliable. The exception to this was the ceremony on the first of January. We all watched from a wooden stand in the Forum as my father climbed the steps to make the sacrifice at the top of the Capitoline Hill, and then we cheered him as he came back down the hill and entered the Senate House as Consul. Well, I cheered when I was told to, as I couldn't see over the front wall of the stand. I don't suppose it was that interesting, and my most vivid memory is of hiding under the wooden benches of the stand with a little boy from the family of one of the other officials, playing soldiers with a couple of wooden toys. But here is the important thing - every year these ceremonies, and all the fuss and excitement associated with them, were passed on not just to other men, but to their families, and so we all shared in the glory of the top office. It does not feel the same nowadays, because the top man in Rome is always the Emperor. My brother was brought up to compete with everyone else from his generation. Now all the young men of Rome's leading families must accept that their education and upbringing are directed towards them being second best. I find it difficult to see the point of this.

The next year, because my father was no longer in office he was around more. Normally, he would have gone and governed a province and I have no idea why he did not. On consideration, I suppose his health was already weakening. But he did get us front row seats for the triumphal procession of Pompey the Great, who was a highly successful general returning to the city after a long campaign in the East. That procession - and I have now seen many triumphs - is one of my most precious memories.

In my mind, it is a long golden day at the beginning of autumn, with the sun winking on heaps of shininess, carts piled with gold, furniture and statues. There are prisoners-of-war in strange and colourful clothing, soldiers marching in endless rows, some singing, some waving, some looking as though the city was a little disappointing compared to the places they had conquered.

For me, the most exciting of all were the animals never seen before, and best of all - an elephant. Felix had described elephants to me (though he had never seen one before either) and I knew that the mighty Hannibal had ridden on them when he fought us in Africa, but seeing an elephant took me beyond my imagination. For the first time, I realised that things in the stories told by Nanny and Felix could appear right in front of my eyes, and all because I was a Roman, living in Rome, the greatest city in the world. After the soldiers, and animals, there came carts holding great sheets of wood with maps painted on them showing the places that Pompey had conquered, countries with strange names like Cappadocia and Pamphylia. Felix fortunately had come prepared and helped me spell out some of the words and tried to explain where all these lands were. Also on these carts were written lists of all the towns conquered, tallies of the money taken, the names and captains of all the pirate ships that had been captured, accounts of how Pompey had distributed that money and how much each soldier had received as his share of the booty. Oh, and the noise was terrific, chants that rolled along the crowd and bounced off the shifting mass of heads, cheering in thundering waves, the tramp of the soldiers, trumpets ringing out at every opportunity. The noise and the numbers overpowered me as did the thought of how far away all these places were, and I felt so bewildered by it all that

I started to grow afraid, even though I did not know why. Only the thought of Nilla's scorn if I cried kept me strong, and after a while, I found that if I concentrated on admiring the animals and gold and maps, I could push the fear to the back of my mind.

When every soldier had passed there was a pause then the mighty hero himself came along on his chariot. I felt a deep sense of disappointment. The figure in the chariot was quite old with a face that was pleasant but a little wide, beaming his self-satisfaction at us all, and he was painted red. He could have been - well, my father, or rather, my grandfather, and I was embarrassed, because I had thought he would look like one of my Greek heroes from mythology. Fortunately, he had one saving grace - when I asked Felix about the magnificent red cloak that gleamed with gold embroidery and jewels sewn along the edges, Felix said that it had once belonged to Alexander the Great himself. I was impressed for just long enough for the general to pass, and then asked Felix why the red-painted face. Felix didn't really know but in all triumphal processions, he said, the victorious general had to have his face painted.

"There are lots of things which only happen during triumphs," explained Felix, automatically going into his schoolroom voice. "Do you see the man behind Pompey, perched on the back of the chariot? Do you see him leaning forward and talking to the general?"

I could indeed see this and thought it was very rude to interrupt the general during the most important day of his life.

"It is his job," said Felix. "He has to remind the general that he is only a mortal man, so that the general doesn't get too proud and offend the gods."

I thought it a little mean of the gods to not allow this man just one day without interfering - after all, if you are a god, why would you be afraid of any man? But Felix said it was more to do with us humans showing respect than the gods being afraid. I stared curiously at the back of Pompey the Great as his chariot rattled off into the distance, his red cloak glinting.

Our parents went to the official banquet that evening and I noticed that the whole household seemed to be on holiday. A lot of singing and laughing came from the slaves' quarters and after I had gone to bed, I could hear faint music drifting across the Palatine - we were not the only house celebrating. It made me feel happy and safe. Rome had won. As I fell asleep, I wondered if I would ever see all those lands that Pompey had conquered. A child wonders these things and then, as an adult, you realise that you have come to accept the limits of life. Very few women can claim to be well-travelled. I have never even left Italy, while nearly every man I have known has gone abroad, to serve in the army, or as part of a provincial governor's staff. Some, my brother for one, travelled for education even. Imagine that - you decide that you want to study philosophy, or rhetoric, and announce that you are going to go to Athens, Rhodes, or Alexandria. And then you just go.

Many years later as I told Sulpicia this, she said, "Of course, that is only true for a terribly small proportion of men too."

I looked at her and frowned.

"I mean," she said, "the idea that one can travel to extend one's education."

"But I could not join the army to travel or be a merchant and travel," I pointed out. "Men can do that. Women do not travel."

Sulpicia gazed over my shoulder and into a wider horizon.

"I go to our house on the Bay of Naples every summer and I often visit my friends in Tibur and Lanuvium and Antium," she murmured. "But - yes, I do not travel. Do you think once I am married, I will be able to persuade my husband to travel and take me with him?"

I looked at her but lied. "Maybe. Octavia went to Athens to persuade Marcus Antonius to remain loyal to her brother. And my sister went with her husband to Asia when he was governor."

"We both know that it is not likely to happen," she said. "My husband will go abroad to fight in the army - in which case he won't take me - or to govern a province. And wives are frowned upon there too, despite Octavia or your sister. I shall never go to Athens, Alexandria, or Rhodes."

I wished with all my heart I could have put an arm around her, told her not to be so silly, of course she would… There was no point.

Chapter 4

My father reached the peak of his ambition with his consulship and after that it was as if he had no more strength. He lingered nearly two years after standing down and died in the autumn plague in the consulship of Metellus and Afranius. It was an exciting point in politics, for Julius Caesar, Pompey the Great and Marcus Crassus were planning an alliance that would change the course of Roman history forever. Because of this, you will not find my father's death mentioned in any of the annals. The only thing I have read in which my father plays a part is Sallust's War against Catiline, a work of unparalleled bitterness and gloom, and Decimus Junius Silanus, like every other character, does not come across well.

But back to Pompey, Crassus and Caesar, who moved into power as my father faded. I don't think my father would have been impressed with The Three, as everyone called the alliance. I cannot remember anything about him that strayed beyond the boundaries of what was considered the done thing. He liked a predictable life, I suppose. His death was also predictable. Every winter he had difficulty at some point, sometimes a cold that turned into a month-long illness, maybe a cough which sounded as though the insides of his lungs were being scraped with dull knives. Every few years, Rome suffered a wave of breathing illnesses and fevers, sweeping up from the unhealthy marshland to the south, and that my father fell victim was no surprise. He was a long time dying, wheezing and coughing from his bedroom for days on end. When he suffered these bouts of illness, we were allowed visits where we were strictly urged to entertain without tiring him. We were shepherded back to the Juniatrium by Nanny as soon as she judged that my father needed a rest. We would tell him all our little bits of news and play word games and he would tell stories on his good days. But the good days got few and far between and when we did see him, he could not make the effort to laugh and tease us. He grew thin and old-looking, and though he was propped up on cushions, he would start coughing and be unable to stop, and the doctor would step between us. One morning we were woken very early by Nanny and in a brief whispering procession through the darkened house we were led to say goodbye to him. He lay on his bed with his eyes shut and his chest barely rising in time to the tiny, snatched breaths which wheezed from between his grey lips. Our mother stood watching him, her hair loose and falling down her back, with just a shawl over her sleeping tunic. She looked young and sad, and I felt sad for her for now I knew that my father was dying. I assumed that she loved him as I did and wondered if we would grieve together. We were allowed to kiss him, and then returned to the Juniatrium where Nanny helped us dress to keep us occupied more than anything, and we waited for Felix to bring the news.

I was eight years old and at first was convinced that only my sisters could keep me from dying of grief myself. But it was one of those occasions when I realised how many people I had in my life, people who loved me. I was not left bereft and alone. I had Junia, Nilla, Nanny and Felix and my brother. Brutus was so kind to us all. He was friendly with Silanus of course, and I dare say missed him as one would a favourite uncle, but he had moved out of the family house and set up on his own years before. I am afraid that I never really considered anybody's feelings at the time, I was so taken up with my own. I did not see much of my mother, except at the times when we sat in the atrium watching over my father's body while visitors came to pay their respects. Then my mother sat next to the body, in plain and dark-coloured tunics and wraps, her hair pinned up simply. I had wondered if she would weep and let her hair down and tear at her clothes, but Junia had said, "Of course not, Tertulla. That is not how our mother is." There was never any hint of her being overcome with grief in this very public arena, and any hope I had of being able to cry in her embrace was squashed. I decided she was incapable of mourning anyone, except Brutus, and that was the moment I realised, crossly, that Brutus was the centre of my mother's life.

What I did not know was that there was already another man in my mother's life, and he was as important to her as my brother. I found out about him at my father's funeral.

Now that I have planned my own funeral, I can see that organising my father's was a full-time occupation for my mother and she had probably been working out the details from the moment the doctor told her that my father was dying. My father had no male relatives living, and all his wealth came to us, though not much was left. This is why my own funeral has been planned and money set aside for so long. I have no intention of leaving debts or worries for someone else, and I want to make certain I get my own way. I have requested a speech in the Forum, and I think, given my age, I might get it.

At one point during the days between death and funeral, we were summoned to my mother's room to stand and listen while various aspects of the ceremony were discussed in front of us. Brutus was there and at one point he looked at me and said, "Maybe Tertulla could stay at home with her nursemaid? She is quite young..." and got no further before my mother said briskly, "Tertulla is her father's daughter and will not embarrass any of us." I opened my mouth in indignation to say that of course I wouldn't embarrass them, but Nilla stepped on my foot, and I was silent. Brutus saw my face and smiled. "Of course," he said. It was during this meeting that I learned that my father had left his wealth to us, his three daughters.

"What wealth there is," said my mother, not in a critical way, just stating facts.

"He had many expenses as Consul and did not have the opportunity to make money from a province," said my brother in diplomatic tones.

"Indeed," said my mother. "In light of which, this will not be an extravagant funeral. We shall do everything as it should be, but we are not going to put on a show. I have hired the actors and musicians for the procession, but our own household women will be sufficient as mourners. We shall give away food on the day after the funeral, not hold a public feast. As for the oration in the Forum, there are no male relatives, so I have asked Marcus Cicero to do it, on the grounds that he claims to have been Silanus' friend. And even Cicero cannot demand a fee for doing a funeral oration. We shan't stint on the funeral couch or the incense for the pyre, but we aren't going to be reckless either."

Brutus nodded slowly, looking at the floor.

"Silanus was not an ostentatious man," he said quietly. "I would have done the speech myself, if you had asked me, Mother."

Even I saw the reproach in this and was just a little bit thrilled at watching my mother being criticised. She put out her hand towards Brutus and for one moment there was a smile on her face and a gentleness in her eyes as she said, "I know, my son. I had hoped that you would stand by me though for the whole funeral. I would appreciate your being there at my side. Otherwise, your Uncle Cato will feel obliged to stand with me."

"May we be at your side too, Mother?" said Junia, her voice high and tight.

"You shall walk behind me, all three of you," said my mother, turning to us and speaking with her usual practical good sense. "You shall have Nanny with you. Behind you come our relatives, and Felix will walk behind the family, along with all the other freedmen."

Nilla started and said, "Felix is freed?"

My mother smiled. "In your father's will, along with Aretus. It is an honour, but he has earned it."

I smiled back. I approved of my mother praising our dear Felix.

"And," said my mother, anticipating the question threatening to burst out of Nilla, "Felix will stay on as your tutor, just as Aretus will stay on as steward."

It was only as I left the room that I remembered that my father was dead, and I was supposed to be unremittingly devastated. It was strange. I kept forgetting to be sad. I supposed that this was normal because one could not cry continuously. And I imagined my father smiling at me and whispering, "Chin up, Tertulla!"

The night before the funeral, as we lay in bed in the dark, I asked all the questions my sisters could not answer. Nanny and

Felix had already prepared us by explaining the ceremony, but I wanted to know more.

"Junie?"

The silence that answered me was no deterrent.

"What happens when you die?"

"I don't know, Tertulla."

Nilla said, "Father is at peace now." She had heard my mother saying that, and so had I but it wasn't enough.

"Yes, but does he know that he is at peace?"

Silence. Then Junia said, "I don't think we can know what happens, and it might be so different, being dead, that we can't imagine it. But I think something happens. I don't know what, don't ask, Tertulla! I just don't think a person completely stops, and there is nothing for ever."

I decided that I needed a conversation with my brother who was always reading philosophy. Brutus had spent a year living in Athens and everyone knew that Athens was full of philosophers who did nothing but talk about life and death. But just in case, I lay and looked up into the dark and whispered "Hello" to my dead father; I knew that if he were still somehow out there, he would be blowing me a kiss. Just before I fell asleep, Junia said, "Nanny was crying when we left Mother's room. She was hoping that she would be freed too."

"I don't want Nanny to be freed," I said sleepily. "I want her to stay with us for ever."

It was a grim day for us, though Nanny and Felix as always were there, and Felix, to our delight, wore his freedman's cap for the first time. I thoroughly approve of this tradition of freeing loyal servants at one's death. It is entirely typical of Augustus that he even legislated to restrict the number of one's own slaves one may free in a will. This takes no account of the moment of splendour it brings to a funeral, for the freedmen walk through the city as its newest citizens. It reminds us that the dead still have the power to bring life to Rome. But apart from that, it was to the eight-year-old me a dreary December morning, painted in grey and brown, and the day stretched out in front of me full of the frightening unknown. We gathered in the atrium and prepared to accompany my father's body through the streets and into the Roman Forum, the heart of the city, and then out to the field beyond the city walls where a funeral pyre was ready waiting for him. As we waited, my dull thick tunic and shawl, produced from a clothes chest especially for today, felt strange and too bulky. I hoped I would not trip on its folds. Incense burned in the braziers at each corner of the room, and through the open front doors, we could see a crowd gathering. Eight men made their way into the atrium, bowed to my mother and arranged themselves along both sides of the couch on which my father's body lay. They blocked my view of him, and I felt a sob suddenly burst from me as I realised that I would never see him close to me, properly, again. The musicians outside began to play, the eight men lifted the couch onto their shoulders and slowly they moved out of the doors, my mother and Brutus following. Led by Nanny, we three sisters made our way outside and took up our place in the procession, stumbling a little in our unfamiliar clothes and now all crying. Tears ran down Nanny's face. A group of the household women wailed from some way behind us, a ghastly noise. We wove our way along the top of the Palatine Hill and down into the Forum, crowds of people standing to each side with their heads respectfully bowed. Because my father had been Consul, many distinguished men were waiting for us, including the current Consuls and some of the magistrates chosen for the next year. Naturally, many women came too, members of our family or accompanying their husbands and often both. I stood at the back of the crowd of men with all these women, Junia and Nilla on either side of me holding my hands because I was so young and upset. I could feel the warmth of Nanny behind us standing so close to me I could lean my head back into the folds of her lovely soft cloak and see out of the corners of my eyes her arms reaching down to my sisters' shoulders. Everyone knew to fall silent, and the musicians stopped playing. A man I didn't know stood up at the front of the Platform and began to speak about Father. I didn't know any of the things he was saying, and the person being described really didn't seem like my father at all, but the speaker had a beautiful voice. I started to follow the rhythms of his sentences and almost enjoy the music of the flowing syllables, and so for a while I forgot my grief. But all too soon, we were on the move again, following behind our mother and Brutus as they paced behind the funeral couch. Once more the musicians led the procession, and behind us, if I sneaked a look, were actors wearing masks, each of them representing one of my father's ancestors. These walked in slow and confident strides, making sweeping waves to the crowds who stopped and gazed as we passed.

I followed through the streets of the city and out of the gate in the walls, aware of all the people surrounding me, until we came to a stop and the procession flowed around us and broke up, spreading out to encircle the cleared space where a pyre had been made ready, a huge and neatly constructed box of wood. As the carriers began the task of getting the bier on top of the pyre, people edged closer, and blocked our view, while Nanny and Felix drew us back and to the side a little - I suppose they thought that it would be too upsetting for us to be at the front and close to the pyre and the body on top of it. I tilted my head back a little to look up into the mass of adult faces around me and there in front of me was my mother. Through a gap in the shifting bodies, I saw her face clearly and she was looking fixedly to one side of my father's funeral pyre. I thought it must be that she couldn't bear to watch as my father's body was laid on top of the wood, and almost felt sorry for her, when it struck me that she was looking at someone across the pyre, someone amongst that crowd of men in dull tunics and togas. And before I could start trying to see who it was, torches were produced and brought to the edge of the pyre. I won't describe the rest of it. It is not easy to watch a funeral pyre. It was when we had reached the end of the whole dismal ceremony and evening was falling that the crowd of people started to thin out. Some were leaving, others moving to our side of the pyre, studiously ignoring the hot red centre, and drifting with studied tact and solemn faces towards the small group standing nearest the blaze. Having manoeuvred thus, people carefully stood in irregular groups, waiting to speak to my mother. They shuffled closer, talking in low voices to one another, claiming wives along the way, and practising the words of condolence. Some of the women embraced my mother, one or two whom I knew well took the time to come over and hug us. The men smiled at us awkwardly and said what a fine man our father had been, while behind them his funeral fire glowed and outlined their bodies. Right at the end, I saw that the Consul-in-waiting Julius Caesar was holding my mother's hand and bending his head down to hers and smiling. And in one tumultuous moment I knew.

My mouth open in shock, I quickly looked around and saw to my horror that everyone else was watching - carefully and with blank faces. They knew - they all knew. And then the world shook itself into a show of normality and everyone looked away and murmured about the approaching night and getting back indoors. Caesar strode away from my mother and smiled at me as he passed our little group. And like the fool that the eight-year-old me was, I looked up at Nanny and asked, "Will Julius Caesar marry our mother now?"

Chapter 5

Nanny's eyes widened and in a moment she had taken a sharp look at my mother to check that she had not heard. On either side of me I heard one sister stifle a squeak and another gasp, and Nanny murmured to us all, "Stand up straight, be quiet and don't say anything else AT ALL."

We all shut our mouths so quickly I am sure I heard teeth click, and with blank faces we marched home behind our mother, brother, uncles and aunts, flanked by men from our household staff carrying torches. All the way I wondered about Julius Caesar and why he had smiled at me.

When we got back to the house on the Palatine, Nanny whisked us straight to the Juniatrium and sat us down before even letting us take off the cumbersome mourning robes. Felix, who had walked back with my brother, popped his head in, took one look and disappeared. Nanny watched him go and took a deep breath.

"Listen, all of you," she said, and her face was as stern as Nanny's face ever got. "When a woman is as impressive as your mother Servilia, there is always gossip. When a man is as controversial as Gaius Julius Caesar, there is always gossip. People will put the two together for no other reason than that it sounds good. What I expect you three to do is to avoid such gossip and show that you are not affected by it. Honour your father's memory by honouring your mother." We nodded and I wondered if I was the only one of us to notice that she had not answered my question. I decided then and there that Julius Caesar would be our stepfather pretty soon, and once Nanny had gone, plagued my sisters for details.

Junia was the least upset by it all, having known that "something was going on" as she loftily informed us, "for ages". This was unlike Junia - usually it was Nilla who enjoyed knowing things about people and being superior. But I needed to know. I demanded Junia tell me.

We sat on the floor, huddled, so that we could not be overheard, and Junia began.

"I heard the rumours about three years ago," was as far as she got before being interrupted.

"Three years!" exclaimed Nilla, and immediately clamped a hand over her mouth.

"Yes," Junia said with some impatience. "Look, just be quiet and I'll tell you what I know."

I nodded, Nilla kept her hand over her mouth and Junia carried on.

"There was a scandal three years ago. During a debate in the Senate House, our Uncle Cato was attacking Julius Caesar, I can't remember why, apparently he has always hated Caesar. During his speech a messenger came in and delivered a note to Caesar and he seemed to be taking more notice of it than what Uncle Cato was saying so Uncle got annoyed and asked to see the note. And Caesar let him see it. It was from our mother, arranging a time when she and Caesar could meet and apparently the note said, 'in the usual place', so whatever it was had been going on for some time."

For a long moment, Nilla and I absorbed this.

"And before you ask," continued Junia, "I know this because I was in earshot when Uncle came round to see our father later that day, and he didn't trouble to lower his voice. I could hear him and Mother and Father arguing in Father's study, and you know what Uncle Cato is like when he gets angry. I stood in the garden as near as I dared and heard everything he said. And he was so angry, he called Mother all sorts of names. He shouted at Father for not keeping Mother in line…yes, I know, I thought that was funny too."

"What did Mother and Father say?" asked Nilla, eyes so wide I thought she looked like a frog.

"Mother said nothing and Father told Cato that nobody could judge someone else's marriage without proving himself a fool and wasn't it time that Uncle Cato got married again and showed the rest of us how to do it properly. And Uncle Cato left. After that Mother and Father spoke in whispers, and I crept away."

I said in confusion, "But Uncle Cato is married."

Both sisters looked at me with their older-than-you faces on.

"Uncle Cato is married to Aunt Marcia now. But years ago, he had to get a divorce from Aunt Atilia because she was immoral," said Nilla, her usual air of knowledgeableness fully restored.

Ignoring Nilla was hard, but I concentrated on that all-important word "immoral" and what it might mean. I wondered if I dared ask if Mother was immoral too, but fortunately Junia carried on.

"Father was telling Uncle Cato that it was none of his business. Which it isn't," she explained.

I thought that Julius Caesar and Mother between them seemed to have made it everybody's business. And nobody had answered my original question, which was still important.

"Will Mother marry Julius Caesar then?"

Junia and Nilla looked at each other and shrugged.

"Julius Caesar is divorced," said Nilla. "I suppose he could marry Mother. She is rich and beautiful."

"But she won't be having any more children, and Julius Caesar only has a girl," said Junia slowly. We all knew what it meant to have only girls.

"Should we ask Brutus about this?" I asked as we reached the Juniatrium. What would our brother make of this, with his lofty ideas?

"No, we shouldn't," said Nilla firmly. This surprised me. I had expected Junia to be the one with objections. Nilla, I thought, would like to dig. She liked knowing things. She saw my face and went on, "Brutus is a prig, Tertulla."

"What do you mean?" I demanded, not liking to admit that I wasn't sure what a prig was.

"He is quick to condemn people," said Junia quietly. "I have no doubt he knows, but he won't be - sympathetic."

Nilla added, "Our brother has views on the proper behaviour for women. That's why he hasn't married yet. He hasn't found a woman prepared to be treated like a kicked dog."

I was shocked. "Brutus doesn't treat us like that – does he?"

Junia looked up at me. "Tertulla, he pays some attention to you but barely notices me or Nilla. He is only our half-brother. I'd be surprised if he thinks of us from one year's end to the next."

This was interesting - I decided to watch Brutus and how he behaved with different people before I returned to the subject. In the meantime, I asked, "What are we going to do?"

"Nothing," said Junia firmly. "Tertulla, women like us - "

"Girls," said Nilla.

"- girls like us don't do anything," continued Junia. "We get married and produce heirs."

I thought of my mother who always seemed so strong and in control of her own life. And yet, just as Junia had said, our mother had grown up to get married and have a child, then marry again and have us…

"Do you think our mother married our father for love?" I asked.

"Nobody marries for love," said Junia. "We certainly won't."

"But she must love Julius Caesar," said Nilla wickedly.

As you can imagine, the three of us kept our ears open for anything we could learn about Julius Caesar and there was a lot to be gathered. Everyone was obsessed with the man. You may be sceptical about what an eight-year-old hears, and I agree. But Nilla was eleven and Junia approaching marriage, and between us we gained a lot of information.

Gaius Julius Caesar, born in the same year as our mother ("Ha!" said Nilla, as though this proved that the two must be in love), clever, good at public speaking ("Just like everyone else in Rome," said Junia) - and attractive. Interestingly, he had a formidable and highly respected mother and I immediately felt sorry for him. The best story was garnered by Junia on a visit to a suitable friend - we were allowed on such visits - and she could hardly wait to get us all together into the Juniatrium and free from Nanny so that she could convey her intelligence. It was gossip of the finest order, combining sex, nobility, religion and a pithy afterword from the man himself.

A young patrician called Publius Claudius Pulcher had tried to seduce Caesar's wife - "Seduce?" "Kiss, Tertulla. Which is really wrong if it is someone else's wife" - and as if trying to make it as difficult as possible had decided to do it by breaking into Caesar's house at a time when no man was allowed in the place. At the festival of the Good Goddess a select group of the highest ladies in Rome were invited to take part in the ritual at the house of the Chief Priest, who just happened to be Julius Caesar.

"He is Chief Priest?" said Nilla with justifiable incredulity.

"Yes, apparently he ran in an election a couple of years ago and bribed everyone," said Junia, full of her oracular knowledge. For once, Nilla and I tried to listen respectfully, but I could not keep quiet for long.

"Why did he want to be Chief Priest?" I asked and annoyed her. She hurried on.

"Oh, I don't know, Tullie, ask him! The thing is, because he is Chief Priest, the rites were held in his house and all men were banished for the night - you know that everything male is either put out of the house or if it is something like a picture or statue, it is covered up." This sounded nowhere near as bizarre as some of our religious practices, so I just nodded and fixed my eyes on her to make her go on.

"So, in the middle of the rites, there was a huge outcry that a man had got in, and Caesar's mother immediately put a stop to the rites and summoned Caesar, and the Vestal Virgins all had to carry out a purification, and there was lots of gossip. Then it turned out that the intruder was Publius Claudius Pulcher, and he wanted to seduce Caesar's own wife, during the actual rites." This was all said very quickly so that we could not interrupt, and when she stopped and looked at us, it took a moment for me and Nilla to produce obedient gasps.

"So Caesar divorced his wife, and this is the thing that was being quoted all over Rome - he said that he did not think that she really had succumbed to Publius Claudius, but Caesar's wife had to be above suspicion."

I noted carefully that use of the word "succumb", appreciated the pomposity of the final clause and then moved on to a more immediate question.

"But everyone knows that Caesar has been seeing Mother for years, long before this all happened. Why had his wife not divorced him already?"

My sisters looked at me pityingly. I scowled defiantly at them but felt myself reddening under their gaze.

"Yes, well, it isn't fair," I muttered.

"Don't be such a child, Tertulla," said Nilla loftily, and so that conversation ended in tears and Nanny said she was embarrassed to find us fighting like that. The thought of being sent to our mother to be judged filled me with alarm, so I immediately and uncharacteristically begged Nilla's pardon.

This was the start of my interest in Caesar. My theory that he might be my real father came later. As a child, I assumed he would now marry my mother and replace the father I had just lost, and much as I had loved Silanus, Caesar was a much more interesting figure. I felt no disloyalty, I was just on the hunt for another father and Caesar, I thought, would do the job nicely. I wondered when I would see Caesar again given the life I had as a child and in the sort of household I inhabited. There was not much opportunity. We were allowed out of the house, but we were carefully chaperoned, and all journeys were planned, destinations scrutinised. We had friends, we had playmates, we had outings, but I realised that for an eight-year-old girl to seek out a man who would be Consul of the Roman Republic was utterly ludicrous. I had to be patient and every time we walked down into the Forum I wondered if this would be the day when I would see Caesar, surrounded by clients and petitioners, striding across the stone flags to the Senate House, or to one of the treasuries or the Records Office. I wondered if I would recognise him. I wished that I had looked more carefully at the man who was holding my mother's hand at the funeral, bending slightly to talk with her. My memories were only of dark hair and a sort of boniness about the face. Realistically, of course, it was very unlikely that I would ever see anything, for politicians of Caesar's status were often so surrounded that it was difficult to catch a glimpse of them. I also wondered if my mother would have the nerve to invite him to our house maybe for a dinner with friends. She was beginning to branch out I noticed. She and her female friends were beginning to hold small gatherings, not quite parties but definitely suppers, during which people would talk or a poet would be invited, sometimes a famous musician. I wondered if there was any chance of being in the atrium on the evening when Julius Caesar came but I should have known better. My mother was very much aware of her status, and she would not have invited Caesar to our house while the memory of my father prevented her. She was expected to be in mourning for a year and any entertaining that she did during that year was discreet and confined to close friends and family. In other words, she made sure that she was above suspicion.

It was a long time before I saw Julius Caesar again and when I did, the man in front of me was so different from my memory that I had to look again. The only thing that remained the same from my memories was the dark hair, though I realised that here was a face of great intelligence, a face that had lived. The eyes were slightly sunken, the grooves from nose to the outermost corner of the mouth were pronounced, and the corners at the sides of his jaw were almost angular. When he smiled everything about his face lifted — eyebrows, corner of eyes, even those grooves from nose to mouth. The cheekbones suddenly came into their own and he was utterly entrancing. The secret dream that had lain inside me so deep and dark that I had not even noticed it, flowered into life, and I wanted more than anything to be his daughter.

I have only spoken of this to three people, and the most sympathetic was Sulpicia. Several years after we first met, I had invited her to the house on the Palatine and because it was such a beautiful day, sunny but not too hot, we were sitting in the little courtyard garden and drinking wine - rather daringly of course, with no man to guide us and tell us when we had had enough. It was very well-watered of course, as I am not that daring and find that drinking wine in the middle of the day and in the sun is foolish.

"You were - what? - just eight years old?" she asked. "Did you feel resentful towards your mother at all? You loved your father very much, didn't you?"

"Yes, I did, but I cannot remember ever feeling that my mother had betrayed him. Certainly, I felt no resentment towards her. It was just one of those things that happened when one is in the adult world."

"I only saw your mother a few times, when I was a child," she said. "It is hard to imagine because Caesar is part of history to me. Your mother though was a real, living person. I find it almost impossible to imagine them together. When did you think that Caesar might mean more to you?"

Clever Sulpicia. Straight to my secret, without my having to say it.

"A couple of years later maybe, I think. When I was about ten. Junia was getting married, and we had started to read some of those terrible Greek romances together. They sparked sentimental feelings, and I missed Junia and needed something to occupy my thoughts. I was certain of it by the time of my betrothal with Cassius."

"What did your sisters say?"

"I never spoke to them about it."

This was a surprise for her. She had once said how honoured she felt that I thought of her almost as a sister, when she knew of the relationship I had with my real sisters. Now, I was admitting that I had told her something I had never confided to them.

"I don't know why," I said.

Sulpicia frowned. I can see her now as she looks down into her wine-cup, formulating the words.

"How does a little girl come to an idea like this on her own? And then to speak of it to nobody? To live in silence, just - thinking - or is "hoping" a better word?"

"It sounds strange when you put it like that, but no, not until I married Cassius. He was adamant that it could not be true, and barely had I mentioned it to him when - other things happened. He needed it not to be true, I think."

"Did you ever dare ask your mother?"

"Yes. Once."

And despite our friendship, I could not tell even Sulpicia what had happened there. She did not seem to mind. She left it to me to decide when and how to give her more - if I ever wanted to talk about it. I thought I would, one day, but I was fooling myself.

Chapter 6

Caesar was Consul the year after my father's death. It was a turbulent time for the office. He achieved it through bribery and the influence of his friends Crassus and Pompey, and only his uncritical supporters were not upset by this. Demonstrations and opposition marked his year of office, and my mother and her friends were always talking about what had recently gone on in the Forum. Caesar's consular colleague was hostile to him, an awkward situation which ensured that he could achieve little, and the rest of the Senate argued constantly with whatever was proposed by Caesar - or Pompey or Crassus. Each of The Three had his own designs, his own goals for Caesar's consulship, and they did not bother to hide this, which of course annoyed everyone who ever thought that we should abide by our ancestors' ideals. But this year, in return for their support, Caesar made sure that his allies were rewarded. Pompey got his reorganisation of the East ratified by a reluctant Senate, while Crassus struck an extremely good deal for his colleagues in the business community who were often frustrated by the Senate's innate snobbery. On their own these measures made perfect sense - Pompey was a superb organiser, and Rome's treasuries needed a successful and happy business class, but the fact was that The Three just ploughed through the system to achieve their aims. Our Uncle Cato, defender of every tradition, good or bad, was at the front of the attack and at one point was arrested, which annoyed my mother. She felt that although she did not like Cato very much, he was still her half-brother and therefore it reflected badly on her. The day she heard about the arrest, she spent long hours in her room writing letters, and messengers sped from and to our house. I don't know if it was our mother's pleas which did the trick, but Cato was released after a day or so.

I still held hopes that Caesar and my mother would marry. I didn't like the idea that she might still be his mistress, not when she was so beautiful and clever and highly born. It laid her open to gossip and she was too proud for that. And if she married him, we would have an interesting stepfather, a man once more at the head of our household. Since my father's death, I had missed a male presence in our house. I have no idea why I felt this, but in the back of my mind was the suspicion that we were turning into a version of the Vestal Virgins - an all-woman household, tending to a small set of tedious tasks forever. Life would be much more exciting if our mother married again. Caesar's daughter would become our stepsister which could be interesting, and I was confident of my ability to become a favourite stepdaughter, just as I was certain that I had been my father's favourite. My mind strayed on - Caesar was friends with Pompey, the general I had watched in the triumphal procession, so maybe I would meet him and ask him how he came to have the cloak of Alexander the Great. And to please Caesar, Pompey would bring out that cloak and let me wear it just for a few moments, so that I could imagine that I ruled the world, the hero of ages. Needless to say, things did not arrange themselves according to my dreams.

My brother Brutus was just starting out on his Forum apprenticeship and had arranged to shadow several eminent men as a way of gaining experience of the law courts and Senate. Naturally, my mother knew all these people and was just the right person for him to try out his thoughts about a political career. He often came to dinner and if there were no other guests, the three of us would attend too, mostly confined to listening while our mother and brother discussed the events of the day. Nilla frequently found these conversations tedious, Junia spent most of the time looking into the distance as she contemplated goodness-knows-what, and I attended carefully. Brutus said that I sat like a mouse at a hole in the kitchen wall, ready to scuttle out and swipe any crumbs which fall. The day I remember was a day of particularly rich pickings for the mouse.

We all knew that something extraordinary had happened for earlier in the day my mother had been out and come back to the house in a rage, swirling shawls and veils all over the atrium, and snapping at the maids trying to gather them up. Our steward Aretus tried to manage the situation, but she was brusque even with him. This was not typical behaviour: my mother kept calm in every situation and was unfailingly polite. She always said that that only a person with no intelligence treated the staff badly. I had never seen her behave towards the household like this and it says something that Aretus and the slaves were taken aback. I made sure that I was completely out of sight around a corner, and heard her loud angry footsteps head off towards her room.

When, a few hours later, Brutus arrived, I was in a frustrated welter of impatience. I made sure I was in the atrium when he arrived and dragged him into a corner so I could demand that he tell me what had happened. That was the good thing about Brutus in those days. He never told me to run along or refused to let me know what was happening. He was a little distracted and impatient that day, but he explained. It was good stuff - I saved up all the mouse-crumbs, ready to relay them back to my sisters. Brutus looked at me, almost smiling, as he stood and said, "I want to see Mother so go and tell your sisters. Give us some time before you come into dinner."

I nodded and tried to keep the excitement from showing. I watched as he crossed the atrium towards the corridor leading to my mother's room, stopping for a brief conversation with Aretus on the way. Dinner would be late, I thought as I scurried back.

"Caesar has given his daughter in marriage to Pompey the Great!" I announced, standing in the middle of the Juniatrium, and relishing the drama as the faces turned towards me reacted in horror.

"He is at least thirty years older than her," said Nilla and stopped to calculate it exactly.

"Why?" asked Junia. But in a few moments, she had worked it out for herself.

Pompey's career as a soldier had been meteoric and triumphant. His political career unfortunately had been lame. All his attempts to become part of the core of the political classes had been thwarted by people like my mother and Uncle Cato, who all remembered that Pompey had started his career as a young, bloodthirsty and rule-breaking brigand.

Eventually Pompey was reduced to drastic means, an alliance with Caesar and Crassus, and the dubious distinction of being one of The Three. Now, it appeared, Pompey also got Julia, Caesar's daughter, who at the age of seventeen was indeed many years younger than her new husband.

"She is only two years older than me," said Junia quietly.

"It gets better," I said, with huge satisfaction, forgetting in my joy of being the messenger of such news that one should at least pretend some decorum. "Mother and Brutus had arranged with Caesar for Brutus to marry Julia and now Caesar has broken off the arrangement and Mother is furious."

"Brutus?" Junia looked at this and saw the plan. "Yes, it is a particularly good match for them both. They are patrician and while everyone knows that Caesar has no money and huge debts, Brutus is very wealthy. It's a good connection."

"Why weren't we told?" I asked crossly. My sisters ignored me.

"I know why she proposed it," said Nilla suddenly. "She has realised that Caesar is never going to marry her, but if her son and Caesar's daughter marry, there is at least an excuse for her and Caesar to meet. But Caesar needs Pompey to be on his side so this is a marriage of politics. I feel sorry for Julia for I am sure Brutus would be a much better husband for her."

"Tullie, did you get this from Brutus?" asked Junia. I nodded. She frowned.

"He has gone to see Mother in her room. We are to join them at dinner," I said and for the first time wondered how Brutus was feeling about all this. It dawned on me that he might well be feeling rejected, hurt. He might have liked Julia - I had not asked. It was with some nervousness that we trooped into dinner that night.

What you must understand is that Brutus and my mother hated Pompey. In one of Rome's long list of rebellions, Pompey had killed Brutus' father, my mother's first husband. Pompey had been on the side of the Senate and People and doing their bidding, but this was no reason for forgiveness. My mother and brother kept their hatred warm as Pompey grew more famous and respectable. But with this latest coup, he had struck at them again.

"This wretched gang of Three is stirring up so much trouble for themselves they will regret it," predicted my mother as she tore the shell off her egg at the start of the meal.

"I am alarmed," said my brother a little more mildly, "that Caesar feels the need to make this marriage alliance. He and Pompey have already made their agreement and Crassus is on their side. Why is that not enough?"

"Because Caesar knows that a buffoon like Pompey is not to be trusted," my mother whipped straight back. "He is a nobody who has made a career out of stamping on all our traditions. His idea of honour is laughable. He is completely cold-blooded and will see no need to keep an agreement if a better offer comes his way."

"You sound like Uncle Cato," said my brother, and as my mother snorted, continued, "I can't support Caesar. I find the idea of three men manipulating the elections distasteful, and their attitude towards their fellow Senators is one of contempt."

My mother nodded, not because she was agreeing with Brutus, but because she saw a way of Brutus gaining an advantage. "You may not be in the Senate yet, but you can still align yourself with those opposing The Three. There are plenty of very respectable men who feel as we do. Cicero, Bibulus, people like that. You need to form a group of your peers as well. You can spread rumour and gossip and stir up your elders as you tag along behind them. Ask them why they are allowing The Three to behave like this. See what they say."

"Appius Claudius detests The Three," said Brutus "and he has a daughter of about the right age."

"Don't run straight into marriage with the first girl who comes to mind," said my mother sharply. "It is unfortunate for you that you have lost Julia, but you don't have to run off wailing into the arms of the Claudii. You aren't one of those heartbroken young men from the comedies."

At which Nilla sniggered, ensuring that Brutus and my mother remembered that we were there.

A very strange affair took place that year and it involved my brother Brutus. It also shows you how influential my mother could be, and I remember being impressed. It started just a few months into Caesar's consulship and after Brutus had been rejected as a son-in-law in favour of Pompey. My brother made himself a thorn in the paw of The Three that year, along with Uncle Cato and others. It never occurred to me that this would get him into trouble because even I knew that Brutus was not yet important enough. The Three were busy fighting the whole Senate and Brutus was not even in the Senate. But one day, when he was due to come to dinner and I had taken up my usual place in the atrium to wait for him, I learned an important lesson in politics. As usual I ran up to him when he entered and flung my arms around him, but this time he did not sit and talk with me. He looked very stern and said today he could not stay.

"I must see Mother now," he said and headed off towards Mother's room. I was upset at first, but it did not take much thought for me to decide to sneak to a hiding-place in the garden, under the window of the room. I had discovered - not by chance but through deliberate effort - that if one stood on the path which ringed our courtyard garden, outside the window of my mother's room, it was quite easy to hear what people were saying inside the room, even if the wooden shutters were closed. Of course, one could not just stand there - too many of the staff would cross the courtyard for one reason or another, and it would be obvious that I was eavesdropping. None of the little benches dotted around the garden were close enough or I could pretend to be reading. But there was a large stone planter of flowers next to the box hedge just to one side of the window. Sometimes the hedge would be clipped into a strict cube or a globe, but given time it grew ragged, and the space between it and the planter was blurred with foliage. Then I could wriggle behind it and be hidden from everyone.

Brutus did not take up any time with niceties and it seemed my mother did not expect him to. As soon as he was in the room, they were talking and it meant that I, taking my time to crawl unseen up to the window, missed the first part of the conversation and had to work hard to understand.

"We must find out who is behind Vettius," was the first thing I heard. My mother. Brisk and in control, of course. Who or what was Vettius?

"Mother," and my brother sounded weary. "We know it is Caesar. Let us not pretend. He is using Vettius to disable the opposition to his preferred candidates at the elections. I have been attacked because it is too obvious to go for Uncle Cato. Curio is involved because he has been active in criticising The Three among the younger set. It is the same for Lentulus. We have been named because we are doing so well at discouraging people from supporting The Three's lapdogs."

Now you might think that a small child would make nothing of this, but when you have been born and brought up within sound of a riot in the Forum, then you catch on very quickly. Did I know anyone called Curio or Lentulus personally? No. Did I know the names? Of course. To me, it all made sense. My mother had advised Brutus to lead a group of younger, ambitious men against The Three, and now he and his friends were under attack in their turn. But Brutus was still speaking.

"Just think, Mother - if there is enough of a scandal, Caesar can get the elections postponed, and rule the summer visitors out. That core of respectable middle-class voters are just what Caesar, Pompey and Crassus don't want - your average merchant from Capua does not care two hoots about Pompey's prestige or which province Caesar gets to govern next year, they care about the economy being stable and the grain supply steady. They like predictability and they hate the element of scandal which people like Clodius bring."

"You don't have to harangue me about it," said my mother. "Clodius is a disgrace, and I cannot imagine what The Three see in him. The furore he managed to stir up over the Good Goddess scandal was destructive and without any gain."

Brutus sighed and said, "Back to my present problem…?"

"I shall go and see Caesar now," said my mother. "I shall congratulate him on his daughter's wedding and ask him to stop attacking you. He will not refuse."

This was the moment. My mother stated what she would do and what the outcome would be, with complete confidence. I stiffened under the window ledge, hardly daring to understand her. My first reaction was awe, then it occurred to me that Brutus must be in a lot of trouble if my mother was going to carry out an uninvited dinner-hour visit to the Consul. I waited for Brutus to try to discourage her. Instead after a pause, his voice, stiff and cold, said, "If you must."

"I am willing to consider any alternative proposal you care to make," said my mother in a similar tone. And then, after another pause, I heard only the scraping of furniture as they rose.

I noticed that Brutus accompanied her as the two of them left a few minutes later, then I went back to Juniatrium where dinner was being served and Nanny had a stiff word with me about disappearing at a most inconvenient time. It was only later when we all supposed to be asleep that I could tell my sisters what I had heard.

"But what has Brutus been accused of?" said Nilla immediately and I had to admit that I did not know. It must have something to do with the elections but that was as far as we could get. We discussed it a little further then went to sleep. Junia however had decided on a strategy. She asked Felix first thing the next morning, as we were settling down to our schoolroom tasks.

"Felix, dear, we know Brutus is in some sort of trouble and we are worried," she explained, looking as sweet and honest as only Junia could. And as she had hoped, Felix could not resist this. Felix had been Brutus' first tutor and he was proud of his pupil. He told us what the staff network knew, which was of course, considerable.

Vettius - I don't think anyone ever told me his full name - was a complete unknown, who had appeared before the Senate with no warning, dragged along to the meeting by one of the most respectable Senators one could imagine, Scribonius Curio. Curio announced that a conspiracy to assassinate Pompey the Great was being planned and that Vettius was his evidence that this was true.

"Pompey the Great?" said Nilla. "That would be terrible!"

"If Pompey were dead, our brother could marry Julia," I said, and Felix shot me a quick and worried glance.

"Let me carry on, all of you," he ordered quickly. "Or don't you want to hear what the Senate did?"

Scribonius Curio was alerted to the plot by his son, who had been approached by Vettius.

"As you all know, your brother has been leading opposition to The Three along with several friends, one of whom is the younger Curio," said Felix. "Young Curio very sensibly made no promises to Vettius, and immediately told his father. Together they persuaded Vettius to come along to the Senate and there tell the gathered Senators all about this plot. Vettius declared that a stranger he met in a bar who claimed to be the secretary of the Consul Bibulus, had given him a dagger to kill Pompey. Vettius had agreed to the killing - presumably he was paid well - but did not want kill Pompey himself so started recruiting likely people to do the deed for him."

At this point seeing the incredulity on our faces he stopped and decided to make an educational experience of it.

"Now you can all see the problems with this story, can't you? So - one at a time, I want you to point out something which you would notice if you were questioning this man in the Senate."

"Why did Vettius think he had been chosen by someone he didn't know to carry out such a dangerous act?" said Junia promptly.

"Why did Vettius agree to come and tell the Senate?" asked Nilla. "Hasn't he condemned himself? Or did Curio promise him immunity?"

"Why did he have to be given a dagger?" I asked. "Is he so poor he doesn't have one of his own?"

"Shh, Tertulla!" exclaimed Nilla. "The dagger isn't important. The strange thing is that the man who gave Vettius the dagger said he was employed by Bibulus. Everyone knows that Bibulus hates Caesar, but would a Consul really plot to kill his co-Consul?"

Felix nodded. "Vettius was questioned in the Senate by Marcus Cicero and gave the names of other conspirators, including your brother. But, as you girls have already pointed out, his story is thin and unlikely, and many people do not believe that these so-called conspirators were ever approached. Your mother and brother saw Caesar last night and I have no doubt that Caesar will make his own disbelief clear in the Senate today."

Even better, we later heard that Vettius had changed his story completely, no longer naming Brutus or some of the other men he had mentioned but adding a few more names instead. When he started accusing Marcus Cicero, friend of Pompey, the Senate began laughing at Vettius and he was taken off and placed in custody for the time being. A couple of days later, it was announced that he had been discovered dead in his cell, presumably by his own hand. No other details were given and the whole affair was dropped, but I remained curious and unsatisfied. I had been at the heart of a political family all my life. My family history was studded with rebellions and prosecutions and wars, and this seemed to me to be the most stupid bit of politicking one could imagine. Who was behind Vettius? Why was the conspiracy against Pompey? I puzzled at it over and over. When I asked Brutus, he was surprised at how much I knew but also quite pleased.

"You have been out recruiting informers, haven't you, Tertulla?" he teased, and I bristled, in no mood for this.

"Everyone in Rome is puzzling over it," I said shortly. "The point is - what was it all for?"

"Ah well, there, I am afraid I must disappoint you and tell you that there is not an official view, although nobody believes that Bibulus is behind it," said Brutus. "But you know enough to make a guess, I think, Tertulla. If the Senate had taken Vettius seriously, what would have happened?"

"The Senate would have held an enquiry and the elections would have been postponed," I said promptly, and he looked pleased. I smirked. Praise from Brutus was sweet. I decided to carry on and said, "And when the elections are postponed then people cannot come into Rome from the countryside around and they are the middle-class voters, the ones who will vote for tradition and stability. The ones who don't approve of The Three."

My brother's eyes widened at hearing his own ideas come back at him from his little sister. I hoped I hadn't been suspiciously clever, but he couldn't resist finishing off the argument and carried on.

"So if the elections had been postponed, Caesar and his colleagues would have had a much better chance of getting their own favoured candidates elected."

I thought. "Then the most likely person behind Vettius is Caesar? Does that really mean that Caesar is trying to get Pompey assassinated?"

"No, not at all - I don't think there is a real conspiracy at all. I think that Caesar and Pompey and Crassus are working together here. They want to scare people, so they set this story going, and sit back to await the uproar. Pompey is popular with the lower classes, and it would cause a furore if it were thought that he was in danger."

I considered this and it made sense. But Vettius didn't.

"Why did they choose someone as stupid as Vettius then?"

"I don't suppose they intended Vettius to be so clumsy." My brother shook his head. "All they have managed to do is make people like your uncle Cato more determined to stop The Three in any way they can."

"What about you?" I asked immediately. "Aren't you horrified that they tried to get you into trouble like this?"

"Yes," said my brother, "but I had to compromise. I did a deal with Caesar. My name was dropped and in return, I do not oppose any of the candidates they favour."

I knew that this would not sit happily with my brother's conscience, but he seemed quite calm about it. He saw what I was thinking and laughed. "Oh Tertulla, that is such a small thing, really. I don't like having to keep quiet, but politics always has its uncomfortable side, and we don't always get the deals we prefer. I shall be able to fight another battle, unlike poor Vettius."

"Vettius killed himself," I pointed out. "He took the honorable way."

"If Vettius killed himself, then I am the Queen of Armenia," said Brutus, then saw my face and clearly wished he had not spoken. "Forget it, Tertulla. Please. The whole thing is over, and I have taken no harm from it."

But I knew that this was not true. Brutus would not have enjoyed being hauled out of the fray by his mother's lover, and Vettius had been killed to bring the affair to an end, leaving a mess of questions which nobody wanted to clear up. It was, I considered crossly, most unsatisfactory. A rather uncomfortable little voice in my head was pointing out that the whole affair showed poor judgement on Caesar's part. I tried out my mind's picture of Caesar-my-stepfather, putting it next to this new picture, Caesar-the-inept-politician. They did not go well together. It was not that Caesar had been deceitful or a murderer, even. It was that he had been so - ineffective. He had taken a silly idea, chosen a fool to execute it and had achieved very little. He had not even been discreet or clever in the way he had tidied up after himself. I was quite offended. I wanted something a little better from him. I could not imagine what my mother thought of him at this time. I was sure that if he had asked her for advice, she would have contrived a much more successful plot.

"I have never heard this," said Sulpicia.

I shrugged. "It wasn't important, especially when you consider the context. Within ten years the Civil War had started, and we all had so much to think about. And it was something that had no repercussions - it died with Vettius himself."

Sulpicia shook her head. "I think the fascinating thing for me is that nobody has ever told me anything negative about Caesar. And your family and friends are the stuff of history to me."

"You make me feel old," I complained.

"That's because you are old," was the inevitable response. "But seriously, Tertulla, take your Uncle Cato. He was someone who defied the usual expectations we have when we encounter another person. As a poet, I am keen to explore characters as complicated as him."

"My Uncle Cato's main characteristic," I said, "was a conviction of his own righteousness. Allied with that was a lack of any passion in his life, and so you get the most peculiar person I have ever encountered."

"And yet he is almost the stuff of myth," pointed out Sulpicia.

"As long as nobody thinks him a hero," I muttered.

Chapter 7

Cato was my mother's half-brother, younger than her by about four years, and they loathed each other. My brother Brutus kept trying to convince her that Uncle Cato had good points, but she was having none of it. Uncle Cato was invited to family events only when Brutus insisted, and to be honest my sisters and I would hope that he was already busy, for he was a very embarrassing uncle. But whatever happened, my brother thought he was marvellous, and it was this blind adoration which began my disillusion with Brutus.

"I have spent a lot more time than you with him, talking to him," pointed out Brutus when Junia once asked him what he saw in Uncle Cato. "I see someone who is living his life according to his principles. He is disciplined and knowledgeable and stands up for what is right. He makes no compromise."

"But that is not normal for most people," said Nilla, who found our uncle's peculiarities distasteful and a serious threat to her making the sort of marriage she felt she deserved. "If we think something is right and Mother thinks it is not, we have no choice but to do things her way."

"People who are under the control of their guardians are doing the right thing by obeying," said Brutus immediately. "That is what Cato would argue."

The air was filled with the heavy silence of his three sisters bristling at him.

"Well, I think that is a very easy argument to make when you are your own person," said Nilla. "We are never going to be free from somebody's guardianship, so according to Uncle Cato, we shall never have to stand up for what we think is right because someone will tell us what to do, and we shall do it and that will be right."

Brutus laughed. "What has Felix been teaching you? Maybe I should complain to Mother."

This threat drew horrified cries from us all, and he laughed again, holding up his hands, pretending to ward off our complaints. "Peace! I would never complain about Felix, you all know that. He is doing exactly as he should in teaching you to use your intelligence. That is of course what your mother wants - and indeed your father when he was alive." Young men like Brutus frequently lapsed into rhetoric without even knowing it.

"Why doesn't Mother like Uncle Cato?" I asked and Brutus immediately put on his cautious face. He quickly looked at each of us, ascertaining that we genuinely did not know and relaxed at our ignorance. "Well," he began, in what was clearly not going to be a proper answer, "they are quite different personalities. That is at the heart of it. They really don't understand one another. Mother was the oldest of the family, and when she and her sister and brother were very young their mother and father divorced. Unusually, the children went with their mother to her new home with a new husband and I am not sure that was a happy time for Mother."

"Doesn't the father usually take the children when there is a divorce?" asked Junia. Brutus hesitated but eventually answered the question.

"Usually, yes, and I think our mother wanted that. But for one reason or another it did not happen. Anyway, it was then that her half-brother Uncle Cato was born. And then her mother died, and the children were all moved on again, this time going to live with their aunt Servilia and Uncle Drusus. And when Mother was about nine, first her Uncle Drusus was killed, in the actual atrium of their home, and finally her father died. That is a lot to take when one is a child."

We were all silent as we worked through this list of tragedies.

"Her other brother didn't grow up hating people though," said Junia and we all sat up and asked once more for the sad story of our favourite uncle's death. We weren't gruesome, but we loved the story, and you will see why.

"Uncle Servilius Caepio was Mother's younger brother, born just before our grandparents divorced," said Brutus settling into the well-known rhythms. "He was a happy baby and a happy young boy, even though he had to endure the sadness that all the children felt when they lost their parents before he was eight years old. And yet, there was a light in him which kept him smiling and drew people to him. He was an exceptional student, and everyone predicted a wonderful career for he was rich, handsome, and loved. In the year when Tertulla here was born, he married and had a daughter and was as happy as any young man of promise can be. He was asked by Pompey the Great himself to work with him as Quaestor and together they planned to sweep the Mediterranean clear of the terrible pirates. But as Caepio travelled to Asia to meet up with his commander he fell ill. An urgent message was sent to Thessalonica where his brother, Uncle Cato, was stationed as a military tribune, and he immediately set off. The weather was terrible and the only person willing to take Uncle Cato was the captain of a tiny little ship. Even hugging the coast all the way, they struggled and were nearly all lost in a mighty storm that hit them in the straits between the island of Thasos and the mainland. But Uncle Cato swore that the gods meant him to get through and gave everyone new heart. They struggled on and reached Caepio just in time - the two brothers wept their farewells and Uncle Caepio died holding his brother's hand."

There was the usual pause as the three faces turned towards him breathed in our dismay and waited for him to carry on.

"And Uncle Cato's grief for his brother knew no bounds. He who had always been so disciplined and philosophical, broke down and wept. The funeral was the most magnificent ever seen there in Thrace, with Cato commissioning the finest perfumes to be burned on the funeral pyre and the finest materials to be used to wrap the body. And afterwards, the little town saw the most beautiful monument to Caepio placed right in the middle of the town square. It was of pure marble and ..."

"And it cost eight talents," we chimed in as chorus to this tragedy. And the tale was over, while we wondered once more how much eight talents really was and what we would have spent the money on.

"As your only brother, I shall expect a very fine monument remembering me when I die," said Brutus. And when I hugged him and said I couldn't bear the thought of him dying, he said, "Well, then imagine how Uncle Cato felt. And maybe be a little bit kinder when you think of him."

I didn't mind being kind when I thought of Uncle Cato, I supposed. As long as I didn't have to think of him too much. The story of his love for his brother however was at odds with the person I occasionally saw. Saw, not met, for Uncle Cato never addressed a word to any of us girls. I had no doubt that he would not have recognised me if we passed in the street, which was just as well for I had no wish for casual onlookers to make a link between us. If you had the misfortune to encounter Uncle Cato in the street, you would think him mad, for he wore only a toga and no tunic, and his arms were completely bare. Nilla wanted to know what happened if the toga slipped, would we see what else he wasn't wearing? Junia always said "Hush!" but giggled and I always said "Ugh!"

Brutus always said that many people admired Uncle Cato for his adoption of a very old custom. He said it in the sort of voice which tells you that the person speaking is hoping that what he says is true but does not really think so.

Uncle Cato was also rumoured to go barefoot everywhere, but I did not believe that. Roman streets were no place to go barefoot if you could help it, for even up on the Palatine there was rubbish you could tread in, and the stones were broken in many places. Everyone was supposed to keep the area in front of their own homes clean but even though you saw all the slaves out sweeping in the early morning, by evening the streets were as cluttered as ever. And it wasn't as if we lived in the Subura, where apparently people emptied their chamber-pots out of the windows. Anyway, every time I saw him, he had sandals on.

But my Uncle Cato caused a scandal when he divorced his wife, Marcia.

Cato had married twice. I barely remembered Atilia, by whom he had a son Marcus and a daughter Porcia, but I went to his wedding with Marcia, who seemed a nice lady. She bore him several children though two died young. I found it disappointing that we never got to know our cousins well, but from what little my curiosity could discover she and my uncle lived together perfectly amicably. And so when, just before my sister Junia got married, our mother summoned us to her room, I was less prepared than I like. As usual, we stood in a row, with Junia in the middle to make sure that Nilla and I behaved. I stood carefully angled so as to be able to see my lovely wall-painting while apparently focussed on my mother's desk. I was so absorbed in my tree that it took me a crucial second or two longer than my sisters to grasp that Uncle Cato had divorced Aunt Marcia. He had sent her to be married to Quintus Hortensius, the famous orator, who was at least sixty and fancied having a marriage connection with Cato. I swung my head sharply to meet my mother's gaze and found myself saying far too loudly, "No!"

"For once, I sympathise, Tertulla," said my mother drily. "What your uncle is imagining I cannot even begin to…" and my mother for once in her life, lost the power of speech, though even as she shook her head, her face was smiling.

We looked at each other, Junia taking our hands and squeezing firmly so that we stood where we were, mute. Eventually Junia asked, "Mama, this will cause a scandal, won't it? Will it affect the plans for my wedding?"

"I have spoken with Lepidus and he is unaffected," said my mother. "Fortunately, most of Rome knows that your uncle Cato dances to his own tune and that we, his wretched relatives, are innocent of any of his follies. But there will undoubtedly be unpleasant comments and some of your friends may see fit to mention it. You will of course ignore them. Nilla, please pay attention - I expect you to be dignified about this wretched affair. Do you all understand?"

An obedient chorus answered this question and we were dismissed. I gave the middle tree a surreptitious pat and trailed in my sisters' wake, wondering if I would ever have enough money to have my room painted with a garden. I heard my mother start to laugh even before I had left the room.

Of course, as I grew and saw my sisters married and prepared for marriage myself, I found it hard to be so casual about what Uncle Cato had done. I imagined my mother's face if Junia announced that she was being divorced by her idiotic husband so that one of his friends could have her. No, the mere thought made me shiver. Fortunately, we had other examples of marriage to inform us, and I discovered that there was more to literature than Homer and Plato. Junia brought home a tattered little scroll lent her by a friend, a genuine Alexandrian romance, the sort of book we had been told to avoid and had hunted for ever since. Felix would have been horrified to know that at night we sat up into the dark hours and read each other the story of Callirhoe and Chaereas.

In this dreadful piece of improbable adventure, young lovers are allowed to marry, are immediately separated and only after going through many terrifying ordeals are they reunited. I think what really appealed to girls of our age was the idea that one could marry someone whom one loved. It was very much at odds with what happened to us and our peers. Callirhoe fell for Chaereas when they met by chance in the street and that was that - such a thing could not happen on the Palatine Hill.

"It was the god of love, Eros, who managed it that Callirhoe and Chaereas approached the same narrow bend in the road and collided with one another," read Junia in thrilling tones. "He just about crawled home, so struck was he with love, while Callirhoe went to the statue of Aphrodite and lay before it imploring the goddess to give her this young stranger as her husband."

"Can you imagine just walking along the road and you bump into someone and then it is as if Jupiter had hit you with a thunderbolt," said Nilla dreamily. "And then all you can think about is that one man…"

Junia and I gazed at her.

"And which man are you thinking of?" said Junia sharply.

Nilla came back to us and smiled. "Nobody of course. Go on, Junia."

"The god had already devised a plan and the whole city at its next assembly cried out for the two young people to be married.

With rejoicing, the streets were decorated and the dancing crowds accompanied Chaereas to his love's house, but when her nurse came into her room to tell her she was to be married, young Callirhoe was struck with grief. Never did she imagine that her husband would be the young man she had given her heart to."

"That really is very badly-written," I said critically but was hushed.

"Darkness covered Callirhoe's eyes," continued Junia, "and her knees buckled, and she fell across her bed. "She is just shy," cried her nurse and quickly she called the maids to get Callirhoe ready to meet her bridegroom. Half-fainting and stricken with grief, Callirhoe stumbled to the door - and there she saw the bridegroom led towards her by his parents - Chaereas!"

We all sighed.

"He ran to her and kissed her and life flowed back into her. It was as if a lamp had been lit inside her."

Junia put down the tattered little scroll and sighed. "A lamp lit inside," she said. "Is that what love is, do you think?"

"We only know a few people in love," said Nilla. "We could ask them."

"Who?" I asked. "I don't know anyone in love."

"Nanny and Felix are in love," said Junia.

"I don't see any lamp there," said Nilla and we giggled.

"Do you think Mother feels like that about Julius Caesar?" I whispered.

"You read that dreadful romance about Callirhoe?" Sulpicia was amused when I confessed.

"Doesn't everyone? Or do young women nowadays consider that terribly old-fashioned?"

"Well, it is old-fashioned, but we all read it," said Sulpicia with a grin. "Pirates, true love, violence and Persians - what more do you want in a good read?"

"What does it teach girls, though?"

Sulpicia looked surprised. "Nothing," she said. "We don't read stories like that to learn - do we?"

"The lovers triumph over all," I said. "That is a dangerous lie to present to girls."

"It is as far from the reality of its readers as a Homeric battle-scene," said Sulpicia. "Should we discourage the reading of Homer?"

Sulpicia is good at wrong-footing me.

Chapter 8

When I was ten years old, my sister Junia got married. This had been arranged by my parents before my father's death, and they had chosen Marcus Aemilius Lepidus, from a good family of course, even if his father had been killed during a rebellion or something. I was hazy on the details, but nobody seemed worried about it. Given the background of many members of my own family - my great-grandfather exiled, my grandmother divorced amidst scandal, and my great uncle Drusus assassinated - it seemed quite normal. Lepidus himself seemed pleasant enough when he came to dinner, years older than Junia of course, but good-looking. His eyes were large and dark, and he had lovely cheekbones, but I was fascinated by his beard. He followed the fashion amongst the younger men to have a small beard shaved into a line that went from hairline and along the chin like the strap of a helmet. It looked as though it was designed to keep Lepidus' hair on his head, so I had to be careful not to imagine what happened in windy weather or I got a fit of the giggles.

The wedding came at a good time for our family, still finding our feet after my father's death in addition, Caesar, had recently left to become Governor of Gaul and would be absent from Rome for five years. He had not married our mother, but he had married a daughter of Lucius Calpurnius, and we had not yet found out a great deal about who Lucius Calpurnius was, and what his daughter was like. My mother's mood did not alter noticeably, but I could not imagine her accepting this rejection at all.

On the morning of Junia's wedding, we all had our roles. My brother oversaw taking the auspices - as far as I could tell, this meant entertaining a friend who happened to be an augur on the roof of our house with cups of hot spiced wine until a bird flew past. Everyone then congratulated the groom, and the men drank more wine in the atrium until the bride was ready. Nilla and I went to my mother's bedroom to help get Junia ready.

Well, to watch the slaves, my mother and one of the Vestal
Virgins get Junia ready. The Vestal had brought her hairdresser
to do the elaborate hairstyle shared by brides and Vestals, and I
was curious to see how this was going to work. I had only ever
seen Vestals so thoroughly veiled and swaddled that one could
not tell what their hair looked like anyway so I was not sure why
their hairstyle was so important. I supposed the gods knew if the
hair was correct or not. I cannot now be certain, but the Vestal
may well have been the famous Fabia, who was accused of
impropriety with a man, but was acquitted and went on to
become Chief Vestal. She was an acquaintance of my mother -
of course - and probably related to us in some way or other. I
took a careful look at her to see if she looked like someone
capable of being improper and decided not. She looked like
someone who had been swathed in voluminous white robes all
her life and did not know how to be interested in men.

Junia looked terrible, as though she had spent all night awake
and then been sick, and my mother took one look at her when
she first entered and made her lie down. Nanny was sent off to
the kitchens to make a camomile and honey drink despite
Junia's muttered declaration that she could not eat or drink a
thing.

"Your breath must smell sweet," said my mother. "A great
many people will embrace you today and you need to smell
good inside and out. Have you washed all over as I asked?"

"Yes," said Junia miserably. "And I have brushed my teeth
well."

My mother bent over her and sniffed. She nodded and then
turned and watched as the slaves unfolded Junia's tunic and the
great square of yellow cloth which would veil her for most of
the day. A circlet of white and yellow flowers had been laid
carefully on the dressing table, and new slippers were tucked
under the stool. Junia was going to look like a bunch of spring
crocuses I thought and knew enough not to giggle at this picture.
I whispered it to my sister as she lay on the bed, hoping to make
her smile a little. It didn't work and I watched in dismay as a
tear emerged from under her closed eyelids and slid slowly over
the curve of her cheek. I wiped the tear away as gently as I could

using the sleeve of my tunic, and crouched next to her, putting my hand on her shoulder, and whispering, "I love you, Junie."

Nanny arrived then with the drink and Junia sat up. The tunic was inspected, brushed, and inspected again. Then from the huddled figure of my sister, the bride began to emerge. Junia was dressed in the tunic, and everyone stepped back while the Vestal's hairdresser set to work. With the familiarity of daily practice, the unremarkable-looking slave in a shapeless grey tunic parted strips of Junia's hair, twisting and pinning and braiding until Junia's pale face was surrounded by spiky plaits sticking out from her head. It looked awful and I was hard pressed to keep my face calm in case Junia caught sight of me. Then a braided cord was woven into the strands of hair around Junia's face, and all the plaits were gradually wound over and around her head. When she turned and looked at us all for a verdict, her hair was coiled in an elaborate and shining crown and her face was framed with the circle of the cord. She suddenly had grown from girl to young woman, and my mother smiled suddenly and gently kissed Junia's forehead. Nilla took my hand, and we slipped through the ring of adults to hug our sister and tell her how beautiful she looked. There were smiles all around us and my mother ordered wine to be brought to the room. The ladies sipped and giggled, while a couple of maids fastened the crown of flowers on top of the elaborate hair and draped the veil over Junia's head and body, tucking and pinning until she was swathed in yellow. She wasn't Junia anymore, but "the bride" a strange and ephemeral character, born only for this one day and different from all other women.

It was time to process to the atrium so that our brother could announce the omens. There was another flurry of activity as all the women in the room examined folds of robes, and re-pinned hair and veils. As I watched I saw my mother staring into space - something I rarely saw, as my mother always knew what she was doing, it seemed - and then she lifted her hands and fastened a chain around her neck. From it hung a single large cream-coloured globe and I thought how beautiful it was - so shiny and solid-looking. I had never seen it before, and I was not the only woman who stared at it. One woman said, "Oh my, Servilia, is that the pearl?" as though they had already discussed the necklace and I thought incredulously "That? That is a single pearl?" But my mother looked over towards Junia and everyone was suddenly terribly busy pushing the bride out of the door. All at once, Nilla and I were at the end of a long line of women, and only Nanny stayed with us.

"Nilla," I hissed. "Mother's new pearl…"

But Nilla muttered "Later."

"Come along you two," Nanny said in her best "hurry-up" voice. "Time to get you ready for the walk to your sister's new house." And she bustled us back to the Juniatrium, where Junia would never come again as one of us, one of the three daughters of Silanus. She would be a married woman, sit in Mother's rooms, and discuss the difficulties of training one's household staff. As we struggled into our own outfits, Nilla looked at me and said, "There are only two of us now." And Nanny clicked her tongue and said, "Your sister hasn't died, you goose."

"You'll be next," I reminded Nilla and smirked at her sudden look of horror. For the time being, the pearl was forgotten.

We arrived in the atrium just in time to miss the auspices. Nanny kept us firmly towards the back of the crowd of people who now thronged the hall, and I just looked, taking in colours and noise and enjoying the feeling of being somewhere where everyone was uncomplicatedly happy. Junia sat in a chair in the middle and streams of people flowed around the room, breaking the pattern to go up to her and say a few words, many of which made her laugh. These were all relatives or family friends, people who had known her all her life and now only wanted her happiness.

"Are we allowed to go up to her?" said Nilla, sounding unsure, a most peculiar state for her.

"When everyone else has had their turn," said Nanny. Felix appeared at our side, clutching a little scroll, and looking very tidy, though Nanny tutted and moved to tuck a stray hair behind his ear. He gently took her hand as it reached out and with a practised move placed it in the crook of his arm. Nilla and I exchanged glances as Nanny blushed.

When the stream of well-wishers had all drifted off to await the formation of the procession, our little group went up to Junia. For one moment I didn't know what to say so I just clutched Nilla's hand as Nanny and Felix gave Junia a kiss on the cheek each. Felix presented her with the little scroll.

"This is from us both," he said. "I copied it out myself. Some of my favourite poems, and ones I think you like too. May you be blessed, my little mistress." And to my amazement he and Nanny both had tears in their eyes. For one moment, Junia's regal pose on her special chair shimmered and she took the scroll, whispering "Thank you both, dear Felix, dear Ursilla." After a blank moment, I remembered that Nanny's name was Ursilla.

The time to go drew near and there was a swirl of draperies as the guests stood well back and let Brutus come forward. He took Junia to the corner where our family shrine stood and Junia burned incense and poured a little wine on the alter as we all prayed for her marriage. Then my mother unpinned a fold of the yellow veil and let it fall over Junia's face, and Brutus led her out of the house to process the few hundred yards across the Palatine to the house of Marcus Aemilius Lepidus.

The flutes and drums began playing outside the front door and grew fainter as the procession set off. Annoyingly, Nilla and I had to wait with Nanny and Felix and only joined the procession once all the grown-ups had gone. As we trailed along, we could hardly hear the music and we certainly couldn't see Junia. The streets on the Palatine are old and narrow and every time the head of the procession turned a corner the volume dropped, only coming up again if we managed to turn into the road before they reached the next corner. The people ahead of us had made a good job of trampling flowers and nuts into the ground which was a little sad. By the time Nilla and I came past, none of the well-wishers standing at the doors of their houses had any flowers or good wishes for us, in fact most of them were just dawdling and gossiping. The crowd outside Lepidus' house meant that we did not see Lepidus welcome our sister. I don't even know if he carried her across her new threshold as is often the custom. By the time everyone had squeezed into his house, the marriage feast was getting under way, with bride and groom sharing a couch for the first time. As family, Nilla and I were allowed to eat near the main table, and I could see that Junia looked a little dazed but not upset. She ate and drank a little wine and her new husband attended her very gallantly, making her laugh a couple of times. My mother and brother shared the couch with its back to us so I could not see their faces. Instead, I studied the relatives of Lepidus on the couch opposite. I guessed they were Lepidus' mother and two brothers. Lepidus' father, my father and Brutus' father were all dead. In fact, Brutus' father had died supporting Lepidus' father in a rebellion - maybe that had been one reason this marriage had been arranged?

Nilla and I were led away home as soon as the feast was over and for several days afterwards saw little of our mother. I hardly noticed this at first, for I was busy missing my sister. It was only when Nilla asked me if I thought that Junia's wedding had upset our mother that I immediately thought of Caesar.

"Maybe," I said in a whisper, as we sat enjoying the sunshine in the courtyard garden, "Junia's wedding has reminded her that she misses Caesar."

I felt very grown-up and daring to be gossiping like this.

"Well, if she misses Caesar, she has at least something worthwhile to remember him by," said Nilla mysteriously. I hated it when she withheld things from me like this, and was just about to retort with some insult, when it hit me. My mind flew back to the scene when we were dressing Junia before her wedding - my mother putting on a necklace - the woman's cryptic comment. It all suddenly made sense.

"Caesar gave her that pearl?" I forgot to keep my voice down and Nanny, bringing a basket of sewing with which we could display proper virtue, gave me a little tap on the shoulder.

"Enough, Tertulla. Don't gossip, especially when it concerns your mother." Ever since that scene after my father's funeral, Nanny had been firm about never allowing us to voice anything negative about our family. I held my tongue until I could creep into Nilla's little bedroom that evening - she had of course immediately moved into Junia's room - and ask her what she knew.

"I just overheard some talk at the wedding, you know, when everyone was in the atrium, waiting around. Everyone noticed that mother was wearing that pearl and I heard people whisper "Caesar". He gave it to her when he went to Gaul. It is very romantic, isn't it?"

Days later, when we remembered to ask Junia what she had heard about it, she told us further details. The gossip was that once Caesar had decided to marry Calpurnia, a girl hardly older than Junia, he had to decide how to break the news to Mother. He had softened the blow with a present of a pearl worth six million sesterces.

"That would console me," said Nilla, and Junia and I shrieked in delighted horror at how coarse and funny she sounded. I did think it was nice of Caesar though - a gift that precious must have told Mother that she too was precious to him.

When I told this story to Sulpicia, it was at the beginning of our friendship, and as we had broached the subject, I made the usual polite enquiry.

"Your uncle says you are engaged," I said. "Who is the lucky man?"

"Paullus Fabius Maximus," she said with no great enthusiasm. "He is currently serving as Quaestor to Augustus, so I don't expect him back in Rome until Augustus has finished reorganising the eastern provinces. Then we shall get married I suppose."

Her tone was everything I recognised in the young women I saw in the generations below mine They were torn between a respect for tradition and their parents, and a desire to explore the boundaries laid on them by life. They tried to put off marriage and childbearing, an attempt which I found fascinating. And they dreaded a repressive husband.

"You may find that he supports your ambitions," I said, knowing that Sulpicia had already formed a desire to write poetry.

"And I may find that he does not," said Sulpicia, her mouth drawing into a tight little line for just a moment. "But I daresay I shall manage. As long as he lets me write I don't care."

Chapter 9

I wondered if now Caesar was married, he would no longer see my mother. I would not like my husband seeing other women, though I was not so young that I did not know that such things happened. Women were divorced for it, but it was different for men. A woman's chastity was all-important while she was capable of bearing children because a husband had to be sure that any child borne by his wife was his. I understood that but pitied men for their lack of security. Why not, I thought, just trust the woman you married? If she was a decent person you had nothing to fear. I stopped short of applying that to my own parents though, because my father had known about my mother and Julius Caesar. Apart from anything else he would have been in the Senate when my mother sent Caesar the letter.

I have often wondered how I could have been so fond of my father Silanus, and yet so eager to replace him with Caesar. I do not know how to explain this to you. He was an excellent father to me, careful to make sure that I knew I was valued. The truth is that Silanus never achieved the dazzling fame of Caesar - and that fame was too attractive to reject. Of course, you may point out that when I first saw him Caesar was not yet even Consul and had not achieved the reputation he later acquired through war, and you would be right. Maybe you suspect that I am embroidering my recollections with what I have learned since and you may well be correct there too. I am not an expert on how the memory works. The truth is that Caesar was the most attractive and skilful politician Rome ever had, and he was my mother's lover.

But the reason I mention this again - the story about my mother writing to Caesar while he was in the Senate - is that it started to have a greater importance for me. I was old enough now to realise something significant about my mother's affair with Caesar. If gossip had Caesar as my mother's lover in the consulship of Marcus Cicero, in other words, when I was five years old, can you blame me for wondering if the affair had been

active when I was born? Or more pertinently, nearly a year
before I was born?

I had little time to discuss this interesting theory, and truth to
tell I was a little scared of broaching it with my sisters. Junia
was now an outsider, which may seem a cruel way of putting it,
but it is hard to carry on in exactly the same way, when your
sister is a married woman. She lived in a different house and
had so many things to deal with in the strangeness of married
life. She also got pregnant quite early on. I found this exciting
if worrying, but Nilla was no help, being obsessed with her own
wedding plans. Before I realised it, Nanny had gone to live with
Junia to help with the baby, and the Juniatrium was already
looking near empty by the time Nilla got married to the
extremely respectable Publius Servilius Isauricus. This time, I
was allowed to get more involved myself, the unspoken reason
being that I should learn as much as I could for my own
wedding. Isauricus himself held little interest for me. He was a
colleague of my Uncle Cato, and so much older than Nilla it
seemed ridiculous. But as she visited Junia, Nilla could see only
the advantages to marriage, a house to run as she pleased and
the relative freedom of being a married woman, once she had
done her duty in the matter of children. Having to bear children
was the lot of every woman who wasn't a Vestal Virgin, and
when hour nephew Marcus was born, we both doted on him.
We weren't allowed anywhere near Junia until she had
recovered from the birth, and she wouldn't say anything about
it. Nilla and I agreed that we would put that subject to one side
and not think about it until we had to. I concentrated on my
studies with Felix and tried to look forward to having the
Juniatrium to myself.

It was also time to persuade Mother to let me have a maid of
my own, I thought, as I carefully got out the wedding tunic for
Nilla. It was January, and Nilla was wearing a light undertunic
as well for the chilly walk through streets dull with winter light.
Fortunately, like everyone else we knew, Isauricus had a house
on the Palatine and the journey would not be long. I peered up
through the colonnade around the garden and hoped it would
not rain. This time, I would be walking behind my sister and I

74

did not want to risk having my new dress soaked. When you are overlooked and at the back of a crowd, nobody notices if you run for shelter. Now I was twelve and attending my sister, people would be looking at me. It was likely that my own future husband would be there as a guest or a curious spectator.

I ran various errands throughout the morning, preferring to be active rather than a spectator. Fabia, the Chief Vestal arrived with the hairdresser, possibly the same slave who had done Junia's hair, though I did not ask. Once more, the bride sat at my mother's dressing-table and the hairdresser took up her place. The braids were pinned into the elaborate circle which transformed Nilla into a long-necked, large-eyed beauty with perfect pale skin and - I was outraged - a pink mouth, lips slightly parted to show off the full lower lip and the tiny dip in the middle of the upper.

I bent as if to whisper something encouraging in my sister's ear and hissed, "You have coloured your lips...."

She could not yet move her head as the hairdresser fussed over the final details but the corners of her lips moved up. She slid her eyes to meet mine and whispered, "Yes. Stop being so young, Tertulla."

I stepped back, but not after a quick "I am so going to enjoy having all the space to myself tonight. I wonder how much space you'll have."

Being Nilla, she did not blush like the rest of us do, patches of red appearing all over our faces and necks - no, Nilla blushed with a hint of pink stealing over the apples of her cheeks. She looked like the painted statue of a goddess, only with the promise of flesh rather than stone under the layers of colour. I puffed out an irritated sigh.

I watched in silence as my sister put on the coronet of winter greenery and tiny flowers, and the yellow veil. Nilla became the bride in front of my eyes and I sighed with envy at how beautiful and different she looked.

We all admired Nilla, though not as much she thought we should, and my mother asked me to see where things were up to in the atrium. Glad to be freed, I skipped down the corridors to the public rooms and found my brother Brutus and the bridegroom sitting to one side of the atrium while people milled around. Isauricus was saying, "and they say he is about to send news of a very successful fighting season back to Rome, in the form of a book, of all things." Brutus looked uncomfortable so I knew they were talking about Caesar in Gaul. Isauricus was holding a scroll, and I realised that this was the record of the dowry. It had never occurred to me when Junia got married that she would bring with her a considerable amount of land and money, but I was much more aware of these things this time. No wonder bridegrooms always looked so pleased with themselves.

Brutus caught sight of me and waved me over.

"Are the women done, Tertulla?"

Isauricus   looked   startled.

"I had better get back to the house and make sure everything is ready," he said and smiled at me. "Junia Tertia, you look very fine today."

I was a little nonplussed at this and found myself saying, "Nilla looks lovely though."

"Then I am a very fortunate man and must go and prepare my home to receive her," said Isauricus. "Thank you for your time, Marcus Brutus and for your sister. I look forward to our future as brothers - and indeed sister, Tertia." And he strode confidently out of the atrium and into the street. I thought Nilla was quite lucky really. At least Isauricus noticed me, which Lepidus never did. Brutus gave me a quick hug.

"You are next, Tertulla, and I shall make sure you get a very special husband."

I laughed, partly because he had guessed what I was thinking and partly because we both knew that our mother would choose my husband just as she had done for my sisters.

"Were the auspices favourable?" I asked, to change the subject.

Brutus looked at me and said solemnly, "They were indeed. I have never seen a wood-pigeon as fine." And we both laughed.

After the offering at the family altar, we moved into the street and walking just behind my sister was a great deal more interesting than being at the back of the crowd, even if I got hit with leaves and nuts thrown by grinning spectators. I knew that the custom was to call out to the bride to wish her luck, and that people were what my mother called "a little free" with their remarks, but I had not realised that people would be quite so vulgar. For a reason which I cannot remember we had no drum or flutes, just a couple of singers, and they could not drown out the things that people were calling. Twelve-year-old me was shocked that complete strangers wished Nilla a successful wedding night - "No pain, no gain!" called out our extremely respectable neighbour (whom I knew to be a Senator) while his wife laughed and elbowed him. I could not see Nilla's face of course, but I thought her shoulders stiffened. Isauricus' house could not appear too quickly. As we reached the house, the crowd flowed to the sides of the front door and cheered as Isauricus strode forward and whisked Nilla up into his arms. She could not help a little shriek of surprise and everyone laughed and cheered all the louder. I had assumed that a man as old as forty would want to skip over that custom, and my approval for my new brother-in-law was confirmed. As I entered the house, I found myself hoping that whoever married me would be strong enough to lift me so easily.

In the Juniatrium when I returned to our house in the early evening, I felt alone. Nanny was living with Junia, helping with young Marcus and waiting for a second baby to be born. Only Felix was around, and as I went down the corridor, I caught a glimpse of him sitting at his desk in his own room. I would not disturb him. I must make a life for myself now and it would begin the next morning when I would go to my mother and ask about getting myself a maid. And I suddenly stopped just as I was about to go into the Juniatrium. What would Felix do once I was married? I could not remember my life without Felix in it. And if Mother decided to let him go or sent him somewhere else, say to run one of the country houses, would she let Nanny go with him? I thought not, for Nanny was still a slave and useful here in Rome. I went to bed that night with a determination to get things sorted. Of course, it did not cross my mind that Felix, as a freedman, might be quite eager to move away from the family.

On the next day, I went with my mother to visit Nilla on her first morning as a married lady. To mark the occasion, my mother went by litter and I walked alongside her with Felix.

"We must get you a maid," remarked my mother as she lay back in the litter, her own maid arranging draperies and blankets.

"I would like that, Mother," I said, and in my mind crossed one thing off my list. Maybe persuading my mother was going to be easy.

Nilla looked well, seated in the middle of a small but beautifully furnished sitting-room. Someone with an eye to colour had decorated it with furniture was in a light wood, and the coverlets and cushions were in dark blues and greens This contrasted well with the pale walls, which had a very traditional style of painting - neat rows of rectangles pretending to be different colours of marble. Nilla looked around and said, "Isauricus says I had better decorate it to suit myself as soon as possible but I quite like it as it is."

In a dark red dress and an air of satisfaction, she glowed in that room. I smiled at her, my frustrations of yesterday forgotten. Then Junia arrived, now waddling a little and the talk turned to babies. Nilla was positively enthusiastic about this subject now and I listened and stored up the information. No longer would I hide from this part of my future. When I got married I was going to be prepared.

The first part of my plan was resolved with the arrival of Kleia, smiling and chatty, from the household of a friend. Girls from our own household had been trained up to accompany Junia and Nilla as they left our home, but Kleia had been suggested because she just the right age and so my mother swapped a kitchen assistant (apparently we had one going spare) for her. I have always approved of this method of acquiring key slaves. It is much less risky than using a dealer, and I have never met a slave-dealer I trusted. Slaves are a necessity in our society, but they are still human beings, and to make a living out of selling them is intrinsically sordid. Kleia suited me very well and I quickly established a close relationship. Part of the success of the relationship lay in my decision that I must accept her as a person in her own right, and so I found out about her as soon as I could.

"Where do you come from?" I asked politely, careful not to sound as though I were interrogating her. I didn't want her to think I was looking for faults.

"I don't rightly know, lady," she said. "Somewhere to the north, somewhere with lots of snow, I think. I was barely more than a baby when I was made into a slave. I was captured with my mother I know that much but she died before we got to...." She stopped and looked at me: maybe she thought I looked sad. "Don't you worry, Miss Tertulla," she said. "I can hardly remember any of that. What I remember is growing up in the girls' dormitory on the estate owned by my old master. It wasn't a bad life at all, we played in the orchards and the gardens. We did lots of work of course, there was this fierce lady trained us all, but she looked after us too, you know? And then I was picked to come and work in the house in Rome. I loved that. This is an amazing place." She stopped as if aware she had been talking too much, and I turned and looked at her properly for the first time. I saw someone folding and tidying my clothes, a little red as if she were worried she had chatted too much.

So - she loved Rome. I considered this - did I love Rome? I had no idea. It was just where I lived and I knew little about it, with my life more or less confined to the top of the Palatine Hill.

"What do you like about it?" I asked her, and she stopped folding and stood with a tunic in her hands, looking into the distance as she considered.

"I think I like the temples best," she said, "So solid you can see the gods living in them almost. They are fixed - you can see that they aren't going anywhere anytime soon."

The city's temples had been part of my life ever since I could remember, trooping down on festive days to make offerings, mostly in the temple of Vesta, my mother's favourite, but sometimes Juno on the Capitoline Hill.

"Do you know Rome well, then?" I asked her.

"Oh yes," she said. "When we first got here from the estate, there were four of us new to the city so one of the house slaves was put in charge of us and for two days our orders were to go all over the city, find our way about. We had a great time."

She smiled at this memory, then started folding once more, placing the tunics in the chest at the foot of my bed.

I watched her and thought. It was quite likely then that Kleia had seen more of Rome and knew more about the city than I did and she was a slave.

I did wonder sometimes after that if I could persuade Kleia to take me on expeditions around Rome - but I knew that this would not do. Just the quality of our clothing would attract trouble and though I could ask my mother for a couple of bodyguards, that would take the fun out of it. I put it to the back of my mind and picked up the scroll of poems next to my bed. Kleia made a tidy parcel of the dirty laundry and left to deliver it to the washerwomen in their lair at the very back of the house.

She stayed with me until she died of a tumour years ago, far too soon for me to get around to freeing her. I never found anyone else who suited me quite as well, because the maid who grows up with you, who accompanies you from your family home to your husband's - that is something which cannot be replicated.

Chapter 10

And now to tell you about Cassius. It was in the autumn of the year that Nilla got married, and I was thirteen years old. Junia had had two sons by now, so everyone was pleased and Nilla was hoping this was a good omen for her as she awaited the birth of her first child. The Consuls were Crassus and Pompey, and Pompey was still married to Julius Caesar's daughter Julia, whom I knew a little through my sisters. They moved in the same circles of young aristocratic married women. Julia was thirty years younger than her husband, Pompey, and the age difference still seemed grotesque to me, but it was not unknown, and it reminded me that we married to further our family's fortunes. Looking back, I seem to have thought of nothing but my own marriage at that time. I had asked all the usual questions of my sisters when I was visiting them, and between them they had scared the wits out of me with gruesome descriptions of their wedding nights. Then they had drawn up a wish-list of suitable men for me with no hint of irony. Neither of them had thought of the man my mother chose. He wasn't already an up-and-coming star, like Lepidus and he wasn't a distant relation like Isauricus. But when I was summoned to my mother's room, I got Kleia to do my hair quickly and took her with me, because I had a feeling I was going to need her.

Gaius Cassius Longinus. Thirty-one years old and one of the junior officials of that year. Good name. Good family. Not related to us. I dissected each piece of information as my mother told me, and then tucked it away for future examination, once more the mouse at the hole, waiting for crumbs.

I was not required to say anything during this interview. My mother finished talking, asked if I had any questions and when I said that I did not, informed me that my future betrothed would attend a dinner in three days' time. She and my sisters and their husbands would be there.

"Will I be there?" I asked in a sudden fit of panic, wondering if once more I would be the third daughter, too young and left in the nursery.

She looked at me with exasperation. "Yes, Tertulla. He is coming to see you after all." Her tone was not quite withering.

I nodded and tried to calm my breathing.

She turned back to her desk, and picked up a wax tablet, pen already in her hand. The audience was at an end.

Once outside the room, Kleia and I looked at each other, then ran back to the Juniatrium, where Felix waited, agog. Of course, the slave network knew exactly what was happening. We all huddled round in a circle, laughing and speculating, and Kleia cried a little out of sheer excitement. I hugged her and said that of course she must come to my new home with me. Felix beamed and patted my shoulder then went off to confirm the gossip with kitchen staff.

Kleia decided that my wardrobe needed an immediate examination, so I was left on my own to go and sit in the garden with a scroll of one of my old favourites, the Odyssey, and I pretended to read it while thinking of Gaius Cassius Longinus. He was almost the same age as my brother, and Brutus had met him while studying under the same tutor. He came from an old family, and a distinguished one. "His family's reputation is that of not standing tyranny in any form," reported my mother. I wondered what he thought of the current political situation - it was clear that Caesar, Pompey and Crassus were still running Rome as they pleased. Was that a tyranny, a tyranny of three men? I wondered if my new husband were the sort of man who would explain it to me or expect me to have no curiosity. I was confident that I could change him if he turned out to be one of the latter. Nilla had once said that being married was quite pleasant once you got used to things, and that her Isauricus was very polite and often charming to her. Junia had said, "I am the mistress of Lepidus' house, and it is worth everything just for that."

Sulpicia hardly ever speaks of her marriage. She married Paullus Fabius Maximus who was a devoted supporter of

Augustus – he even died in the same year as Augustus, which is taking loyalty to a ridiculous limit. Sulpicia dutifully and quickly produced a child, a girl, and I saw very little of her as domesticity held her tightly in its toils. She certainly did not attend as many of her Uncle Corvinus' literary evenings, and we all missed her. Later she told me that it reminded her too much of her former life, and leaving at the end of the evening, knowing what she was going back to, was too hard. Sulpicia was divorced by her husband as soon as another, more Augustan, wife was waved in front of him.

"I was so relieved - and so humiliated, Tertulla," she confided.

Her uncle was sufficiently annoyed to ensure that he got Paullus Fabius Maximus to settle a respectable amount of money on his blameless wife, and she and her daughter moved back into Corvinus' house where the two of them live still. She is as good an advertisement for never remarrying as I can think of.

I still remember that first dinner with Cassius, or parts of it, at least. And I think the memories are accurate though nowadays I sometimes remember things which I later realise are just dreams. Or maybe the slaves are all lying to me to confuse me. But I do remember being overwhelmed with shyness which was quite unlike me. We all met up in the atrium, Mother and I greeting the guests as they arrived. Junia and Nilla arrived together, husbands in tow, and Nilla got special hugs as her pregnancy was now known by all. When Brutus came in, talking to a tall man of his own age, I quickly stood behind my mother, as if this would let me remain invisible while I inspected my betrothed. I decided that he made a good first impression. For one thing, he came straight up to me and my mother, and made sure to smile at me first. I'm sure my mother didn't like that, but I was heartened. He called me Lady Junia too, very proper, and when Brutus said, "Oh we all call her Tertulla", Cassius looked at me for permission to do likewise. I relaxed a little. Then he gestured to a slave near the door and the man came forward carrying something covered in a cloth.

"I consulted widely about a present for you, Tertulla," said Cassius as he drew off the cloth and showed me two little finches in a cage, delicate creatures with beautiful green and red colouring, who blinked sleepily at me and made enquiring chirrups. They were perfect and I could not believe how charming my future husband was. From that moment, I made up my mind that this marriage was going to be a good one, and I even risked a couple of quick smirks to my sisters who, I knew perfectly well, had been unimpressed with their husbands at first acquaintance. My mother pronounced my gift "sweet" and handed them over to Kleia, remarking, "I hope they don't make too much mess, Tertulla." And she sailed off toward the dining-room, leaving me to wonder why she had felt it necessary to say that. We sorted ourselves into pairs and followed her, while Brutus strolled behind us all, saying "Now behave yourself with my friend, Tertulla," just to make me blush. Of course, over dinner Cassius was not allowed to be next to me. Instead, he shared a couch with my mother and brother, while Junia and Nilla had a couch each alongside their respective husbands. I sat on a chair as usual – my mother had decided that none of us would recline at dinner, however fashionable it was, until we were married. I was higher up than everyone else, and sat up straight, enjoying this superiority, and watching Cassius Longinus closely. As the slaves brought around water and towels and we all busied ourselves washing hands, I found myself looking closely at his long, thin fingers, very brown and sort of used-looking. My hands were pale and smooth, small and delicate. I laughed inwardly at the thought of me being considered delicate, and flexed my small hands, imagining them as fit for nothing more that wearing rings and bracelets, and wielding the odd pen or needle. As I looked up again, I found that Cassius was smiling at me, rolling his hands in and out of the towel, then flexing them in imitation of me before handing back the towel with a mock-flourish, never taking his eyes off me. I stifled a giggle and hoped that my mother hadn't noticed as she spoke with the steward about the order in which she wanted certain dishes to be brought in. This was a daily ritual. Aretus would pretend that he did not have ten years or more of running a major household, and my mother would pretend that she was genuinely interested in nothing more than the napkins and whether the eggs were fresh. They seemed to enjoy it, and certainly they fooled nobody so they can only have done it to indulge themselves. Maybe, I thought, I would find myself doing the same sort of thing when I was running Cassius' household. I asked where his house was, and it was on the Palatine of course. I am sure that people lived elsewhere in Rome, but I did not know such people.

"Which reminds me," said Cassius. "With my parents dead and my sister married, mine has become a bachelor establishment, and I wondered if the Lady Junia - Tertulla - would be very kind and bring some staff of her own to help me put the house into the right sort of state. I am going to entertain a great deal I am sure, and I would like my lady to feel comfortable in my house."

And he raised his wine cup to me. I wished that I blushed prettily like Nilla and did not dare look at my sisters.

"I think that is such a kind idea," said my mother approvingly. She too liked Cassius.

"Mother, do you think I might take Felix?" I asked quickly.

"Felix? Your tutor?" My mother sounded surprised, but before she could point out that a highly educated Greek tutor would not be the best choice for running the establishment of an up-and-coming politician, Cassius himself answered.

"Your tutor? That might be just what I need - could he run my library do you think? And maybe he could help tutor my little boy?"

There was a slight pause as my sisters looked at me to see how I took this. Little boy? Why had my mother not warned me? I looked at the floor and told myself that it didn't matter, of course he had been married before, lots of people were. But why had nobody told me? My mother was speaking, saying something I could not hear, and I looked at Junia pleadingly.

"Oh yes," said Junia suddenly, and may all the gods bless her, she said just the right thing to distract me. "Felix is so well-read and really does love books - you could not hope to get a better librarian. He would be an excellent secretary and tutor."

"We all love Felix," chimed in Nilla. "What a good idea, Tertulla."

And my mother had no option but to offer to ask Felix if he would work for Cassius as librarian-cum-secretary.

"When you are married, of course," she said. "I suggest that Felix stay here in the meantime as Tertulla can still use a tutor."

She made me sound like a child and I seethed.

"How old is your son?" Junia again, gently asking the questions I could not.

Cassius was looking at me and raised his cup to take a sip before he answered. I wanted to drop my eyes again - I am sure that a modest Roman girl should drop her eyes - but instead I just gazed at him, not knowing what I wanted him to say. The shock was beginning to wash away, and common sense was repeating its soothing refrain: "It's normal. There isn't anything to worry about. It's normal."

"He is three," said Cassius. "He lives with his mother and grandparents, and I don't intend to bring him to live with me for some time. Tertulla, I do not expect you to step straight into the role of stepmother, especially as the marriage will not take place for some time. In fact, regarding a date…"

I stiffened.

"Lady Junia Tertia," he said, looking straight at me, "I do not have any intention of marrying you until you are at least fifteen, not because I am reluctant, but because I have far too much respect for your brother, your mother and for you. You need to feel confident that you would like to marry me and I think a couple of years will help you feel that confidence. In the meantime, I have been asked to join Crassus' army when he goes on campaign against the Parthians. And as you know I am Crassus' Quaestor this year so I am bound to go with him."

"You're going to fight in Parthia?" I could not keep the note of alarm from my voice.

"Yes, Tertulla, I am. And I shall come back with the jewels of a Parthian queen and give them to you for our wedding," said Cassius.

"I don't care about jewels," I said automatically, and Junia laughed.

"That is true, Cassius - don't bring her jewels, but look for a picture or a book, or…"

"A monkey," said Nilla and managed to wink at me without our mother seeing.

"Or all three," said Brutus and I laughed.

For the rest of the dinner I looked at Cassius and watched how my family reacted to him. I liked what I saw. My mother was formal of course, but as near relaxed with him as with anyone I could think of. My brother was his friend already. Junia approved of his thoughtfulness towards me and Nilla, absorbed in her pregnancy and busy flirting with her indulgent Isauricus, thought that Cassius would do. He had promised to take care of Felix and I felt confident that with Kleia as well, I would hardly know that I had left home. I would arrange for a little room that would be mine, all mine - and I would have that room painted with Parthian deserts and palm trees filled with monkeys…

"Tertulla!" said my mother loudly and I realised that I had been dreaming. I straightened my back hurriedly and felt my cheeks flare up. But my mother just thought it was time for a young lady to retire. Junia got up saying she would have a quick chat with me, and we left the dining room after saying goodnight to Cassius. I was pleased to see that he got up and made a little bow as he said goodnight. He had convinced me of his thoughtfulness and good manners, and I liked the hints of humour I had observed during the meal. I felt quite satisfied.

Kleia had made the Juniatrium look very welcoming by lighting a couple of lamps and arranging a group of chairs around a table with drinks and some fruit laid out, and Junia made approving noises as she sat and popped a grape into her mouth, looking around.

"Goodness, I miss this place."

I sat down next to her and tucked my feet up under me, in no mood for a bout of reminiscing - after all, this suite of rooms was still my life, and it held no rosy glow of nostalgia yet.

"Cassius, Junie - what do you think?"

She laughed.

"Oh Tertulla, he is lovely – why? Don't you like him?"

I looked around the room and spotted my two new finches on a table in the corner. The two birds were sleepy, but one had his glinting black eyes on me and made a quiet chirp when he saw me looking at him. I could not resist smiling.

"Yes of course I like him. He brought me the birds, so he is clever, and he thought about making me feel welcome and at ease. Did you notice how quickly he realised that I wanted Felix?"

"And how he came up with an unbeatable argument," nodded Junia. "Yes, he will do you, Tertia. I don't think we need to worry about him."

There was a strange emphasis on the word "him" and I looked at her.

"Junie? What do you mean? Are you all right?"

She looked a little shaky - her mouth wobbled as if she was overwhelmed that someone had thought to ask her.

"I've been feeling a little low and very tired since Quintus was born. Nanny says it often happens that after giving birth, you feel a bit sad."

"Really?" I was surprised. "I have never heard that. I thought you felt marvellous if you had a baby."

"Well, yes, you do, but it sometimes feels all - a bit much," and she shrugged though her eyes were a little bright. "Take no notice of me, Tullie."

"Nobody calls me Tullie anymore," I said, and forgot that she was sad.

"Do you mind that he has a son already?" asked Junia gently.

I thought. "No. I was a bit surprised because nobody had told me. But it is perfectly normal that he has been married, doesn't it? Is his other wife dead or divorced, do you know? I didn't like to ask."

"Ex-wife, Tullie," said Junia automatically, then thought. "I don't know who she is or was, I'm afraid, but that probably means she isn't very important. Brutus will know. In any case, whichever it is, you are going to be his wife now and he clearly likes you and wants to make you happy. I think that is all that need concern you."

With that, she hugged me, saying that she had better be getting back. And when she had gone, Kleia put me to bed, and I slept with a smile on my face - or so Kleia said. The finches woke me early the next morning and were indeed very messy. I still thought Cassius had been clever.

Chapter 11

When my friend Sulpicia was newly divorced, she circulated a small number of poems amongst her group. The poems were unusual in that, like Catullus, Propertius, Tibullus, and Ovid and all the others, she talked candidly about love, but the difference was that she was a woman and so nothing quite like her poetry had ever been heard before. Corvinus lent me a scroll with the warning not to distribute it any further, and we all kept this confidence. Sulpicia's parents and ex-husband would have been none too pleased at the idea of these frankly hotblooded poems being widely read. Later, after everyone from that group was dead, the poems appeared under Tibullus' name as a posthumous discovery. It was noted that Tibullus had depicted love from a woman's point of view with imagination and brilliance.

"I hope very much for her own sake that these poems are not autobiographical," I remarked as Corvinus greeted me at the party held to honour his niece and her new-found freedom. I looked around but Corvinus drew me over to a comfortable couch at one side of the room and away from the small group of young men already arguing about which Greek poet was the best model to use for Latin verse. Corvinus and I were easily the oldest people in the room and therefore ignored.

"Jupiter, no," he said. "My niece has never been in a situation where she could experience the - ah - ..."

"Bliss of physical passion?" I suggested. Corvinus shuddered. "Good gods, Tertulla, do you have to? I mean they are good poems, don't get me wrong, but do you realise how awkward it is for me whenever one of these young idiots discusses them, or quotes from them?"

"And yet you don't get embarrassed when Ovid trips out one of his poems," I observed.

"Ovid isn't my niece," said Corvinus. "Where's the wine? Honestly, you'd think one of the slaves would have noticed us by now, wouldn't you? Especially as they are my slaves serving my wine."

I looked at the small knot of thirsty young literati in the centre of the large room where Corvinus held his gatherings. With them around, noisy and demanding and so sure of their own rightness, no slave was going to notice us. I sat up straight and used my best "Roman matron" voice to say, "Young man!"

As one they turned towards me.

"Your host and I are thirsty," I said. "Where is the wine?"

The group of young men broke up good-naturedly, one of them coming over to enquire politely after my health, while others searched for the slave with the wine jug.

Later, I put to Sulpicia my question about her poems being autobiographical, and she laughed. She has avoided telling me the truth, but I hope she has experienced the love described in those verses.

Cassius came to dinner several times and brought a small and tasteful gift each time. My favourites, apart from the finches of course, were a silver necklace with a beautiful drop of lapis lazuli hanging from it - maybe I could grow to like jewels after all - and a tiny scroll with a poem by Catullus copied out on it by Cassius himself, after asking the poet's permission. It was a sweet poem about the poet's jealousy of his lady's pet sparrow.

"Catullus is getting ready to publish his collected poems next year," explained Cassius, "So I really did have to get down on my knees and beg for this as a favour. Fortunately, he likes me."

This made my mother look quite sharply at Cassius and I knew what she was thinking. Catullus, that most fashionable and daring of poets, was the darling of a very scandalous set. Junia had met the poet at a friend's house where he was giving a recital and she told the story of how Catullus had actually had an affair with the infamous Lady Clodia Metelli. My mother had not yet invited him to one of her parties, and I knew better than to ask her about him. Felix told me that only my mother should give permission for me to read any of Catullus' poems and so once more I had to rely on my sisters to find out about the new poet.

"What was he like?" I asked Junia impatiently.

Junia thought and said, "Bright-eyed. On edge. Tertulla, some of those poems were addressed to a boy, love poems…."

I found that this did not bother me particularly, because Felix had made me read quite a lot of Plato's dialogues as well as the Iliad and if the Greeks weren't upset about such things then I didn't see why I should be.

"He read a few poems and they were good, in Greek metres and reeking of the smart set," said Junia, sounding old beyond her years. She was not yet twenty.

"And what does that mean?" I challenged her.

"Oh, you know…" Junia waved an impatient hand, as though sweeping away an irritating insect, though I did not know whether that insect was Catullus with his fancy verse or her little sister.

"No, I don't know, Junia," That made her laugh.

"I'm sorry, Tullie, of course it must be frustrating for you. I meant that the people who hang around Clodia Metelli and her brother have their own vocabulary, "in" words, things like that. They behave as though all they have to do is to lounge around quoting poetry and making eyes at each other."

From which I gathered that Lepidus liked Clodia Metelli more than he should.

"The men all wear ridiculous beards, little tufts on their chins which makes them look like they are only just preparing for their coming-of-age ceremony and the women dress as little as they think they can get away with."

My eyes widened at the thought of Junia attending this sort of party. But she carried on, "Not that I see all this of course, Lepidus doesn't take me to such gatherings, I just hear things. Amongst my friends, he is considered daring and fashionable, so a few of them persuade their husbands to invite him."

I was opening my mouth to ask for more details when two things struck me at once. Firstly, I remembered the ridiculous little beard Lepidus had sported when he first married Junia. Now he was more serious about his politics, he had gone clean-shaven. And I wondered if Cassius had got that poem of Catullus for me at one of Clodia's parties. Well, what if he had? And what if Lepidus had once been one of the smart set hanging around Clodia Metelli? If there was one thing my mother had shown us, it was that there was a big difference between love and marriage. If Junia could handle being married to Lepidus, then it was none of my business whether he shaved his beard or not, and if Cassius was agreeable and civilised, then so would I be. And I would not ask too many questions.

Pleased with my own mature insights, I asked both my sisters if they loved their husbands and got an immediate "No" from them both. Though Nilla said that she thought there was a possibility that she might one day.

"I do find Isauricus very charming, and he really is thoughtful and kind to me," she said, stroking the creases in her tunic smooth over the vast bump of her stomach. "He is terribly excited about the baby and so sweet. He saw some little tunics that a woman was selling on a market stall and bought them, so pleased with himself. And they won't fit before the baby is at least two, I would think."

Junia and I laughed - we had never heard of a man buying baby clothes before. We had between us made dozens of little tunics of all sizes for Junia's babies and she had saved up the ones that had survived for Nilla's child. My mother thought that this provided a good example of the sort of thrift that a Roman lady was supposed to display. Yes, about a hundred years ago, I thought to myself.

Cassius was often the subject of the gossip we exchanged, as I had been able to pin Brutus down one afternoon when he was visiting our mother and he answered all my questions. Yes, Cassius had divorced his wife, after discovering that she was flirting - Brutus shot me a quick look there to see how much I understood - with another man. She was still bringing up their little boy at her parents' house, though the plan was that he would come to live with his father permanently once Cassius returned from the East. Brutus had tales to tell of Cassius at school - how he had defended a friend from bullies, how the two of them, Brutus and Cassius, had once fallen out over a speaking competition held by the teacher. Cassius had even fought with Faustus, the son of the tyrant Sulla, when Faustus started boasting about his father at school.

"He can't bear unfairness or hypocrisy," said my brother, smiling at the memory.

"Well, who can?" I asked

Brutus looked at me. "As people grow they find they have to put up with all sorts of things they don't like just to get on in life. Cassius and I for example both disapprove of the way in which Caesar and Crassus and Pompey arrange the whole of Roman government to suit themselves. But Cassius is a Quaestor this year and his job is to serve the Consul, Crassus. He has to work with Crassus and Pompey as best he can and for someone like Cassius that is hard."

I thought about this.

"What about you? You will have to be a Quaestor and work with men you don't approve of, won't you?"

Brutus nodded.

"I shall manage. By the way, Tertulla, did I tell you that I have a job in the Treasury, organising the mint next year?"

I couldn't imagine anything more boring and politely congratulated him.

All this was faithfully reported to my sisters as we met, sewed, and chatted more frequently as Nilla's baby's birth got nearer. I found it interesting that since marriage, Junia's opinions had firmed up and she expressed them more confidently, while Nilla's had barely changed.

"Brutus will enjoy working in the Treasury," said Junia with a critical tone. "Our brother is very fond of money."

Nilla laughed and I said, "What do you mean?"

"I mean that our dear Brutus has a vacuum in his conscience where profit is concerned," said Junia and pinched viciously at a strand of thread which marred a little wrap of yellow cotton.

Nilla, lying on a couch and watching us work, yipped a little shocked laugh and said, "Really Junia, you will puncture all her bubbles."

"I don't know what you mean," I heard myself say, a little whining complaint with just a hint of panic.

Junia sighed.

"Oh dear. I'm sorry, Tullie, I know how much you look up to our brother, but he is not perfect, and you must know that."

"But - you said, "a vacuum in his conscience", Junie - that is horrible! What do you mean?"

"I mean that our brother is a money-lender, Tullie - which he is not supposed to do, as someone hoping to become a Senator. And he charges an illegal rate of interest."

I opened my mouth to complain then stopped. I did not disbelieve her.

"Lending money," I said and could not avoid the disappointment in my voice.

Nilla stretched and said with a smidgeon of malice, "Yes it really is quite low, isn't it, Tertulla?"

I wished she didn't have to enjoy my disillusion quite so much, and said so, but she laughed.

"I don't enjoy you being sad, Tullie, but I don't see any reason not to criticise hypocrisy when I see it. And Junia has a point, it really is time that you knew about Brutus. Have you never heard people talking about what happened in Cyprus?"

"Cyprus?"

"Yes, Cyprus, Tullie. Come on, what happened when old King Ptolemy of Egypt died a couple of years ago?"

"Uncle Cato went out to sort out the transference of Cyprus to Rome - because the old Pharaoh had left it to Rome in his will or something."

"And darling Brutus went with Uncle Cato to get some valuable experience under his belt," said Nilla, sounding very much as though she was enjoying this. I started to feel a little ill.

"Well, Brutus also set up a side-line lending money to the Cypriots as a private concern," said Junia." At an illegal rate of interest."

This I did not understand for my brother was wealthy enough, surely?

"Why does he need the money?" I asked, and Nilla sighed.

"Everyone needs money, Tullie. Nobody has enough money to do everything Rome expects of them. They all have sidelines. Cicero isn't allowed to earn money from his speeches in the lawcourts but is allowed to receive presents and gets property left to him in people's wills. Lots of Senators run businesses through freedmen. And people like Brutus and Crassus make links with the business community and use them to get around the regulations."

"You make it seem as though the whole Senate is corrupt," I said miserably.

"Not the whole Senate," said Junia, as cynical as Junia ever got.

"Not corrupt really," said Nilla. "Just very good at playing the system. Making it work for them."

"I thought we are all supposed to work for Rome," I said.

Junia took pity on me.

"Your Cassius is going to fight for Rome, with Crassus," she said. "He won't be looking to make money by taxing provincials or lending them money or taking on business concerns. He will be brave and fight nobly and return gloriously."

They both smiled at me, and I could not bring myself to point out the obvious danger into which Cassius rode. As if reading my thoughts, Junia said, "And Cassius will be on Crassus' staff and unlikely to be in the thick of the fighting. He will be fine, Tullie."

You can't have it both ways, I thought to myself. He can't fight and be glorious and stay safe and protected.

I have no idea why, but long after the orator Cicero's death, his private correspondence was published. Sulpicia came to me with a scroll which she had found while browsing through the orator's voluminous correspondence.

"Did you known that Cicero and your brother Brutus wrote to each other?" she asked, unrolling the scroll to show me a certain passage she had found.

I knew of course. I had not been very interested.

"Why on earth is anyone interested in reading his letters now?" I asked.

Sulpicia was astonished.

"The people Cicero knew and wrote to are the people who ran the Republic, Tertulla," she said. "To me, that is fascinating. There are letters from Caesar and Pompey - people like that. And many of the letters are private ones to close friends like Atticus and tell us exactly how Cicero felt."

"Isn't it a little too soon to publish them?" I asked. "After all some of these people will still be alive, won't they? I know Cicero's ex-wife Terentia is still around, even if she is old."

"They say Terentia has agreed, even helped gather them together for publication," said Sulpicia. "But the main mover behind it is Cicero's secretary Tiro. He has spent the last twenty years and more editing Cicero's speeches, working on a biography, gathering letters. He is completely devoted."

"I have just bought a new secretary called Tiro," I said, distracted. "Really, the dealers have no imagination. Every trained secretary nowadays is called after Cicero's devoted amanuensis."

Sulpicia waited patiently through my burbling.

"Tertulla, your brother is mentioned a lot and not always to his advantage. I think you had better know."

"Let me guess," I said. "Money."

"There is one incident," said Sulpicia. She had the scroll ready now and pointed. "Read from here on."

I looked and sighed. "Cyprus."

Brutus did not come well out of it.

I knew that while my Uncle Cato was in Cyprus, my brother had gone along too, as a member of Cato's staff. He had lent money to members of the community. He had established an illegal rate of interest. His agent had used Roman troops to enforce the repayment of the loans. And people had died.

Sulpicia saw my distaste and gently touched my arm.

"History is what we make it when we read it," she said. "You won't be able to stop people making up their minds after reading this - but you are not part of it, Tertulla."

"Thank all the gods that my mother is dead," and that was the first time I ever said that.

"From everything I know about your mother, she would have been able to take whatever people said," said Sulpicia. "And nobody will remember Brutus for this." Her voice stopped. Unsaid were the words, "…given what he went on to do."

Chapter 12

Cassius left for the East with the Consul Marcus Crassus in November, and along with everyone else, we went to see the Consul on his glorious way. Up until the point that Cassius was leaving, I had not really thought about what we Romans were doing invading Parthia. I nagged Junia and Nilla into asking their husbands and they came back with some interesting ideas.

Lepidus thought Crassus, who was now in his late fifties, was jealous of his colleagues Caesar and Pompey. Each of them was famously successful in the military field, but Crassus' most successful campaign had been in the slave revolt led by Spartacus, hardly honourable or glorious. Pompey, on the other hand, had cleared the seas of pirates and my sisters and I all remembered going to his triumph celebrating the successful and wealthy years campaigning in the East. Now Julius Caesar was rampaging through Gaul and sending home reports which sounded like adventure stories, though not as romantic as Callirhoe and Chaereas. Crassus, said my brother-in-law, wanted a slice of that glory.

Nilla's husband Isauricus, more laid-back, more tolerant, said that Parthia was the obvious place to attack, and Crassus was setting up an arena which would bring in a lot of revenue, hold back the hordes of Asia and start many promising careers. I wondered if it were as simple as a division of power - Crassus in the East, Caesar in the West and Pompey in the middle would carve up Rome's provinces into three mini-empires for themselves.

Crassus set out from the Forum that morning, accompanied by a crowd of supporters and of course his Quaestor, my Cassius. My mother and Junia agreed to form a party to go and watch the send-off with me, and we took our maids and a couple of bodyguards to set up camp on the steps of the Temple of Castor, enjoying the good mood of the crowd and the thin November sunshine. We watched the little procession accompany the general down from the Capitoline Hill, where sacrifices had been made to ask the gods for their favour on the expedition, and in the middle of the Forum it halted for a little so that men could wish Crassus well. This being Rome, there were catcalls amongst the cheers, but even these were humorous rather than aggressive, and our bodyguard, used to reading the temper of the Forum, saw no reason for concern. It was good to be in the middle of so many and feel able to enjoy the occasion, gaze around at the vast range of people around me, feel a cool breeze as it rippled across the stone roofs and pillars, even smell the scents of many humans in one place. Airy drifts of perfumes mingled with the odours of sweat and cooking food, and it was not unpleasant.

The other Consul, Pompey, was there with his supporters, all ready to escort the general to the gate of the city, and the two men gave no sign of the loathing which gossip said they felt for one another. I quickly spotted Cassius in the entourage, and I thought he compared very favourably with everyone around him, taller than most, and definitely one of the better-looking men present. I was just enjoying this thought, when there was a movement from one corner of the Forum, like the v-shaped ripple on the surface of a pond which shows that a fish is making for its food. For one moment, the crowd around the consuls all looked in the direction of the incomer.

"Who is it?" asked Junia, and a man standing several steps down from us turned to call out to everyone, "It's one of the tribunes, Ateius!" And how he knew this, when he was below us and even we could not see - well, the Forum crowd in Rome is a beast all of its own and can scent a tribune making trouble as a hunting-dog scents a stag.

My mother sighed. "Typical," she muttered.

"Why?" I wanted to know.

"The tribunes have been against this command being given to Crassus," said my mother. "Or some of them have anyway. Your Uncle Cato has encouraged them of course."

There certainly was a lot of shouting going on in the centre of the Forum and the mood was turning. The crowd was still but unsmiling and when several other groups of men arrived, people made way for them quickly. On our temple steps, the bodyguard quietly surrounded my mother and sister and me, and we retreated several steps up, ready to make the temple itself our refuge if necessary. After more shouting, the main procession began to surge forward again, but the tribune who had started the fuss had disappeared. My mother immediately sent two of our escort to the Capena Gate with instructions to observe and report back. Once the Consuls had led the way out, the Forum emptied like a jug with a hole in the bottom, and when the currents of the crowd had passed, we made our way back up the Palatine Hill, to the safety of our patrician houses. We heard what happened later.

The tribune Ateius, having failed to persuade the general in the Forum to give up his plans for Parthia, had let the main procession make its slow and stately way to the Capena Gate, from where Crassus would leave the city. With just a few friends, Ateius had run through the alleys and reached the gate first, and when Crassus and Pompey arrived there, they found the tribune had blocked their way by setting up a small brazier, already blazing in the middle of the road. As they approached, he began to call down curses, on Crassus, on arrogant ambition and the whole Parthian expedition, pouring wine into the fire and burning incense, until one of the general's men strode up to him and thrust him to one side. The brazier was extinguished, and all the coals scattered, then Crassus held his head up and trod the ashes into the ground as he strode out of the city. Pompey took great care to avoid the area where the brazier had stood and turned back into the city as soon as was decent. With hindsight, of course what I should tell you is that we all knew from that moment Crassus' expedition was doomed, and it is true that the whole city talked of nothing else for a couple of days. I cannot however claim that we had the faintest idea of the disaster that lay ahead. Rome is a resilient place, and her people are both superstitious and cynical. Nobody wanted to believe that the tribune could achieve anything with his curse, so while we loved the dramatic display and some of the maids enjoyed a good shivery moment of doom, we did not believe it would work. My mother's friend, the Chief Vestal Fabia was upset, but more by the effrontery of the tribune doing such a thing.

"Curses should be left to the proper persons," she declaimed as she sat in my mother's room the next day, eating honey cake bites and drinking wine. I sat in a corner, allowed in to benefit from the conversation of the most revered woman in Rome. I wondered who she thought was the best person to declaim a curse. Vestals are selected from Rome's best families which often means the most traditional, and no doubt Fabia had consulted some ancient archive and formed an opinion on how the state should deal with curses. "What tribunes don't realise," the Vestal declaimed, "is that they are still new arrivals and have no connection to the state religion."

"Tribunes have been in existence for several hundred years," pointed out my mother. I looked at her and felt sorry for Fabia. My mother was planning to enjoy this conversation. "And" she continued with enthusiasm, "they enjoy sacrosanctity, which is a religious state, surely, just like that enjoyed by you Vestals."

Fabia sniffed.

"It is certainly not the same, and I am surprised to hear you say so, Servilia," she said with some emphasis. There was a pause, then she continued in a lighter tone, "Oh you are teasing me of course. But really, do you think it is the role of a tribune to curse a general entrusted with a mission by the Senate and People?"

"No, of course not," said my mother. "Tribunes are there to protect the interests of the plebeian population and in my opinion can act as a useful check on the authority of individuals who gain too much power. As is usually the case, their office has become corrupted. They have some useful attributes, like sacrosanctity, and this has been exploited to the extent that their original role is forgotten. Look at all the people who have used the office to gain personally."

"Servilia, name for me one man who has achieved office and then not ensured that he benefits from it," said the Vestal. "It is practically ingrained in our system. We emphasise honour and family to our young men then show them a way of increasing the one and enriching the other. Who is not going to grasp that way?"

"My brother Cato for one," said my mother with a sigh. "And he is so thoroughly objectionable that any cause supported by him is immediately rendered more likely to fail."

There was a pause as both ladies drank their wine and no doubt thought pensively of the awfulness of my uncle Cato. I decided that it would be acceptable to ask my question.

"Lady Fabia, who should be allowed to pronounce a curse?"

The Vestal looked at me and smiled.

"Someone who has thought about it a great deal more than the tribune Ateius," she said. "If Marcus Crassus now fails in Parthia, who is to blame? I hope for the sake of the tribune himself that Crassus succeeds."

"Junia Tertia is now engaged to Cassius Longinus who has accompanied Crassus," explained my mother. "She has a vested interest. Cassius promised to bring back the jewels of a Parthian queen for her."

"Well, if he does, the temple of Vesta would also be pleased to accept a suitable expression of thanks for his safe homecoming," said the Vestal, in practical tones. "Maybe your young man can see his way to mending the roof of the House of the Vestals properly."

My mother laughed. "Fabia, I cannot believe that you put up with a leaky roof - yours must be the richest temple in Rome."

"And that will only continue to be the case as long as I make sure of it," said Fabia and gathered up the folds of her robes to leave.

I decided a few visits to the Temple of Vesta on Cassius' behalf would not come amiss.

The months after Cassius' departure dragged, and my mother's way of distracting me was a restocking of my wardrobe. Prior to this, all my clothes had been made for me in the house by our seamstresses, using material chosen by my mother. I had simple tunics, and a child's toga to wear on formal occasions. Often these had belonged to one or other of my sisters - despite our wealth, there was never extravagance in my mother's household. "There is no point in having money, if you do not hold onto it," she would say. Now I learned how to make and wear the married woman's dress over my tunics, and we also started weaving a series of lengths of light cloth in different colours to use as the shawls and wraps that all women wore over their dresses. The dress was longer than I was used to, and Kleia and I experimented with belting it and pulling the material through the belt to fall in elegant folds and allow me to walk without tripping. I was also very aware of my chest for the first time as Kleia belted the dress under my breasts and was concerned they didn't really do the folds justice. Draping all these layers of material was an art in itself, though Kleia said she thought that it was not as tricky as draping a man's toga. There were times when I enjoyed the feeling of being elegant and grown-up, and times when I felt bulky and constricted by the endless wrappings. Kleia was also sent to learn hairdressing from my sister Junia's maid Phoebe who was especially skilful. I wore my hair tied up in a small knot at the base of my neck like everyone, but Kleia got clever at weaving ribbons in and out of the braids, and even worked out how to make bunches of curls which I thought looked very pleasing as they hung on either side of my face. I asked for scarves, belts and hairbands as presents for birthdays and festivals, copying Nilla here. Isauricus had spoiled her from the moment they were married so she had an impressive collection of accessories. I knew every one of her dresses, but she had the knack of using different shawls and jewellery and hair ornaments so that her whole outfit looked different. Kleia kept a note of our favourite Nilla "looks" and we made cautious experiments.

"When we are sure of the date of your wedding," said my mother, "we shall visit the Emporium and choose some cloth for you."

This was a treat to look forward to indeed - the Emporium lay at the foot of the Palatine Hill, just south of the Forum, and was where the best cloth merchants had stalls. Here was where you could even buy silk, the cloth that shimmered and was as light as feathers on your skin and was rumoured to be grown on trees in the far East.

"When she takes you, go to Barates," said Nilla knowledgeably. "He used to run a string of shops in Antioch, in fact still does. His material is the best."

"Antioch," I said, imagining a far-off desert town, surrounded by camels and elephants, just like the creatures I had seen at Pompey's triumph. Barates probably was used to the burning heat and a dry land. I wondered what he thought of Rome, where the Tiber was always flooding and the marshes to the south of the city sent us damp, diseased air at the end of each summer. Barates however did not wear a turban and bright robes like the people in Pompey's triumph procession. He was barbered and attired in a tunic which shimmered every time he crossed the shaft of light which came into his shop from a high window. Barates saw me noticing and smiled at me, commenting in his excellent, slightly accented Latin, "That light alone is worth the rent I pay for this shop, Lady Junia. Look at how the silk here shines as I move it in the sunlight." And a lazy length of pale green rippled across in front of my eyes, as Barates' assistants stood one at either end, twisting the fabric carefully and making waves with it.

"Ah but today we need material for a dress, Barates, the first dress this young lady will wear. A dress for a new bride," said my mother.

"And I know just the thing," said Barates. He gave a polite little nod of his head, turned and whispered into the ear of one of the assistants, and as two men carefully rolled up the silk, sliding it into a wool bag to protect the precious fabric, Barates hovered by the entrance to the back storeroom. It was not long before the assistant came back with a bolt of light blue wool, pale and very fine. Instinctively my hand went out to stroke it, and Barates smiled as I hesitated. "Please Lady Junia, Lady Servilia - feel the wool. So soft and light, and, if I may say so, a perfect colour for you, Lady Junia. A young bride must of course be respectable, but she must also make her husband proud, I think."

"Your own weaving?" asked my mother, stooping to examine the quality of the weave, so fine one could hardly distinguish the individual threads. Barates nodded.

"I have a factory in Antioch," he said. "And my brother farms the sheep. My cousin dyes the fabric. We make sure of the best quality from beginning to end."

My mother smiled. "An excellent recommendation then, Barates," she said. "And you are right, the colour is just right for her. Do you like it, Tertulla?"

I loved it. Over a white tunic, it would look stunning, and I said so. I then stood by and respectfully watched as my mother and Barates bargained over the wool. It was a most amicable battle, and neither side triumphed, but no lives were lost either. When we got home and unwrapped the blue wool, tucked inside was a long thin ribbon of the green silk, a gracious and thoughtful present.

"I know Barates," said Sulpicia.

It was early on in our friendship, and she was young, about the age I was when I first went to Barates. We decided to go back to his shop together, where I would buy her a wedding present, even though her fiancé was not due to return to Rome for several years.

"I think I met him when my brother and I were children," said Sulpicia as we strolled down the slope of the Palatine towards the Agrippan Shops. Barates had gone upscale and moved around the corner into a very elegant new complex.

"Barates? Or your fiancé?"

"Both," said Sulpicia.

I couldn't see any difference between Barates' old and new shop in terms of size, and the helpful shaft of light was missing. But it was the smart place to be, and Barates had several assistants dealing with customers in a cramped space. If this was success then I was glad for him, though the old man was showing his years now.

He saw me and came over himself to greet us.

"Barates, I have just realised that we have known each for nearly thirty years, and you have not changed a bit."

He smiled and made a gesture that involved sweeping his hands back and giving a slight nod - respectful but not servile. Barates knew his worth.

"Lady Junia, the time has flown but we are the same. Now - it is too crowded in here, so why don't you come to my office and have some honey mint tea?"

I introduced Sulpicia as we were ushered into a large room behind the main showroom, its shelves packed with bolts of cloth. Although the assistants were in and out, one corner was set aside for a table and chairs and we sat and watched the back and forth of men and material, while Barates disappeared to see to the mint tea. Sulpicia sat and watched everything, and I enjoyed her energy and interest.

"The colours, Tertulla!"

"I know. If I too were a poet, I might try to describe it but…."

Sulpicia laughed. "Have you ever read a poem about cloth? Do you think anyone would want to read it if I wrote one?"

"Barates' shop is worthy of poetry," I said looking around. "Imagine where all these lengths started out - in fields as plants, on the backs of sheep, in the Far East spun by magical insects…"

"And then through the sorcery of dye, they take on these colours," Sulpicia joined in. "Look at that yellow, Tertulla - so deep and rich - how on earth does anyone produce a colour like that?"

Barates heard her as he came in once more with a tray of three steaming cups, and the scent of mint and honey swirling around him.

"Well, ladies, while we let this cool, I shall tell you," he said. "That yellow is made by mixing saffron with a lichen which grows in my country, Lady Sulpicia. My brother gathers the lichen in our home town of Antioch, and when it is ground and added to the saffron, oil and water, it produces that yellow."

I suspected that it was not that easy, but for the purpose of poetry one did not need more than an exotic moss and saffron. I was almost certain that urine would be involved at some point to fix the dye, and that was not at all poetic.

But because of that ribbon of green silk he gave me so many years ago, I always bought from Barates until the day he left Rome to go back to his home city for good. In the meantime, he proved a good friend and a business partner. The silk wore out of course, but I kept a scrap in my sewing basket for sentimental reasons. I don't know where my sewing-basket is any more. I have not sewn for years. My eyes and fingers long ago gave up on such fiddly work. Kleia will know where it is. Oh, but Kleia is dead of course. Nearly everyone I ever knew is dead. Thank all the gods for Sulpicia.

Chapter 13

In the years of Cassius' absence, Rome did not fare well. Normal political life seemed to be in abeyance, as if we were all waiting for someone - Crassus or Caesar or Pompey - to step in and take charge. The Three might have been generally hated, but they were the best hope when it came to sorting out the upheaval into which the city descended. My brother-in-law Isauricus had just reached the important office of Praetor and frequently voiced his frustration, because there was no point in holding a law-court, as the Praetors were supposed to do, while there were riots in the Forum The Consuls, his superiors, seemed unable to do something as straightforward as supervise the usual elections, let alone quell the violence. At the start of the next year, Rome was left with no Consuls at all. Instead, individuals like Clodius (the naughty young man who had tried to seduce Caesar's wife) with their own gangs of supporters, established themselves at the heart of political life and seemed quite prepared to wage war in the centre of Rome itself. Aretus would send runners down to the Forum in the morning to find out what had happened during the night, and whether it looked safe for ordinary people to visit shops and temples. He and my mother bought four more bodyguards, and armed them with cudgels, which must have been illegal. But everyone did this, and it would have been foolish not to take some steps. Isauricus was thankful to leave for his province, where, he said, he might get something useful done, and while he was away, Nilla stayed at various of the family villas south of Rome, and my mother, Junia and I often visited her, though Lepidus insisted on staying in the city throughout this time as he was supporting his brother Paulus. Paulus was already working towards a Consulship of his own, regardless of anything else going on, and Lepidus knew that he would benefit if his brother reached the Consulship. Their focus on their goal as things fell apart was both astounding and to be expected.

Fortunately, another distraction my mother lined up for me was not dependent on being in Rome. It was a course of lessons on household finances. I did not anticipate this being at all interesting, especially as both Junia and Nilla had not enjoyed their tuition, but as often happened I was the exception. I have since then been grateful on many occasions for my ability to manage my own finances. First, I learned how my mother's secretary kept the household accounts, and how Aretus kept overall control of expenses by being the person to whom everyone had to go to seek approval for expenditure. If the cook wanted a new pan, then Aretus had to nod, like Jupiter himself overseeing the deeds of men and gods. Every year he - Aretus, of course, not Jupiter - conducted an inventory and recommended to my mother what needed to be replaced, slave clothing, bedding, towels, old furniture. He and my mother had worked out a scale of expense for various occasions so that the cook knew the budget for a dinner party with family and close friends, a wedding feast, a birthday. All sorts of details were unfolded for me and the amount of money we spent as a household was frightening. I asked where the money came from, and this is where things grew fascinating.

"My father was very rich and so my dowry was considerable," said my mother. "It is all invested, though some of it went to fund your father's campaign for the consulship. Unfortunately, your father did not govern a province and thus get the chance to make back some of the money."

I also learned that my brother Brutus was extremely rich as he had inherited not only his father's fortune but that of my Uncle Caepio, my mother's brother who had died so tragically early, and had adopted Brutus in his will to ensure the smooth handover of his wealth to someone in the family. A portion of this went on the dowry of Caepio's daughter, but the remainder was all Brutus'. I asked my mother where her father's fortune had come from and she said briskly "He was a very successful governor of Gaul," and changed the subject.

As you may imagine I was not content with this and as always Felix was the one who elaborated on my mother's skimpy explanations, telling me in more detail the truth about how

Rome governed her provinces. Roman politicians often went out to rule provinces of our empire after they had served their offices, and took this as an opportunity to make money, through war, confiscation and taxation.

"Running for Consul is very expensive," said Felix. He was about to say more but stopped. I knew that my father had probably done something during his campaign which was not strictly legal - bribery, I guessed. Even Felix was not going to explain any more about that. It was another secret of the Senatorial classes. Bribery was illegal, but it was endemic, an expected part of election campaigns. A very drunk minor poet once pointed out to me at a party that only the Latin language has several words to name the different agents who conduct illegal bribery at an election. I asked him how he knew that no other language in the world had such words, but he just waved his hand to dismiss my question, so I found someone else to talk to.

What Felix did tell me was the story of my grandfather's time in Gaul.

My grandfather was Quintus Servilius Caepio and he was proud, arrogant, and greedy (Felix did not say this of course, I worked it out for myself). He was governing in Gaul when he heard that the tribes were hoarding a huge amount of gold and silver in a town called Tolosa. This treasure already had a story all its own, for it had been taken hundreds of years ago from the holy shrine of Delphi by an army of Gauls rampaging through Greece.

"Now Delphi," said Felix, "was full of treasure from all the pilgrims who came to ask the Priestess of Apollo for prophecies and advice. Even Croesus the king of Lydia who owned so much gold that he could fill the ornamental lake in his garden with it came to Delphi."

I briefly wondered about asking Felix how big this lake was but decided to let that go.

"What did he want to ask the Priestess?"

"He was planning to invade his neighbouring kingdom and wanted to make sure that he would win."

"What happened, Felix? Did he beat the neighbour?"

"No - the neighbour beat him. You see, when Croesus asked what would happen if he went to war, the Priestess told him that a mighty empire would fall. And what he didn't realise...."

"...was that the Priestess meant his own empire," I finished.

"Exactly," said Felix approvingly. "You have been taught well, Junia Tertia."

I giggled and agreed, before turning to the crucial point.

"Then the Gauls stole the treasure from Apollo and brought it back to their own country - and my great grandfather decided to steal the treasure from them?"

"He claimed the treasure for Rome," said Felix in tones which made it clear that he did not approve of my use of the word, "steal", at least when it applied to a Roman governor. After a pause, he went on, "and sent it back to the port of Massilia in the south of Gaul, so that it could be shipped to Rome. But - the treasure never reached Massilia. It vanished into thin air and so did all the men guarding it and the carts transporting it – everything. Later, your great grandfather was accused of stealing it and he was fined heavily and had to go into exile, but the treasure never reappeared. It was said that it was cursed because it had been stolen from the god Apollo."

I was intrigued and a little concerned. "You mean my family's wealth is based on stolen and cursed gold?"

Felix was soothing. "No, no, your great grandfather was unjustly accused. No doubt the treasure was stolen back by the Gauls and hidden away. But because your family managed to pay the fine, and seemed unaffected by the loss, the rumour sprang up that they were being funded by the treasure."

As you can imagine this gave me a great deal to think about, for even if my family were not rich because of some amazing treasure from long ago, I had to look at where our money came from. I asked Brutus - poor Brutus, he must have dreaded visiting in those days for wondering what questions he was going to face.

"When I marry Cassius, I shall have a dowry, won't I?"

"Yes, set aside for you by your father before he died."

"And if Cassius dies where does that money go to? Do I get it?"

"Yes, you do get it, though I won't tell Cassius that you are already planning what you will do after he dies."

"Suppose I die?"

"Then it goes to your children. Look, Tertulla," said Brutus, "what is this all about?"

"I am not really sure," I admitted. "It's just that I realised recently that I don't know where our money comes from, and I thought I should."

"Why?" asked Brutus. "You always have had - and always will have - someone to look after that for you. Mother and I do it now, Cassius will do it when you are married."

"Mother had to learn how to deal with money, didn't she?"

"Mother has always had to be independent like that," said Brutus. "She was orphaned at an early age, and then her guardian died. She grew up with her aunt and grandmother advising her and they insisted that she and her siblings all learn how money works. And she has in turn taught me. I must have a certain amount of land and holdings as you know to compete for my place in the Senate, and I make sure that I keep a close eye on what is happening to all my investments, as well as having excellent stewards in all my properties. And our Uncle Cato has been particularly good about giving me opportunities as well. Is that the sort of thing you need to know?"

Oh, I know all about our Uncle Cato and his opportunities, I thought, remembering Cyprus. But I was not going to challenge Brutus about this. Instead, I addressed Brutus' final question. "I think what I need to know first of all is exactly what I own - or have in my dowry anyway."

"We can arrange that," said Brutus. "Let me talk to Mother and I shall prepare a list of your assets and go through it with you."

My mother was pleased, I think, that I wanted to know about finances and so it was in her room that she and Brutus and I sat as I finally learned my worth one spring day in the year after Cassius went to the East.

My dowry was an interesting mix. I would bring a full wardrobe and all the possessions which a young married woman would need, two slaves for the use of me and my husband, a tile factory in Etruria and a tenement block on the Aventine Hill. My mother would also give us one of her houses on the coast at Antium, south of Ostia, to be a country escape. I was impressed.

"Cassius must know the sort of family into which he is marrying," said my mother.

Brutus said mildly, "He does know. He is from a similar family."

My mother looked at him and pronounced, "However much you like Cassius, and I admit he is a very likeable man, his background and ours do not bear comparison. He is moderately wealthy, his forefathers are irreproachable and he is plebeian. We on the other hand have ancestors who are nothing short of illustrious and we are patrician. He is doing very well for himself by marrying Tertulla and there would be no harm if you reminded him of this next time you see him."

"Next time I see Cassius, I shall be heartily glad that he has returned alive from the East and shall make sure he knows that. We can get round to a comparison of family trees later."

"I thought that I wasn't patrician because of Father," I said a little tactlessly, but too interested to care.

"You are my daughter," said my mother and that was the end of that conversation.

However, the next time the rents on my Aventine tenement came in, my mother showed me the books. She had an agent who did nothing but go round our various properties in Rome, checking for repairs and gathering the rents, and he reported directly to her every month. I was allowed to sit in on that meeting and listened avidly as he discussed tenants in detail and asked my mother for funds to repair the internal staircase. I wondered if I should see this tenement place, but Brutus said no. I did wonder about actual cash in my hand - would I have any money, myself, from this dowry? Or did everything go to Cassius?

"Your dowry goes to offset the expenses of having a wife and family," said Brutus patiently. "Cassius will make you an allowance out of it."

"I had not realised that I was so expensive a pet to keep," I said peevishly. But I did not forget to check on the level of the allowance by asking my sisters. Needless to say, Nilla was indulged and Junia was expected to be frugal.

Early in the New Year, as I waited in vain for letters from Cassius ("The shipping lanes have closed for the season and the official couriers are certainly not going to be allowed to take personal letters," said my mother), Nilla gave birth to a healthy baby boy, and my mother basked in satisfaction over her three grandsons, produced so soon after marrying and with no harm to babies or mothers. Not that she doted - my mother did not pick them up or coo. I did though. I liked my little nephews. Sometimes I wondered if I should suggest visiting the boy who would become my stepson, but Brutus once more said no.

"That is a decision for Cassius alone," he explained. "And at the moment he will probably have far too much on his hands to even think about such things."

When I look back on incidents like this, I cannot quite work out why they annoyed me. Brutus' argument was valid. I lived in a world where my husband would take it for granted that his wishes should be respected. Nonetheless, Brutus' reply needled its way under my skin and into my brain. It took a long time for me to work out why it had made such an impact on me, but it was so simple and obvious once I had - it was the increasing difficulty I had with Brutus' patronising attitude to women, foreigners, people who had opinions contrary to his own... I suppose as I got older, I saw the flaws in my brother more and more. This is perfectly natural of course, and in many cases does not lead to a diminution of love or respect. In the case of my mother, my respect for her grew warmer with understanding of her faults and by the end of her life, I loved her without reserve. The reverse was true for my relationship with Brutus. Gradually, I reduced the number of times I went to him for advice. His pomposity made these conversations tedious, and he never forgot if one did not take his advice.

He formed a good alliance at around this time, by marrying the daughter of the Consul Appius Claudius, then going off to Cilicia with him to help govern the province. I knew exactly where Cilicia was, it was on the way to Parthia and so the province heard the news from the East quickly. I begged Brutus to relay the bulletins about the army's progress against the Parthians, and when he played the superior male by questioning the extent to which I would understand military affairs, I got so frustrated that I shouted at him.

"You" and I may have emphasised the pronoun unnecessarily, "have no excuse for not writing to tell me what is happening, as Cilicia at least is a peaceful province."

Brutus said very priggishly that Rome was grateful for his service, wherever it was. But he did take care to include news of the Parthian campaign whenever he wrote to my mother.

One sad event took place in the summer after Cassius left for the East and gave me another insight on marriage and a woman's lot in life. It also had political implications that were quite important. Poor Julia - Caesar's daughter, from what I knew of her was a good and beautiful person. Nobody ever said anything which could be seen as the merest whisper of criticism, and Junia, who knew her quite well, confirmed the general opinion. Death in childbirth at an early age was the danger every woman had to consider as she headed towards marriage, and I grieved for her young life and the life of her baby. She also formed the link that bound two such different men as Caesar and Pompey, and everyone saw The Three as suddenly vulnerable. They were physically separated, Crassus and Caesar at either ends of the empire, with Pompey in Rome. Communication alone would be a huge problem. Their enemies took advantage.

Four years before Caesar returned from Gaul, violence raged in the centre of Rome. Gangs belonging to the various factions fought in the Forum throughout the spring and summer, as accusations regularly turned into riots, and men died on the steps of the temple where my sister and mother and I had stood to watch Cassius follow his general to Parthia. We got used to staying on the Palatine and keeping a slave on the roof of the house to watch for the thin lines of smoke which tracked the violence. The usual election of Consuls was postponed repeatedly, and to my mother's disgust the men eventually elected were spectacularly useless. Nobody really noticed this though because Rome heard the first tales of Parthian disaster at the end of the summer, and immediately little else mattered. You can imagine the panic that the news stirred up in a city which had already spent so long struggling with its own atmosphere of blood and hate. But our defeat in Parthia was shameful and total. I cannot remember how many men died, but three legions lost their standards to the enemy, the general and his son were among the dead and the Parthians did not even respect their enemies' bodies. One rumour went round the city that the head of the defeated Crassus had been cut off and taken to the King of Parthia who ordered it to be used as a prop in the performance of a play.

Brutus wrote a full account to my mother which she let me read and to my surprise he included a short note to me telling me about Cassius - how his advice, ignored by the general, had turned out to be right, how Cassius had led the quarter of the army which survived back to Syria, how he had then set about securing the borders of that province and was being praised by everyone for his determination and clear thinking. In the absence of a governor, Cassius took over the defence of Syria and held off the Parthians successfully for another two years until he was relieved of duty and allowed to return to Rome. It meant that he was away much longer than I had hoped but his courage brought him nothing but praise from all sides, and my brother-in-law Lepidus said that his future career was practically guaranteed now.

"If any of us have any career ahead of us," said Lepidus mournfully. We - my mother and me - were at Junia's to see the boys and have a family dinner, and as always, politics was the main topic of the conversation. My mother, even though she had been exceptionally politically astute since her youth regularly asked her sons-in-law for their views and thus flattered them into talking more than they did with their wives. It annoyed Junia, though not Nilla. Lepidus in particular warmed to my mother's attention and he would stroke his chin thoughtfully when my mother asked him a question. Fortunately, he also appreciated that she was worth listening to herself, so avoided patronising her. After all, as Caesar's mistress, one never could just dismiss my mother.

"I do admire your mother," said Sulpicia.

Everyone did.

Chapter 14

What then had Caesar been doing? What was happening in Gaul while Rome felt the sting of disaster in the East, and I wondered if Cassius would ever come home? Well for one thing, he saw my mother every year when his army were in winter quarters and the Gauls were quiet. It was three days' journey by ship to the town of Luca in Cisalpine Gaul, if the weather was not too bad, and every October, she would announce that she was going to the country for a rest and did not need anyone to accompany her. It took me a couple of years to realise that she did not in fact go down to Antium or Lanuvium or the bay of Naples, and as usual I would have drifted along in ignorance if one of my sisters had not enlightened me. Then, I was embarrassed because the two of them, Caesar and my mother, were so old. Nowadays, I imagine them meeting in an anonymous house, lent to them by a discreet friend, and feel quite benevolent towards the two of them, mere fledglings in their forties. In between these brief holidays, Caesar fought the Gauls a lot, but you can read his own accounts of that, if fighting long-haired natives is what interests you. I have read them, and they are to my mind a depressing accounting of the number of lives it takes to gain an Empire. Nevertheless, at the time I pored over each dispatch as it arrived. I still had hopes that one day I would find out that Caesar was my father. I now realise that I was very lonely at times during these years, knowing that I would marry Cassius but having few people to talk with about it. There was Kleia of course, but she was a slave, and my sisters were living their own lives. When I did meet up with them, they had their concerns about husbands and children and households to discuss, and naturally for them all these things were more important.

I finally complained bitterly to Junia one day and she gave me an uncharacteristic reproof.

"Tertulla, you really do have to learn patience. There is no point whinging at me like this - I cannot bring Cassius back, and

I cannot make the Parthians suddenly retreat, I cannot do anything you are demanding! You have a betrothed husband who is to all appearances suitable and pleasant and has been attentive as far as he is able. To whine that he does not send you letters when he is at this moment in the middle of the deserts beyond Syria, holding back the Parthians, is ridiculous, and for one who prides herself on her intelligence you really should be doing better!"

She ran out of breath there, and I just sat and gaped for this was my Junia who had helped me since I could walk, always gentle, always sweet. At last, I ventured,

"Are you feeling well, Junia?"

"Because that must be the only reason why anyone should ever contradict you or tell you the harsh realities? We really have spoiled you, Tertulla, haven't we?"

I felt lost. The tears were threatening, which usually would have annoyed me but not now, when my Junia had called me spoiled and accused me of being unable to face up to reality.

"I'm sorry" I said in the smallest voice I could remember using to anyone bar my mother. And then, because there was still some defiance in me, "Though I don't really know what I am apologising for." And she laughed but just when I thought she was all right once more, started to cry in sobs which spilled out of her like the thick sputtering of an over-full lamp. My confusion vanished as I put my arms around her until she had cried it all out on my shoulder. That took quite some time, as well. I shushed and murmured and rocked - and it felt wrong. I was not the one who gave comfort, but now I was nearly sixteen I had better learn how. Eventually, she quietened and I called for some wine. I drew back and wondered if she had something more to tell me - and she did.

"I had a miscarriage several days ago, Tertulla," she said quietly. "It was very early and I know that it happens to so many women - but I'm feeling so shattered and empty and useless…"

"You aren't useless, Junie," I said quietly. "I wouldn't know what to do without you. I'm really sorry about your baby."

"Thank you dear," she said, and she sounded like a mother, immeasurably older than me. We did not go back to my own querulous complaining of course. We talked about family, about how Nilla was doing at being a mother, how Junia's own two little boys were growing, how Brutus' marriage to the almost colourless Claudia, now he was back in Rome, was looking under strain. Riots ravaged the city, hordes of Parthians battered the eastern borders, and Caesar burned down thousands of Gaulish homes, but we were the daughters of Servilia and lived on the Palatine Hill, and our task in life was to keep our bloodline going.

"Junia?" I asked. "Do you ever think of our father? Silanus?"

"Yes," she said. "Enough to know what his name is without being reminded. It isn't just me, Tullie, something is wrong, isn't it?"

"Nothing's wrong," I said and kept quiet.

I am now going to pass over a year or two of riots and scandal, mainly because the events did not touch our family in any great way. I have been through two civil wars since, and I have a sense of perspective. I am going to talk now about the year before Caesar crossed the Rubicon river and started the first of those civil wars. This year was special for my family in many ways, and we shall begin with my least favourite family members.

My brother-in-law Lepidus, he of the much-stroked chin was very proud that his brother Paullus was Consul and together they undertook the repair of the famous Aemilian Hall in the Forum. It had been first built by their distant ancestor, and Lepidus knew that he could use this to his advantage in his own campaign to be Consul in a few years' time.

My uncle Cato was in the forefront of the fight to thwart Caesar in his desire to stand for the Consulship again while still governing Gaul and was as embarrassing as ever. My mother was quietly doing all she could to persuade people to support Caesar, and my brother Brutus stepped up to defend his father-in-law Appius Claudius in a notorious lawsuit. The usual stuff, the oil-and-bread of Roman politics.

More unusually, my sister Junia became the target of scandal and gossip which was most unfair because she was guilty of nothing, of course. It is a strange little story. It began when

Marcus Cicero wrote to my mother. Marcus Cicero was always on the fringes of our acquaintance, and everyone knew him. He was from a rural Italian family, perfectly respectable, but nowhere near us in ancestry or wealth. He made himself important by becoming the most influential public speaker of our time and had even reached the heights of the Consulship. He had been the silver-tongued speaker who gave my father's funeral oration. I knew my brother liked him, and later I found out that Cassius wrote to him regularly and counted him a friend, but in the context of my life then he meant little. He was in demand at dinner parties because he had wickedly amusing conversation and often one would hear about his latest crack while gossiping with friends. Even in those times, we gossiped. One could not live in uncertainty all the time.

Cicero's letter reported that he had met a man called Vedius Pollio who carried a portrait of Junia in his baggage.

"A picture of Junia?" I exclaimed.

"Don't interrupt, Tertulla," said my mother. And carried on, as calmly as if she were discussing tonight's dinner menu.

Cicero was governor of Cilicia at the time and had taken an instant dislike to this Pollio.

"He claims to be a friend of Pompey, which I do not believe," wrote Cicero, "and he goes everywhere accompanied by a trained ape driving a small chariot, would you believe? His baggage was opened and inventoried by mistake by a clerk who immediately informed me of what he found. Your daughter's image is just one of five portraits of highly born Roman ladies, and you would not believe the other things listed on the inventory. He could not explain why he had these portraits, and I am completely at a loss as to what he thought he was doing. I shall end this by telling you that the man claims to have made a fortune breeding wild donkeys…"

My mother did not laugh when she read this but immediately sent for Junia, who said she had never even heard of a Vedius Pollio. And there it might have died a death, but Cicero also informed the families of the other four women and the story of course got out. Junia's husband, my idiot of a brother-in-law, was very embarrassed and decided that Junia must give him an explanation. When she had none, he was so horrible to her that poor Junia ended up on our doorstep, in tears, saying that Lepidus had told her to go. My mother, who until this had not taken the matter too seriously, became terribly angry; she went over to speak to Lepidus immediately while I comforted Junia.

"I just don't know what I have done!" she sobbed, lying on a small couch in the Juniatrium, while Kleia brought handkerchiefs and drinks and some water and towels for when Junia had finished crying. I stroked my sister's hair and thought sadly how stupid Lepidus was. Could he really have lived with Junia for seven - no, eight - years and not know her at all? Thank all the gods that Cassius was not like that. I mentally made a note to pay another visit to Vesta's temple and leave an offering.

When my mother returned and announced that she had informed Lepidus of his error, and that Junia could now return to her home, Junia started crying all over again.

"You had better stay here for a few days," decreed my mother. "It will do Lepidus no harm. And I am writing to Cicero to let him know what I think of his gossiping."

Junia stayed one night then went back to Lepidus and later reported to me that he had apologised gracefully. As far as I could tell, neither of them referred to the incident again. It was a sobering lesson for me though, for if someone as sweet and truly virtuous as Junia could be thrown into such turmoil by other people's gossip - well, what chance did the rest of us have? I hoped that Nilla was taking note.

Then the oh-so-longed-for happened: Cassius was on his way back. Letters arrived as he crossed over to Greece and then Italy, and spring blossomed as I imagined the ride up the roads from the south, not yet dusty with the summer's heat, but dried up after the rains of a muddy winter. He wrote last of all from his estate south of Rome at Lanuvium, saying he was going to be taking some days to sort out everything before he came back to the city.

"For one thing," he wrote, "I need a bath, a good shave and a haircut, before I dare let myself be seen by you, dear Tertulla. I hope I haven't changed much - or if I have, it is for the better.

And what about you? I have been away more than four years and you have gone from thirteen to seventeen - or are you eighteen already? I don't even know your birthday, which feels strange. You must let me know, for I owe you so many presents...."

I tried to answer this letter straight away but was in completely the wrong mood, so nervous I could not hold a pen properly let alone think of witty and grown-up things to say to him. Eventually, I did something I hardly ever did - I consulted my mother. I went off to her room to ask if she had a moment.

"Of course," said my mother immediately, twisting round on her stool, and looking at me with no surprise at all. "Cassius has written to you, hasn't he?"

I found myself walking past her to the far wall and stood looking at my favourite tree. Behind me my mother waited.

"I don't want to get married," I found myself saying, and for a moment I was both appalled and overcome with panic. I reached out my hand to the tree and wished with all my heart it was real and that I could climb up into it and disappear. Tears blurred the image.

I was not surprised at all as I felt my mother's arms around me. I turned and managed to gasp out two little squeaks into her shoulder which she correctly interpreted as meaning that I was scared. Without saying anything she held me and stroked my hair, while I choked on my own panic. After a while, when the sobs had grown less jagged, she took me to the couch, and we sat with arms around one another, just like the mothers and daughters in the paintings and sculptures. A handkerchief appeared and soon we were ready to talk.

"Did this happen with my sisters?" I asked and was a little surprised at my mother's laugh.

"You girls! Can you really do nothing without reference to each other? Yes, of course this happened with your sisters, but for once, Tertulla, we are not going to talk about them, nor shall we compare you to them. You are your own person, a young woman about to be married and quite naturally fearing what is unknown. It happens all over the world thousands of times every day. You are normal. But because it is you, it is also the first time this has happened - ever. And so, you are right to feel unsure. But look at it like this - marriage for you will be a liberation."

I thought about that one. Had Nilla or Junia found freedom through their marriages? But with an effort I thrust that thought away. I was Tertulla, the third daughter, and I was going to be different, as I always had been different. I was - possibly - Caesar's daughter.

"Is," and I blushed but had to ask, "is sex liberating?"

My mother looked at me and her face softened as she smiled.

"It isn't the sex itself, though that can be extremely - pleasant," she said, a small pouting laugh carving her lips upwards. "It is the trust that a kindly marriage-bed can produce between you. You have to trust someone who knows you so closely, he has to trust you because you will bear his children, and you have to trust him again to honour you by bringing up those children with you."

I had heard similar rather pompous speeches before.

"I know but - does the pleasure mean that he will keep loving me?"

My mother sighed. "It doesn't work for everyone."

We both thought "Junia" I am sure.

"Tertulla," said my mother. "I am more confident about your marriage to Cassius than almost any other I can think of. He is a sensible man, he has a sense of humour, he is kind. Put all those together and you will have a husband who will treat you well in bed and out. He wants you to have a true marriage, where both of you work together for the benefit of the family."

"Like you and Father?" I ventured.

"Your father is an excellent man," she said, and if she thought that I did not notice the tense of her answer, then she was mistaken. Inside me, my heart gave a little thrill.

We talked on about marriage and the opportunities it gave a woman, how she had run the family side by side with both her husbands, how they had trusted her to look after her own finances. "Money is important, Tertulla," she said. "Always control it if you are able."

The best piece of advice was that about finances. Cassius never had time, poor man, to do anything but entrust the money side of our marriage to me, and that has been a blessing. Men respect a woman with money. It has ensured, for example that I got through the bad days, and that I never felt the pressure to marry again. My marriage to Cassius was as good as any marriage can be, and I have never felt the urge to find out whether my experience could be repeated with another man.

I thought that having held off the hordes of Parthia, Cassius would come home to a sort of hero's welcome. My sisters and I thought he was wonderful of course but the rest of Rome merely muttered a distracted thanks and fell back to gossiping about what we would do with Caesar. But I cared little, for finally I married Gaius Cassius Longinus, left my family home and was carried over the threshold of my own establishment. Cassius put me down and led me to the corner where his family shrine stood, a brazier and a table next to it. I took up my stand and held my hands over the pottery jug of water on the table and the brazier of quietly crackling flames, palms down and steady until I could feel the heat of the flames. I turned to Cassius and said, "Where you go, there I shall be with you" and with that I took control of my new household and revelled in my new kingdom.

The first few days after my wedding were filled with the tasks of getting to know my new home, of talking to the housekeeper, the steward, the head cook, the laundry maids and so on. Here I appreciated my mother's insistence that we were all well-grounded in how to run a house, as I managed to carve out a role for Felix - secretary, tutor and librarian - and set Kleia to install my wardrobe. But a few days into all this when I was beginning to feel a little fractious and unsure over my newfound authority, Cassius took me through the house and to one side of the courtyard showed me a small and very plain room. It was well away from the atrium but from it you could hear when the fountain in the courtyard was running. As I looked around and saw that it was empty, I wondered what it was for. I looked enquiringly at my new and already adored husband. He smiled and took two steps to stand in the centre of the room, taking up an orator's stance and grinning broadly at me. I could not help smiling back, and he suddenly lunged forward to catch my hands and whirled me around. "Tertulla!" he cried. "Haven't you worked it out?"

I looked at him, bewildered.

"This is your room," he said. "This is whatever you want it to be. You can make it a library. You can make it a sitting room. The steward and the housekeeper know that you will want it to be furnished and decorated exactly as you please. All you have to do is plan it and then tell us what you want." And he dropped my hands to pirouette in the centre of the room, arms spread wide to introduce me to my kingdom. I turned with him, thrilled at having a space that was all mine. Of course, I knew exactly what I wanted to do with it. "I'm going to make it into a garden," I said.

I did not merely copy my mother. I had my own trees, my own birds and plants. My room had a single door and three large blank walls waiting for me to fill them. I needed no windows. Our courtyard garden in the middle of the house was a step away if I wanted it but this was going to be my secret garden. While all the controversy over Pompey and Caesar was going on, the lead up to a civil war for all the gods' sake, I was decorating my perfect room. I hope that you have also noticed that Cassius had once more given me the perfect present. I thought with pity of his first wife, the idiotic woman who had lost Cassius for another man. Thanks to her, I now had this - my very own room.

Chapter 15

I must make it clear; I have never stood for Dictatorships, Triumvirates or Emperors, and yet I have lived through them all. During my twentieth year, the Republic I have always supported withered, and nobody seemed able to stop it. I say "nobody" but of course I mean "no man".

Pompey was rallying forces, said Cassius, but not in Rome. In Rome itself, Pompey and his allies talked and consulted and went round each other's houses to talk and consult: foolish, to my mind. It was clear to me that we needed troops and experienced troops too if we were to stop Caesar. He had several battle-hardened legions fanatically loyal to him after ten years in Gaul. Pompey on the other hand seemed more interested in what his fellow Senators thought of him.

One evening over dinner, I asked Cassius why Pompey was not making more military preparations. Cassius reminded me that Pompey had conquered the East, and this was where his resources were. He had swept pirates from the Mediterranean and organised the whole of Asia. For a moment, I was back more than a decade, watching the triumphal procession and the dazzling cloak of Alexander the Great on the shoulders of the old man riding past in his chariot. I smiled as I remembered how much I had wanted that cloak.

"Pompey is planning to fall back to Greece and give himself time to build up an army, while Caesar, if he crosses into Italy, will immediately put himself in the wrong, and few people will join him. Then we can wait for Caesar to come to Greece and fight him there." Even to me this sounded ridiculous, and I could not believe that my soldier husband, who had actually fought campaigns, was wholeheartedly behind this. The idea that one could save Rome by retreating from it was bizarre. I pointed this out to Cassius and he nodded.

"I can see your point, Tertulla, believe me," he said. "But this isn't like the olden days - the stories you've heard about our enemies attacking Rome, and us needing to stand on our walls and defend our city - those days are over. Can you imagine the damage Caesar will do to his own reputation if he physically attacks Rome itself? There are hundreds of thousands of people living here, many of them the sort of people Caesar has traditionally relied on for his support. His own wife is here..."

I thought, "Caesar's mistress is here," but did not say it. Instead, I pursued the argument.

"Is Pompey relying on Caesar not attacking Rome?"

Cassius blew a wry little puff of air and said, "Yes it has come to this. We are relying on Romans not attacking Rome."

"And will the rest of Italy be safe?" I asked.

"Yes. If they have any sense, every town will let through the troops, no matter which side they are on."

And hope that the right person then wins the war, I thought. If Pompey came back to Italy victorious, then anyone who had supported Caesar would be wise to grovel. I voiced this and Cassius shook his head.

"Too far ahead, Tertulla. I cannot see that far. I just feel that after those years fighting in Syria and seeing an army go down so terribly, so -" he had no more to say but shook his head. "So now, Tertulla, we have to decide - two men are demanding that I give them my loyalty when all I am loyal to is Rome. What do I do? Which man out of Caesar and Pompey is better for our city and empire?"

"Caesar," I said without hesitation. "If I were you I would declare for Caesar."

"Interesting," said Cassius.

I said quickly, "It is nothing to do with my mother."

No," agreed my husband, with just a slight hint of laughter in his eyes, "I did not think for a moment that it had anything to do with your mother."

We were reclining on our dinner couch after the meal, and the slaves had withdrawn leaving water and wine in jugs at hand. I did not drink much wine but Cassius gave me a fresh cup and topped it up with water before serving himself.

"What is it Tertulla?"

I looked hard at the floor in front of me, feeling his arm draped around my waist, imagining how he was looking at me, slightly puzzled, maybe concerned.

"I think Caesar is my father," I said to the floor and felt Cassius tense beside me. There was a long pause.

"Tertulla," he said gently. "I really think that is very unlikely."

His words took time for me to hear them. And I was dumbstruck. How could he not believe me? For ten years I had nurtured this colossal, shameful, exciting secret and now Cassius would not accept it? Once my voice returned, I could not find the right words. My temper flared and I scrambled to turn to face him.

"And what would you know about it?" I said, rude to him for the first time, but instead of getting angry himself, he took my hand in his.

"Is this so important to you, Tertulla?" he asked, and he spoke very gently.

"I have wondered for ten years," I said, and was dismayed to feel the tears well in my eyes.

Cassius sat up on the couch and took me in his arms.

"Tertulla, you are definitely your mother's daughter, just to look at you," he began, and I had to interrupt.

"My mother is beautiful," I said pointing out the obvious flaw in what he had said. He laughed, and with one finger under my chin, tilted it up and said very sweetly, "Tertulla, so are you."

This stunned me. I had never imagined that I was beautiful, like my mother. I had always assumed that Nilla was the pretty one. But Cassius carried on, "Tertulla, for you to be Caesar's daughter your mother would have had to have - er - been with Caesar at a time when nobody in Rome thought she was. Rumours about Servilia and Caesar only started at about the time when Cicero was campaigning for the consulship and you would have already been two or three years old. Yes?"

I did not even have to think back. "Yes."

"Do you really think Tertulla," said Cassius, "that nobody in Rome would have found out about such an affair for three years?"

I knew the answer here and shook my head.

"It isn't the sort of thing that goes unnoticed," said Cassius. "So I think that it is unlikely. But if you want to be sure, Tertulla, you are going to have to ask your mother."

His words sparked a thought in me.

"Did you - when you were thinking about me - did you know that my mother was Caesar's mistress?"

"Yes," he said immediately.

"Did you wonder - about me?"

"Yes. And I checked."

I was silent. I was now very uncomfortable and only wanted this conversation to move on. I shifted on the couch away from his embrace.

"I'm tired," I said, unable to think of anything else. "I must go to bed now. Goodnight Cassius."

He smiled at me from the couch, lifted his cup of wine to me and said, "Goodnight, my beautiful wife. Sleep well."

I went to my room, my Painted Garden. The decorators had worked on it over the summer and it was the most perfect room ever made. Do you remember that my mother's room had a single wall painted with a garden scene with three trees? I took that idea and extended it. When you enter my room you are surrounded by a wild garden and it is all seasons at the same time. Here there are no fences or walls, for it is open to everyone, and it beckons you to walk in. The trees are hung with quinces, pears, pomegranates and apples. Lower down grow small bushes of herbs, prickly rosemary, thyme, sage and comfrey, while wildflowers nestle around the foot of each tree. The artist painted fallen leaves of yellow in little piles on the ground here and there to contrast with the silver grey of the sage and the mossy brown of the tree trunks. In the grass are all my favourite flowers, chamomile and daisies and irises, with rosebushes blooming deep red and pink. There are birds flying in the blue sky, and on the ground is a tiny golden cage with my finches, the ones that Cassius gave me the first time we met. They were still alive when they were painted for this fresco and as I sit in this room today, I see them in the cage and remember how happy they made me.

I have never had the paintings changed though they have had to be refreshed a few times over the years. It is still my favourite room, and I sit there every day in the biggest, most comfortable chair I can find. I don't have a desk anymore, but my secretary Tiro has the most perfect little lap-desk especially made for him. I sometimes wonder if, when I die, I will finally step into the walls and walk in my garden and Cassius will be waiting for me. I do hope so.

"Oh Sulpicia!" I cried as I read the title on the small scroll she had just placed into my hands.

"I had to," she said. "There are too many shades of green in this room to ignore. Happy birthday, dear Tertulla. Am I allowed to guess at the number of years?"

"You are not," I said and devoured the few lines she written for me.

Poem in honour of my friend's garden
This is a room of all seasons,
where leaves turn from green to fawn
and edge into winter.
When Tertulla walks in this garden
she smiles at sparrows and painted parrots,
plums and pomegranates.
A palm tree lords the olive.
In her garden, home and abroad,
Tertulla meets the world.

Chapter 16

But back to the year of my marriage, back to everybody watching as Rome moved from uncertainty to doubt to fear. Pompey and Caesar and their friends pushed back and forth: should Caesar be recalled from Gaul? Should he be allowed to stand once more for consul? If so, was it legal for him to stand for that consulship while still in Gaul? I found these questions almost amusing, because in my experience, if the Senate wanted something to happen, then it happened, legal or no. They could always find good reasons.

My memories of Rome during that December are dark as the entire city seemed to hold her breath. I remember thunderstorms which of course everyone took as portents, even though they are common enough at the end of the year. Many people from the north of Italy decided to take refuge in the city, for surely Caesar would never attack Rome herself? They poured in, and the extra numbers made the city uncomfortable. The temples were thronging as every head of household made their way to appease the gods with sacrifices. Some people packed their families off to country houses and relatives, although it was hard to say where would be safe. The Senate met frequently, trying to find a compromise that would suit both men, and messengers rode up and down the Flaminian way as reports went to and from Caesar's stronghold of Ravenna.

Several of the tribunes had long been supporters of Caesar and they made it clear that they would use their office to push forward Caesar's plans, if they could. Cassius thought it was too soon to declare one way or the other. There was, he said, just a chance still that Pompey and Caesar might come to an agreement. I pointed out that this was unlikely, but Cassius said, "Tertulla, I have to try."

One morning just before Saturnalia, Barates my favourite cloth merchant was shown into my Painted Garden. He looked strange in such a different setting, and I could not imagine why he had come. It turned out that he had a proposition.

"I am about to leave Rome for a while, Lady Junia," he said. "I have run down my stock, and my nephew will stay to keep an eye on the shop, such as it is. But I do not feel that there will be a demand for luxury cloth for a little while here. I shall winter near Brundisium, and when the seas are safe in the spring, I shall sail home to Antioch."

I could not blame him. I wondered for one moment if he had come to offer to escort me there too, then dismissed this silly idea immediately. His offer was very practical however, and I had no hesitation about trusting him to carry out his promise. I sent him off to Antioch with a substantial amount of money. There he was to invest in low-risk businesses and administer them, lodging all the paperwork at the biggest temple in the city, so that Cassius or I could access it if needed. It was a good deal all round, for Barates earned a percentage of the profits, and the temple was to benefit in the event that the world we knew collapsed. That money stayed in Antioch, administered by Barates' family, for many years and was one source of my current wealth.

As events moved nearer and nearer to conflict, my family decided on our policy at a dinner held by my mother at the house at Antium. Although the house had been given to me by my mother at the time of my wedding, anyone in the family could use it, and given where it was situated, they did. Lepidus liked it very much, so much so that he bought a house nearby, which of course meant that Junia didn't stay as often as I would have liked. This was typical of Lepidus. He always managed to do whatever he did in such a way that he put my teeth on edge. Cassius and I kept a small staff there permanently and anyone from the family travelling to the Bay of Naples by sea would spend at least one night there. We even had a sitting-room decorated especially for my mother, not as fine as hers on the Palatine, but pretty enough, with stylish vases of flowers seeming to float on walls painted to look like panels of white marble. Once Saturnalia was over but before the new year brought in new officials, we all made our way there, from Rome via Ostia. I left a day before everyone else, bringing half a dozen slaves to get things ready, setting out at dawn to get down to

Ostia where we had booked our usual little boat which spent the summers sailing to the Bay of Naples and back, and the winters shuttling between Antium and Ostia. Once at Antium, a little convoy of carts took us to the western cliffs where our villa huddled into a green hill and overlooked the end of a sweeping beach, beautiful for walks in the summer and lashed by salty gusts of wind in the depths of winter. Once I had enjoyed the small suite of baths, I slept soundly in preparation for a busy day ahead. My main concern was to make sure that our cooks had everything they required to prepare a special dinner. I knew that the staff would be able to prepare the guest rooms without supervision, but getting decent ingredients was not always easy in the winter. Fortunately, we had brought most of what was missing from the local market, and I eventually felt that nobody would go too hungry. The guests started arriving as darkness was looming from the small hills inland, and there was only time for baths and meals served as and when the guests needed them. By the time Brutus and his wife Claudia arrived, everyone but myself had gone to bed and once I had greeted them and ensured they had everything required, I too retired for the night, exhausted and slightly resentful that hardly anyone had thanked me.

I had planned that the grand dinner would start early on the next afternoon because I knew it would be a long meal, a business meal. The family would use it to make final decisions and plan for the years after this madness had played out. None of us were naive enough to hope that Rome would survive the years ahead without fighting. I could not tell you what we ate at that meal because although I had sweated over the menus and the organisation, the food itself was completely unimportant. There were three couches and my siblings and I, our spouses, and my mother made nine diners, the perfect number. Plato, I thought, could have written a jewel of a dialogue about us all, witty and philosophical talk flowing with the wine. Instead, my brother Brutus started off the discussion, though I could tell that Lepidus wanted to. Isauricus was uninterested in being in charge, but he watched everyone else with his usual amiable smile, at ease because his decision was made.

Brutus made the mistake of starting with philosophy, asking us all what a philosopher should do in a situation like this and was interrupted straight away by my brother-in-law Lepidus, to a silent chorus of eye-rolling around the table.

"Brutus, this is not about philosophy," he said, and sounded sharp and tired at the same time. "I don't even know the difference between an Epicurean and a Stoic. We have got to work out who is going to win this particular battle and whose side we should choose - it is as simple as that. I know what I intend to do - I am going to follow Caesar. The man has leadership, he has charisma, and the masses are behind him, as well as his army. The Senate have treated him appallingly, but those men he has led in Gaul for ten years - I tell you they will follow him. They don't care about Rome or principles or what a philosopher should do. Pompey may have had years of generalship but he's old and he is out of touch. He hasn't fought for years, and frankly, Caesar is the better soldier. I vote for Caesar."

It sounded very straightforward when let us put it like this and Isauricus, though he said nothing, nodded his head in agreement. Brutus looked sulky, but Lepidus ignored him and looked at my mother.

"Servilia," he said, "I would like to hear what you think."

My mother shrugged, as though she knew nothing of these things.

"I agree completely with your picture of Caesar," she said. "I agree with what you have said about Pompey. If I were a man, I would not be here now for I would have ridden north and joined Caesar already. I believe - and I'm sorry to say this, Brutus - that Caesar has right on his side. Maybe a philosopher would disagree with me but a man must fight for his place in our society and Caesar has been insulted for long enough. He is the most competent and intelligent man of his generation and the Senate have never been prepared to recognise this. However, there is little that I personally can do except to make sure that anyone from this family who supports Pompey will be pardoned by Caesar should Caesar win." And she looked at Brutus. There was a silence. Brutus who had been looking at the floor lifted his head and exchanged a look with my husband. I knew what this meant. Very politely and with determination, my brother and Cassius were going to range themselves against my mother and my brothers-in-law.

Brutus said, "I shall be going to Cilicia to join the new governor Publius Sestius as soon as I can arrange a ship. Sestius has asked me to serve on his provincial staff there. He has not yet declared himself one way or the other, but I trust him to be honourable if we end up on different sides."

My mother nodded.

"In many ways," she said, "this is a very sensible arrangement - Lepidus and Isauricus will go and join Caesar. Brutus will go to Cilicia and observe, and Cassius, I am assuming that you will join the Senatorial majority and follow Pompey. Eventually, you will all find yourselves in Greece as I think it likely that Pompey will withdraw there as soon as Caesar makes his stand, and that is where the fighting will be. We women will stay in Rome, or here at Antium. However - we must remember that Civil War is a disgrace, a pollution, and the gods are not going to forgive us easily. Whatever we do, we must pray and sacrifice and keep as many friends as is possible. It may well be that you will meet each other on the battlefield. May you all be protected and return safely."

I think every head bowed as she spoke. It felt as if she were a priestess intervening for us, for our divided country. This was my mother at her best.

She continued with a brisker, practical tone to her voice, once more the materfamilias, planning for her household.

"This villa will be our base, girls, and I include you, Claudia, of course; there is room for all of you and your children. We shall keep a boat down at the harbour on standby in case we need to go further south, but I do not believe we shall be targets. Caesar and Pompey have more important things to do now. It may even be useful to be able to meet with people in Rome from time to time. You men must all send keep us and have no fear that we will be working in whatever way seems best to make sure that as many of you as possible will be safe and that your property is safe too. Whatever happens this family will carry on, our resources will be preserved, and we shall bring up the next generation. Naturally I hope that Caesar will win this particular battle but, if he does not, I think that we have the authority to plead our case and make sure that we can survive no matter who is in charge. That is crucial. I have three grandsons now and they must have a future."

There was a silence around the table as she spoke and for a moment the mention of grandsons distracted me. The ironic side of me sighed that my mother had not seen fit to mention her little granddaughter, another Servilia; another side, female and anxious, looked at my sisters who had fallen pregnant so quickly after their marriages and hoped that there was nothing wrong with me. When my attention came back to the discussion Isauricus was speaking.

"I think that this is the only sensible way to proceed, Servilia," he said. "Brutus, Lepidus - along with Cassius, I think that we should all four of us make an agreement along the lines of Servilia's suggestion. Let us fight where our hearts and consciences dictate and hope for peace when this is all over. Let's agree that we will not hold our choices against each other."

To my relief they all nodded. My sisters and I exchanged smiles, and my mother picked up her wine cup.

"A libation," she said and, pouring just a drop of wine onto the marble floor of our dining room, she prayed that the gods would look after us all, bring us home safely and that peace would be established. I fought to keep pictures of a bloody battlefield in Greece out of my mind.

When they had all left, Cassius and I stayed in Antium. I had no wish to return to Rome and watch everyone teeter on the edge of their ambition. But I am perfectly sure that similar scenes were happening in houses all over Rome that winter, and the new year was not very old before Cassius decided that he must return to the city. I did not have to wait long for his first letter.

Cassius Longinus to his beloved Tertulla, greetings.

We are just twelve days into the new year and the unsurprising hour has come - Caesar has declared war by crossing his troops over the border from Gaul into Italy. As to whom he has declared against, I do not know - Rome? Surely not - I am convinced that Caesar is a patriot at least. Is it against Pompey, a man who was once his own son-in-law and with whom he has worked on many occasions? I feel sure that they would work together again if there were not so many people determined to divide them. No, Caesar is declaring war on the Senate, a lumbering mass of self-importance which refuses to see that change is needed. Tertulla, I still don't know how to choose between the two sides - and yet I have chosen. I shall do as your mother has suggested. I am going to pay a brief visit to you at Antium, then I shall declare for the Senate and Pompey. And go where I am sent.

He stayed three nights and two days before he went on to join the Senate in retreating to the ports on the south-eastern coast of Italy, from where the crossing to Greece is quickest. We spent one night and half a day in perfect companionship, then quarrelled, then made up. We had been married for just six months.

I felt nothing more than a slight feeling of depression that Rome had not been able to avoid this crisis. Cassius had been asked to help command Pompey's fleet and when he left me, we were prepared for a long separation. Just as he had done in Syria under the doomed Marcus Crassus, my husband would do whatever he was asked to do, because he was a good soldier, a faithful officer and when it came to it, a leader trusted by his troops. Over the next months he sent me many letters some of which made it all the way to Antium, where I stayed and welcomed anyone who would visit. My mother was a frequent visitor as Rome was very unsettled, my sisters less frequently as they and their husbands owned other estates where they would stay. I organised a small group of trusted and active slaves who became our messengers during that time, travelling from Rome to Antium, to Lanuvium, Tibur, and so on, round all the towns south of Rome where the rich have their country homes. The letters I wrote to and received from my sisters were honest, full of our fears, and the fears of women left behind during a war are looked on as trivial by the world. I rarely want to be reminded of them nowadays. What I shan't bore you with are the accounts of battles and marches and perilous sea-crossings. I am more concerned with how I and my family survived.

There were shortages in Rome over the next few years, especially during the many times when Caesar was not in the city, but my family were prepared. We were rich, but we had planned as well. I had made my own private arrangement with Barates, of course, and I never told anyone about this, not even Cassius. Cassius had made some radical changes to his banking arrangements, emptying his account with the Forum bankers he used, and distributing the money throughout Italy and further abroad. Trusted staff like Felix were sent off to several of Cassius' properties with money and valued possessions, packaged for discreet storage. Barates aside, I made Antium the centre of my own network of wealth - which I appreciate was my husband's by law, but it seemed sensible to give me the oversight of several concerns. We agreed to sell the tenement block in Rome that had been part of my dowry. I used the money to buy some land on the road leading from Antium towards Rome and set up a recently freed slave who used to belong to my sister Nilla's household. He was going to use the land to farm vegetables, and my sisters and I were his primary customers, whether in Rome or in Antium, a useful arrangement which served us well during the years of uncertainty and unpredictable shortages. Antium also became the repository for my favourite pieces of art, and our library. If war brought unrest, then there would be riots, and riots in Rome meant fire. I wasn't going to risk our precious collection. Looking around, I saw many people doing similar things, and with an air, unlike me, of having done it all before. I had not run my own household until after the heyday of the gangs in Rome and thinking back I realised how many times my mother had consulted Aretus about making sure that our possessions were safe. For people like my mother, this was just one more era of uncertainty. She had seen her uncle assassinated in the atrium of the family house when she was a child. She may not have seen a battlefield, but her experience of violence and loss had been extensive.

Chapter 17

Nilla's husband Isauricus travelled with Caesar that year, and
headed south through Italy, gathering support, and ensuring that
Pompey and his supporters crossed over into Greece from
Brundisium. Nilla stayed at Rome, and soon tired of the city's
uncertain atmosphere and shortages. As spring turned to
summer, she decided to come and stay, and I found myself glad
of her company and that of my little niece and nephew. My
sister informed me that she was now going to avoid further
pregnancies if possible and that she was also enjoying her
husband's absence. I dreaded to think how far Nilla could go in
the search for enjoyment, but she laughed at me and said that I
had a disgusting mind.

"All our husbands enjoy sex whenever they want with
whoever they want," she said in a very forthright, Nilla-like
way, and I struggled not to blush and give her the satisfaction.
But she was not looking to embarrass me, she meant it.
"Tertulla, I know which of the staff Isauricus uses when he
fancies a change," she said, "and I don't like it, but I have to
endure it. I have done my job, provided the children, one of
each, healthy and beautiful." She was right - little Servilia was
a lovely child, all dark eyes and shining curls, while Publius was
a sweet-tempered quiet little boy, not as boisterous as Junia's
pair, but thoughtful and already doing well at his studies.

"You once said that you might grow to love him," I said trying
to sound cool rather than petulant.

"So I did," agreed my sister. "And I am fond of him. He is a
civilised and attentive husband, and he is discreet. I decided that
I too can be discreet and civilised. Indeed, I am far more discreet
than Isauricus and I make sure that I do not fall pregnant and
provide him with a slave's bastard."

A slave? Nilla used slaves? As I gaped at her, struggling for a
reply, Nilla sighed and told me not to worry about it so much.

The forces following Pompey and most of the Senate retreated
down the spine of Italy and left from Brundisium to gather in

Greece. To most of us it looked like a retreat and we did not understand it. Caesar chased them, waved a contemptuous farewell, and announced that he was coming back to Rome, before setting off to the other end of the Mediterranean. The city, under my brother-in-law Lepidus, declared Caesar a Dictator, and became enticing once more. Nilla and I returned to the Palatine Hill. I wanted to see Caesar now he was the aggressor, the man who started a war, and even Dictator.

"We needed to ensure that everything carries on as normal," Lepidus said at dinner on my first night in Rome for several months. The whole city was in a state of excitement awaiting Caesar's return from the south of Italy.

"Normal?" said my mother.

"As near normal as we can get," said Lepidus with an air of one who had said this many times over the last few days.

"We have no Consuls to hold elections," put in Junia. "And Caesar is effectively in charge anyway. Installing him as Dictator so that he can hold elections makes sense." Lepidus looked at her approvingly as she parroted his opinions loyally, and I sighed inwardly at his stupidity in not appreciating her for the person she was.

"And that is all he will do as Dictator?" I asked, curious rather than apprehensive. Rome had not had many Dictators but my mother could remember the last one, Sulla, and the executions and terror.

"He isn't going to be a Sulla," said Lepidus clearly irritated by my question. "We couldn't think of any other way he could hold the elections safely and legitimately. He will enter the city, take the office of Dictator and hold elections using the Dictator's power, then lay down the office again. Ten, twelve days at the most - this is going to be a proper legitimate Dictatorship. It means that the consuls and other officials elected will be..." He floundered and I helpfully said, "Legitimate?"

"Quite," said my brother-in-law and finally smiled. "Gods above, I shall be glad when this is all over."

"Lepidus will be going to govern Spain as soon as everything is settled there, Caesar has promised him," said Junia, looking proud, and rightly so. The governorship of such an important province was a huge compliment to Lepidus.

"And who is to be Consul after these elections are held?" I asked. My mother looked as though she was tempted to roll her eyes.

"Tertulla, really - Caesar, of course."

Of course. The general had an army, but he needed official status in Rome, to justify what he was going to do. Caesar had claimed Italy, was off to pacify Spain and after that would have to face Pompey himself. One question remained - if Caesar left Rome to do all this, who could be entrusted with Rome itself?

"What about the other Consul?" I asked, and this was the right question this time. The answer was obvious from Nilla's smug face and her husband's sudden modest ducking of the head, as if he had decided to peck at the leftovers on his plate.

"Congratulations, Isauricus," said my mother, also looking smug, as well she might. Her plans for keeping the family successful were going well. I smiled at Isauricus, who looked bashfully pleased with himself, stuck my tongue out at Nilla and called her "The Consul's wife" for the rest of dinner. She was going to be unbearable but I didn't mind. We weren't children anymore. And I liked Isauricus. It was only when I reached the dark and quiet of Cassius' understaffed house on the Palatine that I allowed myself to feel just a little left out.

An invitation to dinner at my mother's house a few days later was unsurprising, but when I entered the house to find that Caesar was guest of honour, my heart lifted with excitement. It was as good as Cassius being home, and in a year when even dinner parties had been few and far between, this became even more special. It was the first time I had ever been in the same room as this man for a private occasion, the first opportunity to find out how his normal speaking voice sounded, watch his mannerisms, observe how he and my mother behaved with each other. Was I still in love with the idea of being his daughter? Or did I dismiss such ideas as being a part of childhood and best left there? The gods above know that I had other things to think about. All I can tell you is that every time I saw him my only wish was to have him acknowledge me. I had thought of such a moment, fantasised of the gradual hush in the room as people looked from me to Caesar and back again, the dawning surprise and shock, the looks of envy from my sisters.

I need hardly tell you that none of this happened. It was a family dinner, just like any other, but with a guest of honour, paying his debt of gratitude to my brothers-in-law. I was the wife of Caesar's opponent, only there because of my mother.

Lepidus and Isauricus, it was clear, were in high favour, rewarded and proud, and Junia and Nilla reclined with their husbands, glowing with the shared triumph. My mother smiled at nothing in particular as her plans knitted together in a pattern she had drawn up years before. I, on the other hand, kept my head down, conscious that my husband was serving Caesar's enemies on the sea around Sicily, although nobody was so tactless as to mention this. Caesar though did ask after Brutus, and my mother replied with no embarrassment.

"He has moved on from Cilicia now of course, and has reached Pompey's camp in Dyrrachium," she said. "He has his tame philosopher with him and writes that he spends his day in discussion and study." She could not help a smile as she finished this and Caesar laughed - not ironically, not with any bitterness, but openly.

"Servilia, how did you come by such a son?" he asked, and my mother answered immediately "In the usual way." The two of them laughed with one another and we were all spectators.

Now as I look back, I am looking on a god, the Divine Julius and father of Augustus, grandfather of the current Emperor, by adoption at least. He is a distant and stellar figure to the young people of my family, and the first thing they will tell you about him is of the comet that was seen in the sky after his death. Well, we all spent that evening with a mortal, a special man, but a man. I know that I risk sounding like one of Catullus' love-lorn idiots, singing their desire in verse as they tell their beloved that they just want to gaze upon their beauty, but I ached to be Caesar's daughter. And after that night, as happened every time I saw him, I thought about nothing but him for several days. Then the longing would quietly fade into the background, and I would get on with my life until the next reminder of him.

Throughout most of that year I stayed in Antium, and often with me was poor Claudia, my brother's wife. Brutus' marriage had been entirely cynical, and was childless, so Claudia was left adrift and wondering what to do most of the time. She was quiet and for the first couple of years of knowing her, I could not start up a conversation that lasted more than a couple of exchanges before she faded away. Junia had more success as it turned out that Claudia loved children and was willing to play with her newly-acquired niece and nephews for hours on end. I kept trying to find a way through to her, eventually asking her to help me plan a new garden at Antium, which occupied the summer months. It was there that the news arrived of the death of her father. Appius Claudius was one of the most arrogant, appalling aristocrats Rome ever produced, so it was as well that he fell ill and died before Pharsalus. Had he survived, he would never have been able to beg Caesar's pardon afterwards. Claudia wept dutifully rather than bitterly, and then touchingly devoted herself to supporting me as I worried over Cassius.

The first great battle affecting us all was that of Pharsalus, more than a year and a half after Caesar crossed the Rubicon river. It took that long for Pompey and Caesar to meet in battle, and I do not criticise them for this hesitation. Up until the point where Caesar crossed from Italy to Greece where Pompey had been gathering troops and resources, there could have been an end made, a reconciliation between the two who had been political allies and related by marriage at one point. Nobody wants to be the man who starts a civil war. When you gather whole armies of men, how do you persuade those men to take that first step in the charge towards one another? The truth is that if you are a woman watching helplessly from miles away, nothing justifies a battle, let alone a war. In the end, we - Claudia, my sisters and I - were fortunate. Our brother was the only one of our close family to fight at Pharsalus and he survived. Lepidus was away governing Spain and Isauricus was the Consul in Rome, looking after Caesar's interests in the city and Italy. Cassius (and I privately thanked the gods for it) did not even fight in the battle, serving with the fleet as he was.

Claudia, Junia, my mother and I - were all at Antium and sitting in my sitting room, which overlooked the garden to the rear of the villa, when the messenger from Brutus arrived. I still have the letter. My great-nieces and nephews look on it as a relic of one of the most famous men in Rome's history. If I ever let them read it, they would be disappointed. Only Brutus could have found the time to write such a pompous piece of prose and on papyrus too - apparently, he had gone to war with a full supply of office materials as well as a secretary and one of his philosopher friends. Nobody who knew Brutus would have found this surprising. The messenger automatically gave the letter to my mother, who held it out to Claudia and said gently, "Read it out to us, please, dear Claudia."

"To my wife Claudia, my mother Servilia and my sisters, greetings," the letter began dutifully. "Yesterday following victory in battle at Pharsalus on the west coast of Greece, Gaius Julius Caesar also received my surrender and granted my appeal for clemency, along with those of many others. Tertulla, I urge you to write at once to your husband and tell him, encouraging him to do likewise. Our cause is lost, and Caesar is the best hope now for Rome. I have already dined and discussed the future with him, and I am confident that this is the way ahead for us all. I shall not write about the battle itself, as civil strife should be forgotten not celebrated, but afterwards one of Caesar's senior centurions found me and told me that he had been detailed to escort me to Caesar straight away. "And I must also tell you, sir, that even before the battle the General was concerned for your safety. We were all ordered not to engage you if it were at all possible during the fighting." Naturally I am flattered by this show of concern for me. I know that Caesar has always been a friend to our family, and despite his enmity with my uncle Cato, I wonder if the respect Caesar has for Cato also affected this decision to single me out for consideration."

Claudia paused here and looked around at us all. Junia and I were making sure we did not look at one another for fear of sniggering, while our mother after a moment's silence merely said, "Do carry on, dear Claudia. It is most interesting to think that my brother Cato may actually have been of some use during his dreary life."

At that, Junia could not keep in her reactions. A strange yelp escaped her, and she put her hand over her mouth and looked down, struggling to keep composure. Claudia reddened but carried on. It is a very boring letter so I shall not quote any more of it. Enough to say that my brother was pleased with himself and was safe. I was relieved however that he said that he had made a point of pleading for Cassius. Later, when I was alone with my mother, I asked her if she believed the centurion's story.

"Surely in the midst of battle, there is no time to stop and enquire names? I know nothing about real battles, and Cassius has told me hardly anything about the fighting he has been in, but surely everything is horrible and confused."

"It will make a good story," said my mother calmly. "Tertulla, it may be utterly unbelievable, but men need their battlefield myths. Caesar's forgiveness will become part of his legend."

"I know that in Homer's Iliad warriors regularly have long and complex conversations, and two of them, I remember even discover they are distantly related."

"I hope your brother can endure being in a supporting role in Caesar's story. But if Cassius is forgiven too, Brutus may find it more bearable, and Lepidus and Isauricus will be rewarded for their faithfulness. Our family will survive. Survival, Tertulla - that is all that matters today."

Cassius, being no fool, made no hesitation after Pharsalus. The war was lost, so he joined the lines of those asking Caesar for pardon. He wrote to me that he had successfully surrendered and was travelling to join Caesar in Egypt where he expected to be given a command of some sort. Cassius was not looking forward to this as it would inevitably result in fighting not just fellow Romans, but also the men with whom he allied himself at the start of the conflict. He was however resigned to it as an inevitable outcome of civil war, and his military experience made him too valuable to be ignored.

The first official news after Pharsalus was of a horror. After the battle, many had escaped, including the general Pompey, who made his way to Egypt, only to be cut down on the beach as he landed. The Egyptians thought that Caesar would be pleased with the gift of his enemy's severed head. Instead, Caesar was upset enough to stay in Egypt re-establishing the monarchy to his own satisfaction. The young Pharoah was deposed and his sister Cleopatra installed in his place. Egyptian politics of course were notoriously complicated, violent and distasteful, but in addition, rumours were soon reaching Rome that Cleopatra was Caesar's mistress. She was twenty-two and he was fifty-two, and my mother was not best pleased.

Pharsalus also brought with it a new sense of purpose for us as a family, because we were now united and firmly on Caesar's side. The men of the family could work together. After Pharsalus, the remaining opposition to Caesar fled to different areas of the Mediterranean, unable to agree with each other of course, the curse of the Republic's political system. Despite this fragmentation, there were enough troops to make the opposition a serious threat to Caesar. Pompey's sons had a powerbase in Spain still and my Uncle Cato gathered several legions in North Africa. In the East, a King Pharnaces of somewhere-or-other invaded our province of Asia and I pictured the Mediterranean Sea as a long thin lake with burning towns on every shore.

Chapter 18

News took a long time to reach us over the winter months, but when spring brought the grain ships once more, we learned of the romance and danger of Caesar's mission to Egypt. The extraordinary story of his first meeting with Cleopatra - her delivered to him hidden in a rolled-up carpet - was the favourite of the Forum. One enterprising group of street actors quickly developed a short comedy which they performed wherever they could make a space. In their version, a small but very well-trained dog shot out of the carpet roll and pretended to bite the actor playing Caesar. Junia and I managed to arrange several shopping expeditions and found the group performing somewhere in the Forum every time. Eventually the actors moved on to take their satire for a tour of the Italian towns, and the show made it as far as the Bay of Naples. The story is still told regularly in comedies and history alike. As far as I was concerned the most important news was that Cleopatra was pregnant by Caesar. All at once, my need to be his child swept over me and I was glad that I was sitting when Kleia told me, her fingers flying in automatic swooping darts as she braided and pinned my hair for the day. I felt my scalp prickle as hot and cold waves broke over my head, and my whole body tensed with the need to shout out my disbelief. "He couldn't!" rang out inside me, followed by, "Of course he could." As Kleia held the mirror up behind my head, angling it this way and that, I realised that I had a sibling whose mother was queen and goddess to her people. One day I might have a god for a brother. "And do you think," asked my treacherous common sense, "that circumstances will ever let you meet your brother and be acknowledged?"

"You don't often get so annoyed," observed Sulpicia. "What was it about this particular incident?"

"It was the stupidity - as with the Vettius affair," I said. "All I could think was "Dear gods, what is wrong with him?" Rome was not a happy place after Pharsalus and he should have returned, to soothe the thousands of people who lost sons, husbands, and fathers...."

"And instead, he stayed in Egypt," said Sulpicia. "And had an affair with Cleopatra."

"Oh yes, he had an affair with a foreign, worse an Eastern, Queen." My voice grew higher as I felt the outrage. "And because he got entangled with her, he met opposition from her co-ruler Ptolemy, and found himself under siege for several weeks. Of course, he fought back and won, and Ptolemy was killed in battle - but it should never have happened. Egypt needed a diplomatic solution - Caesar turned Alexandria into a battle-ground."

"Alexandria was always going to be a problem," said Sulpicia. "Egypt is a problem still for us. Look at our relationship with Egypt over the last fifty years and it is one of turmoil. We need Egypt's wealth but despise its history and culture. We admire Alexandria's founder immensely but not its people."

This is still true of course. Rome has always despised the East.

Once the situation in Alexandria was settled, with no more damage than the death of a pharaoh and the burning down of a wing of the Library of Alexandria, Caesar then decided to go on a trip along the Nile river with Cleopatra. The Roman world twiddled its thumbs, and rumbles of dissatisfaction rolled around the Mediterranean. In Rome, the mood of the city grew sour, and the problems which usually accompany war - money shortages, food shortages, bereavement - loomed larger. My brother-in-law Isauricus was glad when he had finished his Consulship. Unable to bear the constant gossip and threatening unrest in the city, I decided to go to Antium, and remained there until Caesar returned in the late summer. Then of course I crept back, ready to trail in my mother's wake for the chance of a glimpse of him.

I was back in my marital home on the Palatine - I disliked staying in the house on my own but my sisters were both away on their country estates - when my mother came, not for a visit, but to take me out. Because Caesar was in the city - and there were precious few periods when Caesar was actually in Rome - there was a buzz of activity all over Rome. We may have grumbled about our leader hardly ever bothering with Rome, but we loved it when he was there. He arrived with a head full of plans each time, and the sound of hammering would announce his presence to those who did not know already.

I had no idea what was driving my mother, but she looked very pleased with herself and less calm than usual. I was missing Cassius and thought grumpily that it was all very well for people who got to see their lovers, but did she have to make it so indecently clear that she was still enjoying Caesar so much at her age? My mother was now in her fifties, and people had long been using phrases like "still handsome" to describe her. I knew that everyone mentally compared her to the unseen but oh-so-young Queen of Egypt.

Once ready we made our way down to the Forum and found that an auction was going on with Caesar himself in charge. During those years, Caesar held civil offices as well as military power, and now he was Dictator once more, an office which had the advantage of enabling him to get things done quickly. He always had official guards, the lictors, around him, and occasionally used a bodyguard of hand-picked soldiers from Gaul. The Rostra, the speaking platform at the end of the Forum was crowded with men, Caesar to one side seated in a ring of lictors, a couple of soldiers at either end of the platform gazing out over the crowd, men in plain tunics running up to Caesar with piles of wax tablets, and a secretary desperately trying to order everything at a ridiculously tiny wooden table. My mother stopped at the edge of the crowd and gazed at the platform until somebody noticed her. That was all it took. The secretary looked around and signalled, and one of the plain-tunics ran down the back of the platform, appearing a moment later pushing through the crowd to us. To my surprise, he led us around the crowd to a set of chairs discreetly laid out near the front of the platform and off to one side. On guard were a couple of soldiers who withdrew behind the chairs.

"We are expected then?" I muttered to my mother as we made our way towards these chairs. "I still cannot get used to seeing soldiers in the Forum," said my mother conversationally.

We sat and Kleia went off to organise drinks from a nearby stall, while our small knot of attendants disposed itself around us, and the crowd stared through our human shield. My mother gazed straight ahead and said quietly, "We might as well enjoy it while it lasts."

After a few moments of wondering what we were doing here, I tuned in to the calling of the auctioneer and gradually it dawned on me that what was on sale was property. Houses, estates, blocks of flats, workshops, inside and outside Rome, even works of art. Everything was being sold on description only, with the successful bidders taking away a set of wax tablets with which to establish their ownership. I had never seen anything like this before. I saw my mother nod at the auctioneer to establish her claim to a block of flats on the lower slopes of the Esquiline Hill, and that, it appeared, was that. The auctioneer closed the sale as quickly as he could, nobody had the nerve to bid against my mother, and once the small bundle of wax tablets had been delivered, we left. I could not resist just one barbed question.

"So, which of Caesar's enemies owned those?"

"Domitius Ahenobarbus," said my mother. "And you need not look so virtuously disapproving, Tertulla. The Domitii are hugely wealthy and his dependents will not starve."

I found this answer lacking. What would have happened to my property if Cassius had been captured or killed before he could beg Caesar's pardon? My mother understood my silence.

"To the victor the spoils, Tertulla," she said. "You know this."

"We don't have to benefit from it though," I muttered.

"No," said my mother. "But Caesar offered me the chance to buy excellent property at a decent price and I took it. My grandchildren will benefit from it. The Domitii will suffer a manageable loss for a generation or two."

I wondered if Domitius Ahenobarbus had grandchildren, but in fact my mother turned out to be right. The Ahenobarbi climbed back up after this setback and are once more near the heart of power as I write this. And as far as I know none of them ever remarked on my family's acquisition of a rather nice house on the Esquiline Hill.

I felt the gaze of every person in the Forum as we walked back towards the incline that took us back onto the Palatine and I hardly dared to think of what they were all thinking - that my mother was collecting her reward for years of service.

"You need to develop a shell, Tertulla," said my mother.

"Like yours?" I thought but did not say.

When my mother also acquired a luxurious villa in the heart of Campania from another of these auctions, she did not tell me for a long time. I only heard when someone mentioned that the original owner was none too pleased about it.

One more thing came out of those auctions, and it was horrible, shaking me more than I could have thought. My mother's comment about needing to develop a shell to protect oneself from the nastiness of life became even more appropriate. As usual, this story begins with my mother entering the room. The moment she strode in, I knew there was a problem. She was so angry the rage radiated from her and she could not even sit or tell me about the matter at first. I grew quite concerned, but at last she managed to tell me. It all revolved around a foolish man and a nasty little joke. Marcus Cicero, fresh from being pardoned by Caesar, was back in Rome, and found much material for his dinner-party witticisms. As it turned out one of those barbed little comments was at my expense. Someone mentioned that my mother had bought some property at one of Caesar's auctions and Cicero said,

"And what made it even more of a bargain was that she had a third knocked off..."

Not even a good joke, of course, and the meaning was nasty. My name meant "a third", so clearly my mother had pimped me to the Dictator in return for the houses she bought. As Cicero's sayings always did, it went all round the sitting-rooms and dining-tables of Rome.

Fortunately, I was sitting down when my mother finally managed to explain this to me. The feeling of hot, shameful nausea which swept over me was appalling and I fought to stay still and not be sick. I was aware of nothing around me for a few seconds, until to my relief Kleia was there with a damp cloth on the nape of my neck and a soothing, rolling stream of nonsense words. When I could speak, my voice shook.

"That is vile. How could he?" Inside I was desperately trying not to think of the word "incest", surely the most appalling word in the sight of the gods and conjuring up images of horrors such as Oedipus in the plays by Sophocles.

"He is a fool who has made his way by being clever with words," said my mother, now sitting and restored, for the great part, to her usual self. "Cicero is the sort of person who cannot bear to leave a joke unvoiced, however cruel. Considering that he has had to beg pardon from Caesar before, one might have thought he had learned the lesson. And to think that your brother has always valued Cicero's advice and friendship."

My brother was about to go and govern part of Gaul for Caesar and, I thought, would be far too busy being grateful to notice rumours about his sister. Brutus had ignored us all – except Cassius – after his humiliating turn-around after Pharsalus. I grieved, for despite my sisters' feelings, I still loved my brother and valued his advice. Or some of his advice, anyway. But I realised that he had to recover from the humiliating turn-around and by all accounts Pharsalus had been a nightmare. I could wait while he served in Gaul, a task which Caesar had given him deliberately. Caesar was about to deal with our Uncle Cato and did not want Brutus around. It was the winter after he returned from Egypt and Asia when Caesar set off to North Africa to confront the sizable contingent of determined men who had fled there after Pharsalus. Brutus' governorship excused him from going on this campaign, and he made a good job of managing the Gauls. Certainly they remembered him with kindness years later. I thought it was good of Caesar because forcing Brutus to fight against Cato would have been cruel to him, and difficult for my mother. Well, maybe it would have been. With my mother, who knows?

I suppose I had better relate the end of my Uncle Cato. It had a profound effect on my brother, and my sisters and I forgot it as soon as we could. Three years after crossing the Rubicon, two after the battle of Pharsalus, after he had sorted out Egypt and Cleopatra, and Asia - Caesar finally had to confront Cato, the man who had opposed him for all his political career. The decisive and murderous battle of Thapsus left Cato with no hope and Caesar was marching to confront him at the nearby town of Utica. Rather than subject the town to a siege, my uncle killed himself by disembowelment, an unbelievably stupid way to achieve his aims, I thought. The story went that he was stopped in his initial attempt by his son and household and was reduced to unpicking their well-meant stitches and bandaging, but I do not believe that. Every Roman has the right to end his or her life as he or she chooses, and no family or slave would try to do anything to stop him. Indeed, many would assist if needed. I don't know the full truth of the matter but the story which has prevailed has been framed to emphasise my uncle's stoicism and bravery. I do not doubt that he died courageously and philosophically for the men of my family have a tendency towards noble deaths. The women clean up after them, less philosophically but a great deal more practically.

Cicero, now living in retirement, found the time to write a small book in praise of my uncle, to which Caesar replied with an even smaller book criticising him. My mother bought both books so I read them. Unfortunately, Cicero wrote extremely well, and I felt obliged to agree with some of his account of my uncle, but in neither account did I see a relative whom I could admire.

Defeating the allies in Africa did give Caesar a respite and this time there was no local seducer to lure him. He came back to Rome in late summer and announced that four triumphal processions would be held at the end of September and beginning of October to celebrate his victories in Gaul, Egypt, Asia and Africa.

My brother-in-law Isauricus was sent out to govern Asia at about this time and to my astonishment Nilla announced at dinner one evening that she was going to travel to Asia with her husband.

"But governors never take their wives," I objected.

"It has happened," said my mother.

"Isauricus has been asked to go and govern," Nilla said casually, "so I thought, "why not?" and asked him. I'm going to enjoy myself. Imagine, I might go to Antioch and see Barates' family, get a discount on all that lovely cloth. I've missed him."

It was a long time since Nilla had managed to annoy me so much, but fortunately I was distracted by the arrival of Cassius from peace-keeping duties in the East. He arrived in Antium just in time to enjoy a reunion, and then escorted me back to Rome. Four triumphs would mean a lot of parties and celebration, and he and I both wanted to celebrate. There was a concern that the city would start grumbling again as the African campaign had been against fellow-Romans, people like my Uncle Cato. But instead the mood swung around with the promise of days of celebrations. Everyone loves a triumph. Even my brother-in-law Lepidus had celebrated a triumph the year before, though nobody really knew why. He had not done much in Spain but a triumph is an honour, and Junia was extremely proud.

I had recovered from Cicero's jibe of the year before and did not even bother to mention it to Cassius. Everyone else had forgotten it of course, so I don't think he ever knew what had been said. I was also resigned to the fact that Caesar was acknowledging his son by Queen Cleopatra - this was something Cassius had decided to tell me, I suppose to illustrate that Caesar did acknowledge those whom he knew to be his children. Even this did not stop me picking at the old wound of my own birth, for it was now part of me, lying quiet most of the time but awakening in the sleepless hours of a hot summer night, when not even the sea breezes cooled me.

"Am I Caesar's?" - pick, pick, pick.

"Why doesn't he acknowledge me?" - pick, pick, pick.

"If I had been born a boy, things would be different."

Pick. Pick. Pick.

"Do you want me to tell you that this was all foolish and unnecessary worrying?" asked Sulpicia kindly. "I don't think that you do."

She was right.

"I just want to tell you the truth, however unlovely it is," I answered. "It was a destructive cycle of useless wishing, but it is part of my life, and I don't think I am unusual. I think everyone suffers from something similar."

"Even your Uncle Cato?"

I had to laugh.

"Gods, no. My Uncle Cato never suffered from doubt or unfulfilled desire in his life. But don't emulate him. Not even the gods can help you if you do."

Chapter 19

At the end of the summer, as we waited for the celebrations to start, I was stunned and not too happy to hear that Queen Cleopatra of Egypt had moved into Caesar's villa estate on the other side of the River Tiber. I was not the only one. We may have all gossiped about Caesar and Cleopatra for months, but it had not occurred to anyone that he would bring her to Italy. It quickly became clear that Caesar wanted Cleopatra named an official Friend and Ally of the People of Rome. The People of Rome took one look and cascaded into a volley of jokes, insults and graffiti. To do her credit, the Queen rose above all this and did everything expected of a grateful new ally, and soon we were hearing of her wonderful parties. She had an amazing singer to entertain at these gatherings. She had brought the stars of Alexandria's university with her. She had loaned Caesar the world's greatest mathematicians to help with his project of realigning the calendar. As Chief Priest he had a responsibility for this, and he and the Colleges of Priests had been wondering how to reform it. He needed to for people were complaining that the seasons no longer aligned with the months. Alexandria's scholars were the best in the world and the solution to our calendar was worked out and made ready to be presented to us all along with Caesar's triumphs. We also heard that Cleopatra had brought with her a fabulous mosaic depicting the River Nile, and she was looking to donate it to a temple. Cleopatra was clever and understood how the world worked. Don't imagine for a moment that she did the whole Queen and Goddess act when in Rome. She was willing to accept that she was not in Egypt now.

For days, nobody could talk about anything else. The stalls in the Forum began selling all sorts of Egyptian-themed goods, little wooden beetles painted blue and gold and called scarabs, tiny statuettes, standing stiff-posed and unnatural, supposedly of the Queen in Egyptian dress. Kleia even reported that Egyptian food was now all the rage in the street-bars. As far as

I could tell, to be Egyptian, the food had to be made of lentils and spiced. How authentic this made the food, I do not know. But unusually, the Romans had made their enthusiasm for a foreigner clear, and Cleopatra looked set to be accepted. I remained unimpressed.

Junia and I were walking with our retinues to call on my mother one morning and discussing whether to drop Cleopatra casually into the conversation or whether to pretend that the Egyptian Queen had not intruded on our notice.

"Well, I don't have the nerve to introduce the topic," I said firmly.

"It isn't as if she won't know that Cleopatra is here," pointed out Junia. "Are we really going to just scout around the subject forever?"

I felt I could scout around it indefinitely and not come off the worse. "Why do you want to talk about Cleopatra with her?" I asked.

Junia shrugged. "I am curious," she said. "I am eaten up with curiosity, in fact. I burn with..."

I nudged her in a very unladylike manner, and we both giggled.

"Well," said Junia, "I want to know how our mother feels about this."

The matter was decided when my mother greeted us by declaring that we had all been invited to meet Cleopatra at villa across the Tiber for a morning call. My mother actually called it that - a morning call, as if we were all respectable matrons, gathering over weak honey wine to discuss the preparations for a religious festival. I immediately felt outraged at the idea that the Queen could sit there and command us to visit her.

"Why are you going?" I asked. "Why would you want to meet someone like that?"

My mother turned her gaze on me, but it wasn't going to work as it had done when I was a child, so I stared back. She saw me being defiant and gave a little smile.

"Tertulla, she has invited me. And I must admit to being fascinated by everything I have heard about her - she is so well-educated, she speaks several languages and she rules Egypt.

159

Given her family history, that alone is fascinating. And she is about your age, just a little older. Don't you find it intriguing, and want to meet her?"

Of course I did, but there was an undercurrent of feeling, deep within me, that was dark and hostile to the Queen. She had displaced my mother in Caesar's affections and thus pushed me further away from him. She had produced for him an acknowledged son – everyone knew little Caesarion was Caesar's, even without the name. I also felt instinctively distrustful about Egypt. Ever since Rome began to expand its horizons, we had associated The East with all that was degenerate and exotic, never mind that Cleopatra was Greek, the descendant of Ptolemy the general of Alexander the Great. I wanted to hate her.

"We shall go and see what she is like," decreed my mother. "Naturally we shall not talk about Caesar, and we shall not even mention Calpurnia."

Caesar's wife, it appeared, was to be above discussion with Caesar's mistress, by decree of Caesar's other mistress.

The procession that set off across the Palatine that morning was impressive. My mother was leaving nobody in any doubt. A great Roman lady was calling on the Queen of Egypt, and which of them was the more confident of her own worth was a subject for competition. It was hot - despite the calendar saying September, the summer had only just got started - and even lying in a litter, I sweated. Junia and I followed our mother, and our three litters, trailing maids, made a quite a sight even in a city used to processions. We brought Aretus with us to manage the traffic ahead of us, which he did with the aid of a row of bodyguards. Others walked behind, more for the look of things than for security. The city was peaceful and good-tempered with Caesar back home.

Once over the Tiber, the noise and crowding dropped away and the road was flanked with the estates of the very wealthy. The air felt cooler and smelled fresher and was scented with the flowers grown in the immaculately kept gardens. If you had the money for one of these houses, then you could afford a troop of gardeners. My sister-in-law Claudia had access to one of these estates through her aunt Clodia Metelli, notorious mistress of the poet Catullus. Behind the walls and hedges, legendary parties had taken place, in the years when Clodia's brother ruled Rome through his gangs and his sister had reigned as queen of the literary world.

No more than a mile south of our river crossing, we turned up a track leading through a gate in a low wall which stretched out on either side purely as a demarcation of ownership. Just beyond the gate, a small hut housed a couple of slaves, who started to run down the drive. More slaves were stationed along the way, and we could see the message running ahead of us to the house. We made our way through orchards, then lawns, then a gravelled courtyard lined with topiary in large urns and statues. Long and low, the red-roofed house was no grander than our own villa at Antium, but the grounds were extensive, and behind the main villa would be dormitories to house the hundreds of slaves who, I had no doubt, were in residence.

We climbed out of our litters and our maids flitted around, adjusting folds, and tucking in wisps of hair, blotting the sweat from our faces. I stood still but looked around as much as possible, keen to note down the Egyptian touches I was sure the Queen had imposed on Roman lawns. All I saw was that in one corner of the courtyard a dove looked unconcernedly at the ginger cat that lay, belly flat to the ground, just an arm's length away. The cat's white paws were ready to push against the ground, the whole body in one long line from stretched-out tail to straining neck. Every still hair on that cat signalled attack, yet the dove gazed unmoved then casually turned its head towards us. I tensed as the cat quivered, but there was no need: the dove rose in a turmoil of feathers and noise, and the cat was left behind to start an emphatic grooming. The small drama was eclipsed by my mother saying sharply, "Tertulla!" You may well ask why a cat called my attention. This cat wore a gold collar and wore more in gold around its neck than I had on my entire person. I was aware of course that cats are especially venerated in Egypt if not in Rome. We appreciate their ability to kill vermin but otherwise…. I had not thought, when dressing that morning, that I would be competing with a cat.

My mother gave us one critical sweep of her eyes, then nodded and lead the way to the entrance, where a man waited. I assumed he was wearing typical Egyptian dress, since nobody I knew would have had their chief household slave clothed in a pleated kilt and a gold collar, along with a wig of such black stiffness the only reason for its use must have been ornamental. I resisted the temptation to turn and catch Junia's eye. We were Rome in Egypt now, and our mother was our commander. Our job was to march behind her. We traipsed dutifully in her wake and came into a beautifully cool and dark entrance hall, where several slaves (dressed in plain tunics, thank the gods) used enormous fans to move the air from side to side over a pool of water. The Egyptian led us across this hall and into a smaller room which looked over the front courtyard and was lighter, though still cool. Comfortable chairs had been set out, each with its own little table, and cups and jugs were lined up at the far end of the room with a hovering server ready. Sitting in the largest chair and facing us was a woman of about my own age, dressed in a cream tunic, with her dark hair pinned up in a bun at the back of her neck. Cleopatra. My first impression was of a small face with large brown eyes, a slightly bumpy nose and beautiful skin. Her tunic was linen with both neck and hem embroidered in gold and green, a stylised plant motif. Gold chains were around her neck, wrists and, I saw after a carefully discreet scrutiny, ankles. You would not have known that she was a queen, but you would have immediately treated her with respect. As my mother walked confidently across the room, the Queen stood and held out her hands to us, in a gesture of welcome.

"Lady Servilia, thank you for coming and thank you for bringing your daughters," she said in perfect Latin, with a Greek accent which softened the consonants. I listened carefully, noting the slight whistling through the "r" sound in "Servilia". I also realised very quickly that she had a lovely voice - not too high, and at first a little breathy until she got to the point in the conversation where she was talking in long sentences, and less aware of her speech. Then she pitched her voice deeper and lost the huskiness. She also spoke to her servants in a completely different voice, higher-pitched and peremptory, as was suitable for the Queen and Goddess that she was to her people.

I was so absorbed with looking and listening to her that I barely noticed the introductions made by my mother and was sitting in a chair and being served with cool watered fruit juice before I realised that I had been staring. The Queen of Egypt smiled at me as though to say, "I know, I am remarkable, aren't I?" and I gave a small smile back before busying myself with my drink.

"Now how am I to call your daughters?" asked the Queen and my mother said that we should be called Junia and Tertia. Straight away Cleopatra asked, "So there is another sister? One who comes in between you two - yes?"

"Indeed there is, Your Majesty," said Junia. "Our sister Junilla is currently in Asia with her husband who governs it for the Senate and People of Rome."

The Queen nodded then turned to me.

"And this pleases you? To be called Tertia, "The Third Daughter"?"

"It is our custom, Your Majesty," I said and realised that I had called her "Your Majesty", despite my resolution to avoid addressing her at all if I could help it. It didn't bother me, now that I was in front of her. And she was a queen.

You have heard about Cleopatra's fascination and how she captured men's hearts. It is all nonsense. To my knowledge - and nobody will be able to tell you any differently with confidence - she had two men in her life, was faithful to each in turn and bore children to both. According to our present-day law, if she had been Roman we would have honoured her under the Three-Children Law by granting her legal independence from the control of her head of household. I suppose my current guardian must be my great-nephew, poor boy.

That morning in Rome, Cleopatra was authoritative, there is no doubt about that. She spoke and held herself as one who has been listened to and obeyed all her life. She was also a good conversationalist and as I later found out, well-read. Her ability to make jokes in a language not her own was impressive, and she loved puns especially, begging us to explain word play to her. And I could easily imagine those thick-lashed eyes melting the heart of an aging romantic like Caesar, as she tumbled out of the carpet roll in Alexandria.

But the strange thing was that my mother thought she was wonderful.

At first there were a few moments of slightly stiff conversation – she and my mother carefully did not mention Caesar, which was quite a feat as you can imagine, given that we were sitting in his house. My mother even managed to pull off the extraordinary feat of not enquiring after the health of the child Caesarion while avoiding the impression of discourtesy. Fortunately, there were plenty of safe subjects for conversation. How was the journey here? What did she think of Rome? The latter from me was foolish because as a foreign monarch she had not yet entered Rome of course, but in my defence I was nervous.

"I have to be invited to a formal reception by the Senate before I can enter the city," said the Queen. "Then I am to be confirmed as Ally and Friend of the Roman People. Don't worry," she added looking mischievous, "I shall make sure that I look suitably exotic and regal."

My mother laughed. "Madam, you will strike terror into the hearts of the whole gang of bleating sheep."

Cleopatra laughed and as she did so, I felt myself being reeled in. Her eyes laughed at me, then backed off and beckoned me, so that I found myself laughing with her.

"You are the first Roman women I have really talked to," said the Queen seriously. "And I need your assistance. Tell me about all the people I am likely to meet - not the Senators, but their wives. I realise that that I am not going to be popular but which ones are going to try and undermine me?"

Junia and I must have looked startled. The Queen reached out calming hands towards us and smiled.

"Am I too blunt? Should I have taken more time to lead up to this? I'm sorry, but I'm not always particularly good at patient diplomacy. Junia and Tertia, I am so interested in how you were brought up, maybe one day we can sit and talk about it, and you can teach me to be a proper young lady of Rome - but for now,

I am to meet a great many people and I would appreciate any advance information you can give me. Or is it spying? Would it be very disgraceful for you to spy for me?"

Her smile as she concluded this speech deflected all criticism and Junia and I laughed and promised to be truthful about the ladies of Rome, without becoming the Queen's spies. We described the Vestal Virgins in detail, going through their participation in rituals throughout the Roman calendar, so that Cleopatra would understand their importance in our society. She quickly caught on.

"In dedicating themselves to the goddess they help protect Rome, I understand that," she said. "But surely in so many hundreds of years there have been examples of Vestals who - fell? What happened to them?"

It was polite of her to talk about Rome's history so reverently, given that her own country could trace its history back through many thousands of years. It was also a good question for the punishment of a Vestal is particularly horrible.

"A Vestal who breaks her oath of chastity is buried alive," said my mother. "She is carried on a funeral bier to the Colline Gate and put into a small room, with a loaf of bread and a jug of water, and then she is walled up and left. It is as if she is already dead to us, for it is up to the Goddess Vesta to decide the time of the death."

Cleopatra shuddered dramatically and asked when the last occasion was on which this had happened.

"Licinia, several years before I was born," said my mother immediately. "There have only been a handful of cases, Your Majesty."

Cleopatra nodded, then moved on.

"Now who would you say is the most influential woman in Rome today?" she asked.

My mother thought. "Apart from the Chief Vestal and myself," she began and Junia and I simply could not help it. The giggles burst out, and after a moment, my mother smiled at us before carrying on,

"My wicked children are enjoying my lack of humility, but I argue that humility is not an admired trait amongst the Romans, especially men, and I see no reason we should pretend to it now. Your Majesty, my second husband died nearly fifteen years ago, and I have got used to doing things my own way."

Cleopatra looked on approvingly, and I thought that my mother had always done things her way. Certainly my father Silanus had seemed happy to let her and I am sure that he benefited by it. My mother continued and suddenly Junia and I were brought in on the conversation.

"My girls can help with this, but I must ask you to keep quiet about how you know what you learn from us. I don't want any of us to be accused of mere womanly jealousy and gossip."

The Queen nodded though she looked amused that we were concerned about criticism, and we all leaned forward as though one of the slaves standing at the door might otherwise overhear us and tattle.

"I am going to start with a list of useful women, those who will prove good allies for you, Your Majesty," said my mother. "Terentia, until recently the wife of Cicero is a sister of the Chief Vestal. Terentia is rich, pious, and forthright. The fact that Cicero has divorced her for a fifteen-year-old heiress has not damaged her status, rather it has harmed his. She is an expert on all religious affairs which involve women, and she will take great delight in informing you that she will not bow to anyone. Junia, who should be next?"

"Fulvia," said Junia straight away. "Your Majesty, this lady was the wife first of Publius Clodius, then of Gaius Curio. Both men were at the heart of whatever was going on in public life, and the lady Fulvia was active in whatever project they supported. She is passionate, and if on your side, you will be grateful for it. Her knowledge of politics will be invaluable."

"Both her husbands are now dead though," said Cleopatra. "And in Rome, wealthy and high-born ladies need to be married, I have heard. Status usually comes through the husband."

I felt my mother's backbone stiffen beside me. Cleopatra either had not taken on board what my mother had said earlier, or she was teasing her.

"The first marker of status in Rome is family," said my mother firmly. "Where you come from, what your ancestors have achieved - and what you do to honour your ancestors - these things are vital in every Roman's life."

Cleopatra nodded once more, intrigued. I wondered how different all this must seem to her. I am sure that her family were important to her, but the Ptolemies also had a dreadful reputation for assassinating one another, and brothers and sisters married each other. What would have been incest in Rome was to the Egyptians part of the structure which supported the power of the whole dynasty.

"And give me a third important woman, one whom I should cultivate," said the Queen. "What about the wives of the chief men of Rome?"

This silenced us for a few moments, for under Caesar, many of the chief men of Rome had died in the Civil War or retired from politics. There was no obvious leader but Caesar, no outstanding general but Caesar. The Queen looked at us, brow furrowed.

"What of Antonius? Does he have a wife?"

"He is divorcing his wife and is conducting a very public and scandalous affair with the actress Cytheris," I said.

Cleopatra's eyebrows climbed her forehead.

"I see," said the Queen thoughtfully. I suspected that she understood very well. She had surmised the extent to which Caesar dominated Rome and we were confirming it for her. She was polite enough to not ask about our male relatives, for we would have had to explain the divided loyalties of our family. Instead, she signalled to one of the slaves and our cups were topped up and little snacks were distributed.

"Now," she said, "a little gossip if you please - tell me about Cicero and his new wife, and Antonius and his actress." And we obliged and enjoyed ourselves immensely. It was with some sadness that I heard my mother refuse - very gracefully - an invitation to what sounded as though it would be a very cultural and elegant evening with entertainment from Cleopatra's protege, the singer Tigellius.

"I shall make sure that everyone is terribly well-behaved," said the Queen, arching her eyebrows invitingly. "The philosopher Philostratus will be there to make sure we don't laugh too much." She leaned forward and said conspiratorially, "I have invited Cicero, but Caesar says that he won't come. I think he will, just to confirm his suspicions about me."

My mother laughed and shook her head.

"Let us keep our meetings private, Your Majesty," she said. "I simply cannot be bothered to provide entertainment for the gossips, and Cicero is the worst of them all."

I was a little sad at this. The thought of observing all the great and good of Rome having to be polite to Cleopatra because they had not been able to resist the glamour of the invitation was beguiling. It would have been nice to hear Tigellius as well, who now sang in public only when Cleopatra gave a cultural evening to showcase him.

Later I heard people talk about her as though she were merely the sum of her physical features - her eyes were this, her neck that, her waist... It is all ridiculous. When Cleopatra spoke to you and laughed with you, you did not care what she looked like. She was fun and clever and enjoyed your company. That was all that mattered. Once I heard an elderly poet say that if her nose had been a little shorter the history of the world would have changed. I think it was Horace. He enjoyed a drink and would have loved being so outrageous. He didn't actually mean it of course, poets never mean what they say. My point is - history has nothing to do with women's noses. Events rolled out in the way they did because the men Cleopatra loved saw the riches of Egypt and did the calculations in their heads. No man goes to war because a woman looks at him a certain way or has a particularly fine nose.

"I cannot believe that you have seen Cleopatra," said Sulpicia wistfully.

"Let me guess - your only knowledge of her is from Horace," I said tartly.

Sulpicia laughed.

"That dreadful poem of his! I was about nine or ten when Augustus won the Battle of Actium and Cleopatra was universally trampled as the evil eastern Queen who had bewitched decent Romans."

"A crazed queen plotting ruin for the hills of Rome," I murmured. "She wasn't like that."

"No woman could possibly have been like the one portrayed in Horace's Actium Ode," said Sulpicia. "But they needed to hang their fear and hate upon someone. Women are an easy target."

"You should have seen the look on her face as she watched her sister Arsinoe walk in Caesar's Alexandrian triumph. Cleopatra looked like she was enjoying it. In the end Caesar pardoned Arsinoe, but I don't think Cleopatra would have minded one jot if her sister had been strangled along with the other prisoners."

"Not like your feelings for your own sisters, then?"

"No, indeed."

Chapter 20

Huge amounts of money were being spent on the four triumphal processions, and Rome was going to be amazed, entertained and fed well. My family had seats under the awnings of silk which were raised to shade the Forum for the processions and appreciated the shade though many grumbled at the extravagance of using silk. Barates was back and I daresay he and the other cloth merchants were quite happy. I wondered what Caesar was going to do with all that wonderful material after the triumphs, but never found out.

Not all the triumphs went smoothly despite Caesar's reputation for planning and organisation. The first procession celebrated Caesar's victories over the Gauls, which we all knew about as he had written up his exploits and published them, sending them home in instalments for everyone to gossip over. It was quite difficult to remember that those years of governing Gaul had happened before Caesar crossed the Rubicon and started the Civil War. It was the only "normal" triumph, celebrating a governor's actions over a foreign people. The Alexandrian triumph was harder to fathom - Caesar had indeed helped Cleopatra to fight off the troops of her siblings so that she could claim the throne of Egypt, but it did not feel quite Roman. By now, the Queen was an official Friend and Ally of the Roman People, and as such had a seat in the large and impressive stand reserved for terribly important people, such as the Vestals. Also included were Junia and Lepidus, who enjoyed the distinction of being Consul along with Caesar that year. It was next to our seating and if I turned my head and stared unashamedly, I could see the Queen quite clearly. She looked quite different from the woman we had met, more Egyptian, above the level of mere humans, untouchable. I could see a massive collar of gold around her neck, and she must have sweltered in the stylised black wig. But Cassius was marching in this triumph as a soldier, so I turned back to look out for him and waved, and later he said he wasn't embarrassed by me at all. Unusually for a triumph, the main prisoner, the princess Arsinoe, commanded a great deal of awe and even compassion, a quality for which Romans are not noted. I studied Arsinoe carefully as she made her solitary way past, and she looked nothing like Cleopatra. She was older, taller, and wore no cosmetics, but still held her head imperiously high and with a look of defiance. Her robe, which traditionally should have been tattered and dirty, to show her status as a wretched prisoner, was blue and red, making her a striking figure. She took care to pace slowly, and this gave us time to notice how alone she was. The intelligence of this made me realise that she did resemble her sister in one important way. In the end, Caesar pardoned her and sent her off to live far away in exile at Ephesus. I don't know what Cleopatra thought, but Junia said Cleopatra watched Arsinoe walk past with a look of utter despising on her face.

The Asian triumph celebrating a victory over King Pharnaces, I cannot remember at all. Four triumphs in such a short time do that to an old woman's memory. But the African triumph was memorable for the reaction of the crowd again. This time, a baby was the main prisoner and there was not a woman in the mass of spectators who approved of that, as the cart rumbled past carrying his nurse and the little boy on the long winding route through the city. The nurse sat hunched over the child as if to protect him from missiles, but nobody threw anything, though a little arm escaped her embrace and waved as the baby wailed. "He must have needed changing," whispered Junia, and Nilla replied, "And feeding, poor little thing." I'm sure many men felt embarrassed - Romans do not vaunt their prowess against children. When Caesar's chariot rumbled past for the fourth time that month, the cheering was noticeably less than at the previous triumphs.

"I can tell you why," I whispered to him in my head, rehearsing what I could have said to him, advised him - if he had asked. "You couldn't parade King Juba of Mauretania, because he died in a suicide pact after you defeated him in the Battle of Thapsus. So, you thought that his infant son was the next best thing. You forgot that, to Rome, committing suicide was the noble thing to do in the circumstances. Parading that child would only arouse sympathy. But you also forgot that King Juba had fought alongside Romans at the Battle of Thapsus. You have just reminded us that you fought Romans in that campaign, and you expect us to be happy about that."

Did my dream dim just a little? I shot a quick look at my mother, but of course her beautiful face showed not the slightest trace of distaste.

Games and performances of all kinds followed in the days after the four triumphs, the usual theatrical shows, gladiators and animal hunts. These displays were much better than usual because Caesar displayed animals from all over the Roman world, from Gaul in the west to Alexandria in the east. The star of the animals was the wonderful beast known as a camelopard, which was so exotic that nobody wanted it to be hunted, so it was displayed around the city instead. Junia took her boys to see it and I went too to see if it really was that outlandish. I must admit it was the strangest thing I had ever seen, with its spindly legs and great long neck. The children loved it, for the keeper had trained it to bend down its neck to take fruit and leaves from their hands, and close up you could see a rather gentle face, dominated by huge eyes and long eyelashes. It remained on one of Caesar's estates for years, but it must have been lonely, poor thing.

After the celebrations, Caesar set off one last time for Spain, and fought his last battle. Cassius went with the fleet and served with his usual diligence, and I missed him. I had already had enough of talking to my husband through letters, and the few months I had him back with me had reminded me of how much I liked him. As was becoming almost usual during Cassius' absences, I absorbed myself in the concerns of my sisters, writing frequent letters to Nilla in Asia and receiving the odd letter in return; I visited Junia and my mother; I spent large amounts of time discussing our assets with the steward, safeguarding my husband's property as far as I could, dividing my time between Antium and the house on the Palatine.

In the middle of this, my brother returned from governing Gaul and set us all alight with his behaviour. I first learned that all was not well when Felix told me that he had put a visitor in the Painted Garden.

"Your sister-in-law the lady Claudia," he murmured. "She looks upset."

I was in the middle of going through my accounts in the library and was slightly irritated. Barates had just visited and had gone through my investments in Antioch and while I was pleased with what he had to say, I wanted to check everything myself. However, Felix looked worried, so I ordered some honey wine be brought as soon as possible and went apprehensively to see what the matter could be.

"Dear Claudia," I announced as I entered. One sharp look showed me reddened eyes, no make-up, an utterly woebegone face - what in the name of the gods had happened? I decided that I must get straight to it.

"Claudia, what is wrong? Is Brutus ill?"

Completely the wrong thing to say, as Claudia burst into tears, her cheeks barely dry from the last round of weeping. I sat next to her on the couch and put my arm around her, waiting for the tears to reach the hiccup stage, making the occasional "Sh, sh…" just as Nanny had done when we were children. As Kleia came in with the drinks, I gave her a look, and she set down her tray without a sound, and disappeared to fetch handkerchiefs. It took some time before my sister-in-law could whisper in heart-breaking fits and starts. And I was shocked.

"Brutus is divorcing you?" Not very diplomatic but I really was taken by surprise. Claudia wailed.

Eventually I got the whole story. Brutus had returned from Gaul in May, had barely spoken to her, then left for the country house he owned at Lanuvium. After several days, he had come back, and told her he was divorcing her, then left again.

"Did he not give a reason?" I hurriedly amended, "Not that he has a reason, Claudia, we all know how good and lovely you are, but he must have said something?"

"Nothing," said Claudia miserably.

I immediately thought of my mother and went to the doorway to call for Kleia. I gave her whispered instructions, to get my mother over. And then I went back to ply Claudia with honey wine and pat her back every now and then. Claudia, several handkerchiefs in her lap, sat and let miserable tears trickle down, obediently drinking a sip of wine whenever I told her, until my mother arrived. My mother was not easily shocked, but this hit her. She bit her lips thin and stared off into the distance as Claudia repeated her short and sorry tale, then said, "Claudia, I am going to get to the bottom of this."

Kleia had, bless her, made one of guest rooms ready, even thinking to put a little vase with fresh flowers on the chest, and between us, we got Claudia undressed and into bed. I sat by her side and persuaded her to take another cup of honey wine, listening to her quiet laments and firmly stopping her whenever she wandered into the realms of mistakes she might have made to make Brutus hate her. I knew this was not the reason for what he had done, but a horrible suspicion was creeping into my mind.

My mother was busy over the next couple of days, travelling to Lanuvium and back, while Claudia stayed with me. Sure enough, my brother was being incredibly stupid, and his actions set fair to tear the family in two.

"He wants to marry your cousin Porcia," said my mother between teeth that were almost gritted.

Jupiter, Juno and all the gods I couldn't immediately recall - was he mad? My suspicions were confirmed. He was indeed mad. He wanted to marry someone else, just as I had guessed... but my cousin Porcia?

Porcia was the only daughter of my Uncle Cato, and she was - difficult. Do you remember what I told you about my uncle? Imagine that in female form. I didn't know Porcia particularly well at the time, but she confirmed my every fear in the years to come. Uncompromising, fierce, rude -she was awful. That Brutus had divorced poor, sweet Claudia for her was unthinkable and my mother never forgave him.

Claudia stayed at our house for a month while she recovered from the shock of her abrupt and scandalous divorce, and I sent Felix to collect her belongings from Brutus' house. I could not bring myself to see my brother. I thought that he had been unnecessarily harsh on an innocent woman, and Rome agreed with me. Claudia went to live with her sister on a country villa estate, and I am afraid I let my ties with her lapse. I later heard that she lived very quietly and married a local worthy who I hope appreciated her.

When Caesar came back from Spain, victorious of course, there was one last triumph, and this one could not be disguised as a celebration of victory over foreigners. We all breathed a sigh of relief, naturally, for with the elimination of all opposition came peace, and we needed that peace badly. But to celebrate the dreadful Battle of Munda in Spain, a battle in which 30,000 Roman men died, seemed arrogant, at the least.

"He nearly didn't win," said Cassius. "He said that Munda is the only battle where he fought for his life. If he had lost then, I don't know where Rome would be now."

I doubted that life would have changed drastically for me. Some man or other would have taken charge, Cassius and Brutus would have decided which side they were on, there would have been fighting. I wondered how many women thought such things and never told their menfolk. As I look back now, I can see that Caesar's death was looming. He was moving away from everyone, always heading for the next goal, the next battle, and eventually everybody around him started to resent that. It was as if he was climbing up onto a higher plane than most mere humans.

The victory at Munda put an end to war, and at last I met my stepson, another Gaius Cassius Longinus. Naturally, he was called Young Gaius by us all. He arrived at the house on the Palatine in time to see the triumph for Munda, with his father taking part in the procession, and it was as though he had always been a part of our family. As he was fourteen years old, I had been dreading difficulties. Junia said that her elder boy was beginning to show signs of the awkwardness of growing up, and young Gaius was two years older than my nephew. I need not have worried, for he was the nicest young man I could have hoped for. His tutor was a respectable and very proper Greek, who had installed manners, a sense of duty and intellectual curiosity into his charge. Young Gaius and Aristides were installed in a suite of rooms near the back of the house, and they livened up our dinners with Gaius' enthusiasm and Aristides' erudition. Felix and Aristides started work on rearranging our library as our books were transported back from Antium, and I made sure that a complete collection of Caesar's works was added. New bookcases were installed and in this room of learning Aristides and young Gaius took up their study of rhetoric, planning for the young man's entry into the adult world of the Forum and a political career.

"Whatever a political career looks like in these days," said Cassius, as we visited our new library. Cassius had just heard that he was to be Praetor next year by decree of Caesar and did not know whether to be amused at the ease with which he had achieved this office, or contempt that Caesar was ignoring the traditional path.

"It will save me from all that tedious electioneering, I suppose," said Cassius.

"And I have just bought a copy of "A handbook for candidates" by Cicero's brother," I lamented. "I hope that it will come in useful at some point in the future. Once Caesar has lain down the Dictatorship."

"He has only just begun a ten-year stint," said young Gaius. "Why would he give that up? He could use ten years to get everything ordered just as he wants."

"And is that preferable to returning us to proper Republican government?" asked Cassius.

Young Gaius shrugged.

"If it stops more fighting, I suppose," he said. "My friend says that only a Dictator can impose proper order and stop all the in-fighting that used to happen."

"Your friend?" asked Cassius. "Which friend of yours has such dreadful views?"

"Publius Aemilius Lepidus," said young Gaius.

"Ah, my nephew," I said. "He is just repeating what his father says."

"I suppose I should approve of a boy who listens to his father," said Cassius and gave young Gaius' hair a ruffle. "We shall leave you and Aristides in peace now. What are you reading?"

"Cicero's speeches against Catiline," said Aristides.

Cassius groaned. We left the library.

Chapter 21

Settled for the first time in many years, I became absorbed by a personal matter. I had been married for more than five years and I wanted to have Cassius' children. True, my husband had been absent from Rome for months and years at a time, but now I had him here with me. I focussed on this and maybe it was why I took so long to see what was happening around me. We got so used to Caesar's elevation above the life of normal men that many of us just accepted it. He held the Dictatorship several times, at first for a few days, then for a year, then ten years... And it did not stop there. He had the summer month of Quintilis renamed July. He was allowed to wear a wreath of laurel and a purple robe and had a special chair at all Senate meetings.

"He looks ridiculous," said my brother at dinner one evening early in the year after he married Porcia. "He looks as though he is acting the king, for all the gods' sakes!"

Brutus did not often sound so upset, and I was glad that my sisters and their Caesarian husbands were not there. Isauricus was still off governing Asia and Lepidus was riding high as Caesar's faithful Master of Horse which meant something like Not-the-Dictator-but-quite-important. I thought that this summed up Lepidus beautifully.

"He is not a king," said Cassius quietly.

My unlovely new sister-in-law Porcia snorted. It was a disgusting sound and utterly typical of her. My brother, used to Porcia's manners, continued.

"He wears a special robe, sits on a special chair, wears a crown of laurel, has supreme authority over the entire Republic..."

"And that proves my point," said Cassius. "We are still a Republic."

"He appoints all magistrates of any importance instead of letting them be elected," said Brutus.

There was silence as we all thought of the irony of this complaint, for Brutus and Cassius were both Praetors that year thanks to Caesar.

"It can't last forever," said Cassius. "Caesar is now in his midfifties and has had several seizures. He may not last the ten years of his dictatorship. He may be forced to retire."

"He won't retire and he won't stop at ten years," said Brutus gloomily. "He is going to make himself Dictator in perpetuo. And will it then be too late to complain?"

I was astounded and took a quick look at Cassius. He was wearing his most forbidding face, brows lowered and drawn and his mouth thinned. His face suddenly looked old.

"There is no precedent, nothing constitutional about a lifetime Dictator," he said. "He can't. Where did you pick that up?"

"Cicero," said Brutus. Cassius laughed.

"You can't trust anything he says, Brutus. He is hardly in the thick of political life and hasn't been for years."

"Caesar likes him and talks to him," said Brutus.

"Cicero was a good friend to my father," said Porcia. She rarely said anything without reference to her father, and it usually had the effect, as it did here, of stopping the conversation dead.

I sighed in my head and began brightly, "My sister writes from Asia that she and Isauricus hope to be home in the summer."

The slaves cleared the table and fruit and nuts were brought in. Brutus gloomily refilled his wine-cup, and Cassius looked across at me and smiled. We were hoping that our guests would leave early.

I took little notice of this particular conversation, though its essence was often repeated and explored at other dinners. What I did not realise was that it was a beginning. It later transpired that my brother and my husband had already started to gather people, carefully sounding out each man by asking philosophical questions over dinner. I might have guessed this, for only my brother would use philosophy to work out the killing potential of a man. I noticed of course that they were out together quite a lot but I was just pleased that they got on so

179

well, even if I did not understand why this was so. I cannot truthfully tell you that I knew about the conspiracy against Caesar long before the event, but did I suspect that something was going on? Towards the end, yes, just a little. I think I may even have contributed to Cassius' decision.

It was one evening a month or so after the conversation with Brutus and Porcia, when Cassius was brooding over dinner. Caesar had just been made Dictator-for-life in the Senate, as Brutus had predicted, and Cassius had been one of the handful to vote against the move. As I watched I could trace his thoughts as they ran round and round in his head: Dictator is not a lifelong office…we have just made Caesar a tyrant… what are we to do? And my silent contribution was: do you want your child to be born into this Rome? I was just beginning to suspect that I might be pregnant, but it was very early, too early to say anything. To distract myself I leapt straight into what I knew was bothering Cassius.

"How far would you go to stop Caesar?" I asked and immediately heard the hidden question. "Would you kill him?"

Cassius looked into his glass and gently circled it in his hand, to make the little pool of wine left at the bottom swirl up and around the sides. Normally, I would tell him to stop, the glasses were too expensive to be treated like this but this time, I imitated him as I waited for his reply, watching the soft flowing lines of wine left behind on the glass for a fleeting moment before the colour sank back into itself. Just one tiny change, easily put right. Is this how we would deal with Caesar? The dark wine gleamed in the bottom of the glass, now so dark I could hardly see the red in it - but the red was there, I knew.

"Tertulla, Caesar will not be stopped until he is dead. You know that don't you?"

I did not want that. But I did know it.

"Who will - stop him? You?" I whispered.

"Not me, "said my husband decisively.

And I laughed with relief, and said lightly, "Thank all the gods I am wrong then."

"Tertulla, when are you ever wrong?" he teased and I pouted and did a haughty turn of my head, as was expected. We descended into giggles and toasted each other, and there was no more talk of Caesar, though last thing before I slept, I indulged myself with a dream of telling Caesar that he was to be a grandfather. In this dream, the little Egyptian boy, Cleopatra's son, was not Caesar's, and I was his only chance of having a direct line of descendants. Finally, he admitted that he was my father, and my child was immediately written into his will. My dreams were nothing if not practical.

We woke early on the morning of the Ides of March to the cheerful excitement of a house being got ready for a special occasion. There was no breakfast, as we were all knew there would be special food later, and everyone dressed very carefully. Kleia tried out a new hairstyle - "Nothing too much, mistress, don't you worry" - and then we went to deliver a special present from us to Gaius. The boy was white with nerves but smiled a smile of such excitement as we entered his room that Cassius could not hold back a tear or two. The young man was already dressed in his specially made tunic and his tutor, Aristides, fussed anxiously, ducking from one side to another to pat at imaginary creases. My own eyes filled when Gaius turned to catch his tutor's hands and stop him, saying "I couldn't have got this far without you." For Gaius, his tutor Aristides was the most constant person in his life so far. Poor Gaius, no siblings, no shared rooms, no giggling or gossiping together. Well, I decided, he now had a comfortable and loving permanent home, and I would make sure that he always felt welcome, no matter how many children Cassius and I had.

We walked through the house to the atrium, with Gaius between me and Cassius and Aristides walking behind. A round of applause started as people noticed our arrival and the noise rippled around the high marble walls and columns. Gaius blushed, and people called out their greetings and the favoured few came forward to embrace him briefly. Nobody detained him though, and he was showed to the lararium in the corner. The little household shrine was garlanded and space had been cleared for the offerings. We fell silent and Gaius looked once at his father then stepped forward on his own to take a pinch of incense and drop it into the little brazier standing to one side.

Cassius intoned the usual prayer and then Gaius turned to his father, bowing his head, so that Cassius could take the bulla, the amulet of childhood, from around his neck. And with that Gaius was no longer a child. He took the bulla and laid it on the shrine with a solemn face and squared shoulders. When he turned to Cassius his new plain toga was ready. With his father and tutor to help him Gaius wrapped his new toga around himself, and everyone applauded again. The first part of the ceremony was over, and the crowd broke into groups and chatted while Gaius' toga was fussed over by Aristides. I realised with a start that I should be welcoming people and moved from group to group, slightly surprised to see my brother Brutus. As a Praetor he was usually hearing cases by this time. I was so glad he had made the time to attend this occasion and told him so with a big smile. He seemed almost surprised to see me - typical Brutus - and excused himself quickly, going over to talk to Cassius. I remembered the occasions when he had made time for me and felt a little sad, then told myself to be sensible. Before I had got round all the people there, the signal was given, and all the men gathered and set off in the procession to the Capitoline temples for the traditional sacrifice. I admit that I slipped out of the front door to watch them all barrel along the street, Gaius completely impossible to pick out in the midst of all those togas. I sent my good wishes after him and returned to the house to supervise the next stage.

The atrium was now quiet and slightly dull as I looked around wishing that Gaius could have had a sunny morning for his special day. We set out the tables with food for those returning from the Capitoline temples and tidied up the few scuffs left by the crowd. I went over to the lararium and picked up Gaius' bulla, letting the gold bubble swing gently from its leather cord. I wondered if eventually it would reappear around another child's neck and found my hand hovering over my stomach. With a little shiver, I realised that this child I so hoped for would wear a bulla just like the one I held: and surely it would be a good omen if we used this, relinquished by Gaius just as another child needed it. I almost laughed at the perfection of this idea and made one last inspection of the atrium, humming. Outside it thundered and everyone stopped and looked up. "It's on the right!" someone called, and we all smiled at the favourable omen. It was not too long before the good-natured crowd spilled through the door to sample the food and drinks and heated wine before heading off to the morning Senate meeting. Gaius was led back to his room by his tutor, the plan being to change then head out with a crowd of his friends to see the gladiatorial show being held on the Campus Martius. I hoped that the yawning young man would at least make it to the show before falling asleep. They were not going unattended of course. A couple of our older and more sensible bodyguards were shepherding the unruly gang and I did not envy them that task. Meanwhile, old Aristides would no doubt enjoy some quiet, I thought indulgently, and immediately felt a wave of drowsiness hit me. It had been a full day already it seemed, and we still were hours from noon. I decided that I too would take a nap.

Waking up from deep sleep in the middle of the day is never easy. I knew that I was needed and struggled to wake but my dreams turned dark and clung to me so that I had to push them off to reach consciousness. When I came to, Kleia was bending over me, smoothing my hair back from my face over and over, with such a look on her face that I knew something appalling had happened.

"Miss Tertulla, are you all right?"

"What's happened?" I demanded. "Let me sit up, Kleia. I am all right I promise, just in the middle of sleep."

She said, "Let me get you some water. Wash your dreams out of your head." And she abruptly turned and went over to the washstand, dampening a cloth so that I could wash again, and she seemed to me to stand there just a few moments longer than was needed.

Once I had properly woken up, I said, "Kleia, please tell me what the matter is."

She was ready and said straight away, "It's Caesar, Miss. They are saying he has been killed. In the Senate House."

Prickles of shock swept over me, hot and cold all at once and I found myself saying, "He can't have been killed in the Senate House. It is being rebuilt after the fire."

And then I lay myself down on my bed once more and my teeth began to chatter.

Kleia gently pulled a blanket over me. "Miss, just you stay here - I'm going to get you a nice warm drink. You stay here, yes?"

Her sandals pattered quickly into the distance and into the silence noises gradually crept and urged themselves on me. Slaves were whispering to each other, and was that rain in the courtyard garden? I could fancy I heard running feet in the street outside our front door, and surely there were shouts from outside, as the news ran all around the Palatine? Could I hear my mother, calling out for her dead lover? Across Rome, the news was announced in the gladiatorial games where young Gaius and his friends were, and he would never remember his coming-of-age without it being overshadowed.

The one thing I would not let myself think was that my father was dead. That would have to wait.

When Kleia returned with something warm and honeyed, I was sitting on the edge of the bed once more, for things had to be done.

"What is in this? Nothing to make me sleep?" I demanded as I sniffed the steamy surface of the drink.

"Chamomile and honey, Miss, and a bit of wine," said Kleia quietly. "It will warm you."

I nodded and sipped, thinking over a list of questions.

"We need to make sure Gaius comes home straight away - can we send a messenger to the games he is watching?"

"He is home, Miss, shocked but safe. The bodyguard got him away as soon as the news reached them, and his friends are all being escorted to their homes."

"Good. I had better see him. And Cassius?" I saw her face wrinkle in a grimace and knew immediately.

"They are saying he was one of them," she said. "I'm sorry, Miss."

"One of them," I repeated. "One of them. How many were there?"

"I don't know, Miss, but one other person was mentioned, your brother Brutus." Kleia was hovering fearfully. I suppose

184

she thought I might take it out on her, the messenger, but nothing was further from my mind.

"Of course Brutus would be involved," I said. "But Cassius - what have you done?" My head whirled - Caesar, Cassius, my mother, Caesar, Cassius, my mother. I shook my head, to try to stop the words and knew I needed to do something.

"I'm going to the atrium," I said. "Find Felix and the bodyguards and we shall think about what to do."

"Will there be riots?" asked Kleia.

"Probably," I said and marched out of my room, ready to do battle.

It was a long time since we had faced riots in the Forum, but the old routine employed by my mother sprang into my head and soon we were organised. Two of the bodyguards were sent to watch either end of the street, two slaves up onto the roof to observe. Felix went round checking shutters and doors, and all male slaves were issued with cudgels. I had no doubt that we would be a target. Young Gaius very thoughtfully asked if he should go and check on my mother or sisters and I sent Kleia off with him and Aristides. I would have asked my mother to come to my house, but she was safer staying where she was. Only after they had left, did I think that I had not instructed them to check up on Porcia. Oh well. Porcia was quite capable of looking after herself. And then all I could do was wait. I got some old furniture out from the back of the house and had the slaves put it ready to barricade the main door. I made sure the kitchens were producing food that people could eat on the go. And then I went to my Painted Garden and tried to read and was amazed to find Kleia calling my name once more - I had fallen asleep at the desk. This time, she had better news, in that my mother and sisters were all fine, "though the Lady Servilia was as near dazed as I've ever seen her," said Kleia. I half stood, saying, "I had better go to her," but Kleia shook her head.

"Miss, the master is home. He needs you."

When I ran into Cassius' study, he was sitting with his head in his hands. His fingers were bloodied, and a dagger lay on the desk, smears on its blade. It was the guiltiest scene I could have imagined. I knelt and put my hands on his shoulders.

"Dearest?"

We stayed like that for a few heavy seconds, then he looked up, took my hands in his and said, "Tertulla, it was awful. I should never have agreed, never!"

I was appalled. My Cassius could not talk like this. My Cassius was always right, sure, and strong - what had happened? I looked for signs of injury, but found none, despite the splashes of blood. It must have been Caesar's blood. My guts suddenly cramped, but I told my body that I simply did not have time to be ill.

"Cassius?" I whispered.

He stood and I had to scramble to get out of his way. "Cassius!"

"I must go," he said. Then he stopped and asked, "Is Gaius safe?"

"Yes," I said, but he was already turning, striding out of the study, and as I got up and stumbled after him in an undignified flurry of drapery, I saw him making across the atrium towards the front door. He was leaving again, and he had not even washed his hands.

I stood aghast in the middle of the atrium and watched as the door slave hurriedly opened the door and Cassius vanished into the street. Though I ran after him I did not feel I could cry out after him, ask for an explanation, not in public. There were few people in the street, but they all gazed after Cassius and their faces were shadowed. I felt that all eyes swung round to look at me. I held my head high and whirled round, back into my own house where I called for Kleia and Felix. We sat in the atrium, and I sent out my orders. Young Gaius and his tutor were to stay in their rooms at the back of the house, while Felix sent a couple of the younger slaves down to the Forum to find out news and keep us up to date.

Over the course of that endlessly grey afternoon I found out what had happened: of the awful, bloody, inefficient stabbing; of the crowd of frightened men who pushed each other towards Caesar, like a gang of bullying schoolboys who jostle each other to make sure that someone else is first to touch their victim. I found out about the panicked rush through the streets, many of the assassins still holding onto their daggers, just as Cassius had done. Fear ran through the city quicker than fire, carried by the people pouring out of the gladiatorial games, shouting for vengeance, running for their homes. Towards the end of the afternoon as the sun was already setting, a messenger came from Cassius to tell me that he and the others had gathered at the temple of Jupiter on the Capitoline Hill and so he was safe for the moment. I went blindly to the household shrine to pour the drop of wine and burn the pinch of incense that showed my gratitude that he was safe, and there, still, was young Gaius' childhood bulla. I nearly broke down at the sight of the little gold amulet, handed by a young man to his father with trust and confidence - and then Cassius had stabbed Caesar, putting his entire family into danger. I had no doubt that Cassius was safe, but I and his son were not. I looked at the situation quite dispassionately, wondering if I should feel anger for his thoughtlessness. Cassius the soldier surely should have planned for this, taken steps to leave me protected. Why had he not sent me and Gaius out of Rome? I considered the idea of fleeing that very night and gave orders to Kleia that she should pack some clothes so that if the opportunity arose, we could go immediately. I sent two slaves to prepare our carriage which was kept outside the walls near the Rauduscalan Gate ready to take us to Ostia. We could get to Antium in a day, if necessary. And then I went to Gaius' room to try and comfort a boy just years younger than myself. My father was dead, and soon his father might be.

Chapter 22

At some point in that night, I must have fallen asleep on the couch in my Painted Garden, for I woke in a cold dawn, to find that a blanket had been laid over me. I was quite comfortable with a cushion at my head. I blessed Kleia and wondered if I should bother getting up now that Caesar was dead. I suddenly thought of my mother and this was enough to make me sit up and call for Kleia. When she arrived, blurry and dishevelled, I asked her if there was any news from my mother or my sister or my husband and though she shook her head she said she would check. The household was beginning to come to life and I could hear footfalls and murmured conversations. My back ached and I thought of my suspicions that I might be pregnant.

"Stay there," I whispered. "Please stay safe." And I called for Kleia again.

She came running, full of news but before she could say anything, I said, "I am going to stay with my mother. I need an escort, and an old cloak. We shall walk there as soon as possible. Tell young Gaius to come with us." She and Felix grasped the idea at once, and I could see the relief on their faces. I had said nothing to Kleia about my possible pregnancy, but she was as aware of my cycle as I was and must have wondered. Felix, bless him, would just feel better that I was safe on the other side of the Palatine. As we hurried through the still-grey streets, Kleia whispered the snatches of news. The men who had killed Caesar were calling themselves "Liberators" and had gone to the top of the Capitoline Hill to the Temple of Jupiter Best and Greatest. There were soldiers in the Forum, so while the streets of Rome were crowded, they were, thank all the gods, quiet. Those members of the Senate who had been present at the fatal meeting, had run away. Who was in charge? Nobody had seen the Consul, Marcus Antonius.

"Lepidus," I said immediately. "He is the second to the Dictator as Master of the Horse. My brother-in-law is in charge." So, for once, my brother-in-law would be of use.

We arrived at my mother's house on the eastern side of the Palatine, and with no hesitation, she and I fell into each other's arms. The freedom of mourning Caesar with her made me give in at last, and I clung to her. Felix took young Gaius and his tutor Aristides straight to the Juniatrium, and I was led to my mother's room, its painted trees a little faded now. I was fussed into lying on the couch, with my mother kneeling beside me while Kleia ordered the worriedly hovering Aretus to get a hot drink made with camomile and honey. All the order of our houses was forgotten, I thought, and looked at my mother properly for the first time since I had entered the house. Her hair was down and her face unmade-up, and her eyes were huge and shadowed. Lines I had never noticed were suddenly dragging at her face, and in her anguish - her lover dead at her son's hand - I saw a glimpse of what Cassius and Brutus had achieved with their attempt to restore a properly ordered Rome. In that moment, I knew that this was a disaster for us, for me and my husband and the little speck of life inside me, for my mother and possibly my sisters as well. We had nobody to replace Caesar, and no hope that a combined Senate could pick up the pieces of what had been broken that day. I took my mother in my arms and she cried until the camomile drink appeared. Aretus, bless him, had brought several cups of it, and the four of us crouched there and drank.

"Tomorrow," I thought, "we shall all be in our proper places again. It doesn't matter today."

Sure enough, it was not long before Aretus began to look uncomfortable, and he muttered something about seeing to putting a proper guard on the door. Kleia got up from the floor where she had been sitting near me, and gathered up the cups, slipping out of the door. My mother and I sat on the couch, holding each other's hand and waiting. Time did not really pass so much as appear suddenly to have passed. It was about noon when Junia came in, wrapped in a huge, all-enveloping cloak. She had had the same idea, to make her way to the quieter side of the hill, and I was relieved to see her. With Nilla safe with Isauricus in Asia, my family was all accounted for. Now there were three of us, perched on the couch, and Kleia once more came in with water and wine and some olives, cheese, and pastries. Just looking the food made me feel queasy but I drank some wine. Clever Kleia had added spices and warmed it, and she stayed to make sure I sipped at it, then left once more.

"Where is Lepidus?" asked my mother. "How is he? Is he all right?"

"Yes, he didn't go to the Senate yesterday morning, there was something he had to look at in the camp," said Junia. "I sent a message as soon as I heard, and he went to Caesar's house - but he was too late."

I looked at her. "Too late for what?"

"Marcus Antonius had got there first," said Junia. "He has all of Caesar's papers. Lepidus was summoned this morning to Antonius' house, and they are sorting out - well, everything I suppose. He advised me to come here, and I asked that he come round when he can and tell us what he can."

"He may not have time," said my mother softly. "At times like this, men take action and only come home when there is nothing left to do."

"He will come tonight," said my sister firmly, and to my surprise he did. It was late and we were in no mood for a full dinner but Lepidus was hungry, so we all sat or reclined in the dining-room, sipping wine and nibbling bread, while Lepidus ate heartily. He did not keep us waiting but told us as he ate of his hurried ride back to Caesar's house in the Forum. Of his finding a distraught Calpurnia, and Marcus Antonius ordering a couple of secretaries to pack up Caesar's papers with apparently no concern at the loss of his friend.

"The man has a skin like one of Pompey's elephants," said Lepidus. "I asked him how he let such a thing happen, in a Senate meeting which he was supposed to be attending, and he just said he had been delayed outside the Senate and hadn't realised anything was wrong until the Senate began pouring out, yelling that Caesar was dead. He did not even check that this was true but ran with the rest. And then he thought that he could make something of it, so he went and bullied Calpurnia into letting him have Caesar's records and took them off to his own house. He is closeted there with a set of Caesar's advisers and they are making plans. I've been given my orders. I must see to them."

"But you are Master of the Horse," I objected. "Aren't you the next in command?"

"There is no Dictator anymore," said Lepidus, "and so there is no Master of the Horse. I am not such a fool as to try and set myself up as a successor to Caesar. There is nobody who can replace Caesar."

"No indeed," said my mother.

Lepidus, never one to appreciate a moment that begs for silence, stood up, saying, "If Marcus Antonius does try to take Caesar's place - he is Consul after all I suppose - he will fail. The Senate won't go along with it, and he has a colleague, Dolabella, ready to take up the second Consulship. I am in charge of keeping the city free from unrest, and then we can sort out the Liberators."

"Where is Brutus now, do you know?" asked Junia. Lepidus seemed disconcerted by the intensity of the eyes now fixed on him. He wiped his face with his hand and said wearily, "Brutus is still on the Capitoline Hill. It is the sensible thing to do. They sent a message to me mid-afternoon asking if I thought they should try to address the people and I told them to stay where they were. The mood is too unpredictable. People are scared."

"What will happen?" I asked.

"I don't know," said my brother-in-law. "It's a waiting game now. Antonius will no doubt come up with an idea tomorrow." He remembered his manners and came over to my mother.

"Servilia, I am sorry," he said, and we all knew what he meant. Then with a nod to me and to his wife, he turned and left.

On the next morning I was sick for the first time and Kleia tenderly wiped the hair back from my sweating forehead as I lay back on my pillows. I caught the very knowing glance she gave me over her shoulder as she went out of the door with the covered bowl. I hoped that she would be able to dispose of its contents discreetly. This was no time to be making announcements.

Over the next few days my mother and Junia and I sat in the atrium or in my mother's room, waiting to be told of what was happening to our menfolk. I was not such a rebel that I could go against every rule that had been bred into me but how I longed to take a couple of slaves as bodyguard and go down to the Forum and talk to people. Of course I would have to be anonymous, I thought, then shook my head at my own foolishness. Cassius's wife could not stroll openly around Rome.

We received many reports during the day; friends and family sent messages while our own slaves regularly went out to scour for news and we soon learned that Lepidus had stationed soldiers from the troops he was preparing to take with him to Spain all around the Roman Forum. This was a sensible precaution of course, but it was also dispiriting because once more we had broken the rule that armed troops were not allowed inside the sacred boundary of the city. There were few reports of violence, and mostly it seemed people were just talking and waiting. The slaves found it hard to describe the atmosphere. Even Felix, who came round to inquire after our health, said that he found going into the Forum distressing and odd.

"For the first time, Mistress," he said to me, "I felt afraid. Not because I am a freedman, not because I was on my own, but because I thought that people might recognise me as part of the household of Cassius." He looked at me with an apology in his eyes. "I have never been anything but proud to serve you and your family, Mistress, you know that. I am still, but I am also afraid. I have given instructions to all the household to stay indoors unless absolutely necessary and if anyone does have to go out, they must wear the oldest tunics that we have in the house and give false information about where we come from."

"You are quite right Felix," I reassured him, but the heaviness in the centre of my chest would not leave me. He suggested, very gently, that he pack up some of our most valuable items and send them over to my mother's house, and I agreed.

Two days after Caesar's murder — I should say, assassination — there was a Senatorial meeting called by Marcus Antonius and held at the temple of Tellus, well outside the Forum. It was quite clear that the Senate were unsure as to what sort of action they should take against the - and that was another problem, what to call the people who had done this? They called themselves "Liberators", but if anyone else did the same, this would indicate support for them. Likewise, "murderers" or "assassins" implied condemnation. This gave Cicero a chance, and the orator in him came to the fore as he argued passionately that the killing of a tyrant was no sin, no crime, and indeed was much admired throughout the civilised world. The meeting could not quite countenance this, but Antonius stepped in with a compromise. He proposed an amnesty and this was thankfully agreed by all. Cicero made another smooth speech, messages flew between the Capitoline Hill and the meeting, and in a wonderful piece of stage-managed drama the Liberators met Antonius on the Speakers' Platform in the middle of the Forum. The crowd seemed pleased with the resolve to make an agreement and the day ended with the Liberators being invited to dinner by the Consul Antonius as a sign of goodwill. I could not believe this. Had they all forgotten that Caesar was lying cold in the atrium of the Chief Priest's residence in the Forum? Across the Tiber, the two-year-old Caesarion was fatherless too.

But that was driven from my mind when a messenger arrived from Cassius. I was horrified to read that I too was expected to attend that dinner.

"I can't go!" I cried to my mother.

"You can, Tertulla," she said, quite calmly. "I have been invited too, and so we can go together. Brutus will be there as well."

Her words straightened my back. We were not going to disgrace our ancestors, and if anyone could keep up a pretence of cold civility, it would be my mother. But part of me envied Junia, uninvited because Lepidus could not attend. He used the excuse of needing to keep an eye on his soldiers as they patrolled the city.

We decided not to travel in style in litters with a procession over the Palatine Hill to the house of Antonius the Consul. Instead, my mother and I wrapped ourselves in cloaks and were surrounded by a group of strong bodyguards. It felt that every eye was on us as we hurried, but in truth everyone was going around in huddled groups just like ours, carefully not looking for trouble. Brutus and his horrible wife Porcia were already in the atrium as we arrived, Brutus looking terrible and Porcia defiant. My poor brother, I thought - you cannot have slept since you did this. To my immense relief, Cassius came in just after us and I ran to him, for one moment forgetting my doubts, my horror at what he had done. I just wanted to look at him and check that he was still the same Cassius. But he could not meet my eyes. I fell back, and though he took my hand, I knew that there was now a coldness between us. And I still had to tell him that I thought I might be carrying his child.

Our host Marcus Antonius was unusually subdued for him - he had a reputation as a womaniser and bon vivant and was thought of as loud and brash. He was well-matched with Fulvia, who, as we had told Cleopatra, was one of the most influential women in Rome, and though she was about my age was already onto her third husband. No divorce either - Fulvia's husbands did the decent thing and died, leaving her rich and restless. I wondered if Antonius had noticed this. He had definitely noticed the part about her being rich, for he needed rich wives to support his lifestyle.

Over dinner, I quickly realised that my job as a woman was keep my mouth shut. That must have been hard for Fulvia.

Antonius began the conversation with a brisk, "I am not interested in why you did it and I don't want to know - it's done now and we have to get things back on course."

Complete silence greeted this, and he carried on.

"I'm going to get Dolabella to join me as consul, he was already lined up to take over when Caesar left to fight in Parthia. Two Consuls and no Dictator - I've already persuaded the Senate to abolish the office of Dictator. We can't afford to have anyone thinking he can replace Caesar. Apart from anything else, you can't just replace Caesar. You will have heard that the Senate have declared an amnesty for anyone involved in the conspiracy to assassinate Caesar. And yes, the proposal used those words, conspiracy and assassinate. That is what it was, and that is what you did. We can't get around that. Fortunately, I had Cicero ready to speak for the amnesty, tedious old woman that he is. By the time he had finished, nobody was sure if you had done us all a favour or not. He pointed out the advantages of a smooth transition and avoiding civil unrest. The future is not about choosing sides. I hope you agree with me."

There was a feeling of relief around the table, but I was also privately thanking Antonius for saying that nobody could replace Caesar.

"In fact," said Antonius, "my preference would be for you two to keep your offices, but I have to say I'm not happy with the mood of the place - you may have to consider leaving for your provinces sooner rather later. It depends."

I saw my mother stir at this but she said nothing. I thought it was sensible of Antonius to bring this up sooner rather than later, for I could not see how my brother and husband could stay in Rome now. Later, of course, I realised that Antonius was just trying to get them out to let him run things unopposed.

"You have to know," said Antonius, "that all over the city, it is your names being discussed. Not the others, but you two. And that is because you were not just his friends, you were pardoned by him and promoted by him. It looks - ungrateful."

I could feel Cassius take a breath beside me and I did not have to turn to see his face - that sudden tightening of the mouth. Sure enough he said, "Caesar was not my friend." Too soon, I thought, too soon to start that excuse.

"I'm sure," said Antonius drily. "But it is what people are saying. It upsets them. I am warning you so that you know. Interestingly, very few people are lamenting Caesar the great leader who did so much good - no, they are wondering why he was killed by people he loved."

I could feel Cassius shake as he leaned against me, but he stayed silent.

"What are you intending to do next?" said Brutus and Porcia shot him an angry glance for his timidity.

"I shall organise a funeral for Caesar. I shall squash any attempt to either praise or condemn you and I shall emphasise that the office of Dictator has been abolished."

FIONA FORSYTH

Brutus said, "We need a gesture of trust from you personally. Lepidus, my brother-in-law, sent his son to stay on the Capitoline Hill to guarantee our safety tonight at this dinner."

I felt my mother stiffen next to me as I let out an exclamation, "Marcus? A hostage?"

There was a short silence, during which everyone decided to pretend they had not heard me.

Brutus continued, "I suggest you send someone too. What do you think?"

Antonius grinned. "I'm all for trust. My eldest is only three though. Do you want me to send his nursemaid up with him? Lepidus' lad was a good idea though. The fact that the boy is related to you both will not go unnoticed."

I winced as I thought of Junia's reaction to this.

"Neither boy is a hostage. And of course, you have my solemn promise that no harm will come to them," said Brutus stiffly.

Every woman at that table looked at Brutus with disbelief. When Fulvia spoke, she only echoed what we all thought.

"You really want a three-year-old up there on the Capitoline Hill with you? You don't think that people will despise you when they hear about it?"

"Of course, we don't want that," Cassius said. "He doesn't mean it. Do you Brutus?" And in a clear effort to change the subject, he said, "My son had his coming-of-age ceremony on the Ides."

Antonius said with heavy sarcasm, "Then the Ides was indeed special in your family."

I was watching him carefully, and he very deliberately turned to my mother and raised his wine cup in an unspoken toast. She mirrored him, and I knew they were honouring the shade of Caesar. They would work with Cassius and Brutus for peace, but they would not forgive either of them. That realisation hit me, almost physically, and I bent my head to gather my breath back without anyone seeing.

After a moment of silence, my mother said, "Who is arranging Caesar's funeral - apart from you - Calpurnia?"

Antonius said, "Leave all that to me. I'm thinking to hold it three days from now. Once I have settled the details, there will be announcements. I take it that nobody here apart from myself will be coming though." And so we received our orders. Even my mother would not be allowed to go to her lover's funeral.

The evening ended in the misery of parting once more, watching Cassius slipping his hood over his head as he and Brutus left for the Capitoline Hill. My mother and I left in silence, surrounded by bodyguards, and feeling like criminals rather than the bereaved.

I have never seen Junia so angry as when she came around the next morning to complain about her son being used a hostage.

"He is thirteen and terrified!" she stormed at my mother. "How could you?"

My mother's back straightened and she said reasonably, "I could not do anything, Junia, and you must know that. When did we ever have a voice in these situations? At thirteen, your son is your husband's to treat as he chooses. If Lepidus agreed, then there is an end of it. No harm will come to him. He is with his uncles, and you cannot believe that either of them will harm him."

Junia gave one more flounce then subsided onto the couch next to me, one tear sliding down her cheek.

"I really do not understand my husband," she said sadly. "He truly thought nothing of it. A perfectly reasonable thing to do to one's own children."

"Lepidus lost his father too early," said my mother. "He never had the chance to do something like this for him. He hopes that his boy will be proud to serve."

"I don't know whose side I support any more," said Junia.

"We aren't on sides," said my mother. "We just watch and hope."

By the next day, Cassius and Brutus and the others had ventured down from the Capitoline Hill and returned to their houses. I received a message from Cassius asking me to come back to our house, reassuring me that it was safe to do so. I thought it was far too soon to tell that, but dutifully walked across the hill, and found him in his study, looking thin and tired - "but I have bathed, and gods above, it feels good," he said with an attempt at a laugh. Felix had sent clothes up to the temple but the bathing facilities there were a bowl of water. An enterprising barber climbed the hill every morning and shaved anybody who wanted - "and he charged appropriately. He called it danger money," said Cassius.

He yawned so much I sent him off to bed, guessing that sleep had been in short supply. To be honest it was a relief, because I did not know what to say. He had been away for just three nights, and it seemed as if I no longer knew him. I did not count that appalling dinner at Antonius' house where we had not talked and barely looked at one another. As far as I was concerned, this was the first time we had been together since young Gaius' coming-of-age ceremony, and between then and now my world had shifted. My love was now an assassin, the murderer of a man who had shown him mercy. What else could I call it? They might have called themselves Liberators but nobody else did. That night in his bed, I watched him sleeping, and his face was older, the skin looking fragile as it skimmed his cheekbones and temples.

Well, the story of Caesar's funeral is famous and it is bitter to know that Marcus Antonius outplayed us all. Naturally none of us were there. Caesar was cremated without his lover and without me. Not that he lacked for love - I can see the wave of grief now as it storms through the Forum and crashes on the body laid out there by Marcus Antonius so that all can see every wound. I cannot bear the thought that my father's torn and bloody clothing was shown off to the mob and all for what? So that they could count the holes in the fabric, so that Marcus Antonius could put himself firmly on the side of Caesar without saying so. He was not a particularly clever man, but he got this one crucial ceremony right. It was like an orator coaxing a jury at a murder trial, and it resulted in Caesar's body being cremated by the grieving, outraged mob in the middle of the Forum, a blasphemy in itself; this was the first real trouble since the assassination, and several people were killed.

We had stationed Felix on the edge of the Forum, and the moment he saw how things were going he hurried back. Cassius sent me to my mother's house and left me there while he slipped out of Rome. I despised him while acknowledging the sense of his actions. Needless to say, my brother insisted on staying, arguing that he had done nothing wrong. He and Porcia barricaded themselves in their house and waited. As evening was falling, and the funeral pyre was still burning, our house was attacked and the few slaves that we had left there sensibly fled through the back alley and into the house next door. Brutus' house was also attacked while he was there with Porcia and fortunately his household drove off the attackers. But the mood of the city was quite clear, and so he left. Porcia of course went with him.

Deserted by our menfolk, my mother and I were able finally to pay our respects at what was left of the funeral. In the hours before dawn, we crept down to the Forum with a small band of our most trusted slaves, all dressed in the drab clothes of mourning. We joined a small crowd of people holding vigil as the pyre burned on through the night. Men and women were there in roughly equal numbers, I thought as I looked around, and for all I knew there were slaves as well as free. Everyone was muffled up in cloaks, and hoods shadowed many faces. My mother and I waited a little, hovering while our fear of being recognised battled our need to mark his death. Every now and then, someone would step forward and throw something onto the pyre, flowers, and jewellery, and once a little glass jar of oil, for it cracked audibly and sooty yellow flames suddenly sprang tall among the orange glowing of the pyre's embers. We too had our gifts, but for us the right moment always seemed just out of reach. The crowd was thinning when I took a careful look around and saw that a face lit only by dying ashes is not easy to recognise; we had to step forward and take the risk. In the end, I am perfectly sure that nobody was interested as two more women gave their trinkets to Caesar's pyre. The lapis lazuli necklace, which Cassius had given me when we were betrothed, disappeared at once, but I thought I saw my mother's necklace glow for a moment before it vanished under the heap of embers on which it had landed. For a moment, my heart stopped, for I was sure that it had been a pearl. My whole body tighten as I thought of her sacrifice. I opened my mouth to ask her if that was indeed Caesar's pearl, then shut it again. I did not want to risk hearing her say "Yes".

We left and later I heard that his ashes were gathered up in the grey dawn by a few house slaves sent by Calpurnia. She gave the urn to the Vestal Virgins so that nobody would try to steal the remains, and later, when everything had died down, she placed his ashes in the family tomb. She had the courtesy to write to my mother to tell her that this was done. Calpurnia was an admirable woman.

Chapter 23

I did not sleep for the short remainder of that night, and early in the morning went back to my house so that the slaves and I could clear up. Fortunately, the attackers had not got into the house itself so all we had to do was tidy the street outside, mend some damage to the door and paint over the graffiti on the walls. I felt sorry for our neighbour - some of the attackers did not realise that the walls they were painting on were his and not ours. I'm sure he was thrilled to come back from wherever he'd been to find "Murderer" slopped across his front door. I did not go round to apologise.

Over the next few days, I packed up the house with Felix and Kleia. The items of value I had already stored in my mother's house, and I left a skeleton staff to make sure that the dust didn't get too deep. I instructed that my Painted Room should be cleaned thoroughly at regular intervals. And before I left for Antium I whispered farewell to my two little painted finches in the cage forever standing on the painted wall. "I shall be back soon," I promised. And then I walked out and did not look back.

My mother came with me to Antium. I don't know whether Kleia had told her or if she had just noticed - after all she had had to look at me quite a lot over the last few days. I had felt queasy, particularly in the morning, but I had so far managed to eat a little at breakfast. However, being my mother, she knew, and when we got to Antium the first thing she did was send me to bed and order Kleia to make her chamomile and honey drink and bring it to me. I was grateful. Cassius and Brutus were staying at Brutus' estates at Lanuvium, and I did not want to meet them and listen to their discussions which would inevitably focus on Caesar's assassination. For a brief time, I left all the news-gathering and planning to my mother, and tried not to think of Caesar, to simply enjoy a beautiful spring in Antium. Out of Rome, the air seemed clean and the light brighter. My spirits certainly improved, and though I was sick several times, it did not last long. Our garden overlooking the sea became my favourite place for walking and every morning Kleia would make sure that I had a chair, cushions and blankets so that I could sit and watch the sea. I did feel extremely tired, as if my skin were being dragged down by a myriad tiny weights, and there were moments when I felt as if I were not quite in the same world as everyone else. It was a strange feeling of not belonging, like a visitor who walks through the door and realises that everyone is still busy preparing for them. These moments were disconcerting, and I learned to wait for the world and I to snap back into our correct places. I wondered if the baby was somehow taking me out of my usual life and asked my mother. She looked surprised and said she had never experienced such a feeling when pregnant.

"All I can remember is the indignity of constant sickness for what seemed like months," she said. "I had it with all f-four of you, and really, Tertulla, I am quite envious of you."

I noticed that little stutter on the word "four" and that is when I first wondered if she had had a miscarriage between Nilla and me, but I did not ask her. We were already too preoccupied with other matters. She wrote to Brutus and received replies almost daily. Cassius put in letters to me sometimes and I would make dutiful responses. I did not want to face my feelings for him just yet. And while I was already bored with what the politicians were doing back in Rome, my mother was kept informed as her astonishing list of contacts came into its own. Her favourite was Atticus the banker, gossip extraordinaire, who knew everyone, was charming and witty, and never chose sides. He enjoyed the arts, especially Greek literature and spent as much time as he could in Greece. My mother said that was why he started being called Atticus, after the area of Attica around Athens, where he would stay. He was also a great friend of Cicero the orator, another wit and gossip, and you knew that whatever one discovered, the other would soon know. My mother said there was no point in corresponding with both and she much preferred Atticus. She had never forgiven Cicero for the joke he made about me.

Mid way through April, I noticed a little bleeding for a couple of days, along with stomach aches. It passed and both Kleia and my mother said this often happened during the early months of pregnancy. We were a little worried, then as the days passed and nothing more happened, forgot about it. But on the fifth day of May I awoke early, in the semi-darkness of dawn to find myself bleeding and in pain. Kleia was quickly with me, then my mother, and the two of them held my hands and wiped my face, and afterwards washed me and packed me round with towels and strips of cloth. But with the loss of Cassius' child, I lost the only chance I have ever had of becoming a mother.

I don't remember much about the rest of May, the most beautiful month of the year, except that I lay in my bed, then on a couch in the sitting-room, and finally on my chair in the garden, with Kleia hovering. It would of course be good to tell you that my mother and I were brought closer together, and in a way, this was true, as we certainly talked more, and she was relentless in her care of me. She even called a Greek doctor from Rome to check on me, and though I did not believe for a moment that he had the slightest idea of what I had gone through, he did prescribe a highly effective drink of willow bark and valerian, which helped with the pain and kept me sleepy and slightly dazed. He also suggested baths with lavender oil, and I cannot smell lavender to this day without remembering the feeling of being hollow, as I lay in the water and tried to let the warmth and the smell soothe me. My mother would sit with me for part of each day, though she always had something else to go on to after a while. Maybe she found it hard to watch me being so listless and I had no conversation. But she would distract me as she thought best, by reading aloud the letters she had received from Atticus, and so I kept up to date with what was being decided in Rome.

My mother also took on the task of writing to Cassius to explain what had happened to me and an appropriately comforting letter came back from him. I was not interested in this, I am afraid, and it vanished. I am sure that I did not destroy it or throw it away, so I assume that either Kleia or my mother took pity on me. In my reply, I kept my distance from him, not to punish him, or because I disliked him, but because I just could not summon up the will to talk about what had happened to me. Instead, I wrote to him expressing my concern about what was happening regarding him, and this made sure that in future he would not mention the baby. I was trying to be fair, to see the matter from his point of view, but of course I was bitter, then and later, for the lost opportunity. I did not stop loving Cassius, but I did take a break from my life with him, partly because I saw him so little, and partly because I needed the time for recovery.

But I must record some of the happenings outside my own life at Antium and tell the story of the conference we held there if only because it showed my mother in her best light and put every man there to shame.

As Antonius worked to remain in control at Rome, a completely unexpected player joined the game. A teenaged great-nephew, the son of Caesar's niece, appeared in Italy, arriving in Rome to claim his inheritance in early April. He was even adopted in Caesar's will and took Caesar's name, to my mother's disgust. We were in her room at Antium, and I watched the shaft of sunlight coming in through the window with fascination. Every time my mother strode through that slanting shaft of light, the dust leapt and swirled, mimicking her frustration.

"The arrogance!" she spat. "The thought of calling that child by the name of Caesar makes me feel ill."

"You won't ever have to call him that," I said. "It is laughable. If he and his advisers have any sense, they will keep calling him Octavius - or Octavianus, to show he is adopted, I suppose. And anyway, we have more important things to worry about."

"Names are important, Tertulla," she said.

"Of course, Mother," I said, unable to stop my voice from growing tart. "Every third daughter in Rome knows that."

"What?" And my clever mother stopped and stared uncomprehendingly at me.

"Tertia? The Third Daughter? The name that means that we ran out of ideas?"

She scowled with annoyance and flapped a hand at me, dismissing this trivial complaint. "We are talking about men and names really do matter for them."

"Oh, Mother, really, of course, names matter to women too. When was the last time the name "Servilia" in Rome has meant anyone but you?"

My mother's frown was merely puzzled. "There are many Servilias in Rome," she said. "Your aunt and cousin to name but two."

"But only you are the Servilia," I said. "If someone talks about Servilia and does not qualify it, they mean you. Do you not realise that, Mother?"

I took pity on her in the silence that followed this and asked about the boy Octavius. Naturally, she knew all about him.

"He is Caesar's great-nephew, son of Atia who is the daughter of Julia, Caesar's elder sister. Julia married Marcus Atius Balbus, and their daughter married a very nice young man called Gaius Octavius, equestrian but enormously rich and ambitious. Died young I remember, just after getting the Praetorship...." I am afraid I soon stopped listening, knowing well enough that as my mother reached the end of the family tree discussion she would get back to her gripe. "So all in all, a respectable young man, I am sure. And Caesar did not have many male relatives. Clearly the boy was being trained and Caesar intended taking him on campaign to Parthia to see how he would perform. I have heard rumours that he is not particularly strong, although Caesar thought he was clever and would make something of himself if he survived. He can't be more than twenty."

"Taking Caesar's name will be a huge advantage to him if he is ambitious," I observed.

"He is not Caesar," pronounced my mother.

I gave up.

On the third day of June a messenger arrived with a letter from Atticus, warning us that the Senate had decided to meet on the fifth of the month specifically to discuss the idea of giving Cassius and Brutus a special commission to procure corn. My mother laughed drily.

"A complete shambles, of course," she said. "They can't think of what to do with them, so they send them on a completely useless mission to get them out of Italy. Do you really think that people will forget what they have done? That a few boatloads of grain at a slightly lower price will earn the mob's forgiveness?"

"What else can they do?" I pointed out.

"They could realise that the people of Rome are never going to forgive them and that they will always be in danger!" she cried. "Tertulla, people loved Caesar, really loved him, and your brother and your husband killed him. More than twenty men acted that day and who do people talk about? Who is constantly threatened? My son and your husband. Do you hear people muttering about Trebonius? Or Cinna? Decimus, Casca, Cimber? No, nobody talks of them. Brutus and Cassius on the other hand will never be able to enter Rome again."

I could not work out who she was angry with here - the senate or her own son. She sat in her cushioned wicker chair in the flower-painted sitting-room, looking every inch the noble and privileged woman she was, the only jarring note the anger in her eyes as she stared at an empty message tablet.

"I don't even know to whom I should write anymore," she murmured. "They are all fools."

I left her in her unaccustomed indecision and went my own room where I slept for most of the day. At dinner my mother announced that she had ordered everyone concerned to come to Antium where we would all discuss what was to be done.

Early on the sixth day of June, I was in the garden enjoying the early stillness of a soon-to-be-hot day, when the first visitor clattered in through the gate. I let the slaves take care of the preliminaries before stirring myself to go and greet him. He was one of Atticus' messengers and had an account of the Senate meeting the previous day. In the cool of the atrium, I opened the wooden tablets, and found that Atticus had enclosed a small piece of papyrus with a summary of the meeting - the tablet itself, a letter to my mother, I ignored. As I read, my frustration grew. The Senate had sidestepped everything, deciding only that a grain commission for both Cassius and Brutus would be a good thing, and that at some point in the future they could also be given provinces. They had not even got up enough courage to vote on the commissions, and Atticus had appended a note: "Next meeting in six days". In other words, nothing was official. The idiots had not even the courage to do this one insignificant thing. My mother, however, when she read through the letter and note was undismayed and not even angry.

"This gives us time to change things," she said briskly. "We have to get them proper provinces if they are to have a chance."

"A chance of what?" I asked. "They will never be able to go back to normal Senatorial careers."

"At some point," said my mother, "somebody will decide to make them pay. Antonius or that brat Octavius, who knows? In a province, we can gather resources."

This was unthinkable. I found myself whispering, "Resources? Resources for what?"

"Tertulla," said my mother, "they are going to fight. At some point they will have to fight. Or don't you think they should defend their actions?"

I could not say that I thought their action had been indefensible. In fact, I could not see how she could not think their actions indefensible. But the silence grew, and I had to say something.

"I don't want Cassius to fight," I said.

"He will be attacked," said my mother, "there is no doubt in my mind about that. What your husband and brother did has repercussions that they, being men and therefore fools, did not imagine. As usual we must try and steer them in the most sensible direction. This is what life is about for women like us. We are given no power officially and we are always under a man's control, and yet when those men have backed themselves into a corner, they find us already there, preparing to push them out again."

I had to smile at this picture. Oh yes, my mother would be there, ready to push a man to take up what she considered to be his destiny. Later, I would have the energy to do the same for Cassius. My mother smiled back at me, and there was sympathy in her eyes.

"He will be here tomorrow," she said. "Don't expect too much of him."

"I don't expect anything from him," I said, and burst into tears.

Chapter 24

On the seventh day of June, my mother prepared for a council of war. I prepared to meet my husband, and Kleia laboured over my hair and face, trying to hide the weeks of sadness and loss. I decided that the day was going to be too hot for cosmetics and contented myself with the most traditional hairstyle imaginable - a small knot of hair at the nape of my neck. I did not bother looking in a mirror for I knew that my eyes were ringed with the darkness of sleepless nights, and I dreaded the thought of somebody deciding to comment on it. As I sat at my dressing-table and Kleia cleared away quietly, the idea of getting up and moving seemed impossible. Fortunately, my mother entered and came across to take my poor, shadowed face in her hands. "Tertulla," she said, "you have paid the worst price of all, and I am sorry, but I need you in this meeting now." Her energy had its effect and we left for the atrium, where Felix and a young man I had never seen before were setting up chairs.

"Madam, this is Lucius Sestius," said Felix. "He is accompanying your husband Cassius and your son Brutus."

The young man bowed his head respectfully, but said nothing, very wisely, given the mood my mother was in already.

She looked closely at him and asked, "Publius Sestius' son? I believe my son Brutus worked with your father in Cilicia."

"Yes, briefly," said Lucius Sestius. I knew what this meant. Brutus had quickly left Cilicia to join Pompey's forces for Pharsalus. The Sestii had been for Caesar. My mother said "Hmmm", and Lucius Sestius said quickly, "I am currently serving under your son-in-law, Cassius Longinus, and he asked me to take notes of this meeting, Madam." My mother looked around then pointed at a desk set up to one side. He sat quickly and busied himself with unpacking a leather bag, checking the pens and wax tablets as he laid them out. Felix retreated hastily, muttering about drinks, and my mother strode up and down the atrium, her draperies whirling with every turn Her sandals seemed to grow louder as they clacked, almost comically, on the marble floor. I watched Lucius Sestius as he carefully sat still, until, driven to it by the tapping, it seemed, he picked up a tablet and pen. I quietly walked up behind him and read over his shoulder: "Meeting, Antium, eight days before the Ides of June". After a moment, he underlined this. The clacking went on relentlessly and part of me wanted very badly to laugh, but I did not think it would be happy or healthy laughter Poor Lucius Sestius was intimidated enough by the matriarch of this family without having to endure hysterics from me.

My mother must have sensed the tension, for she stopped, and sighed, stretching out both her arms and saying, "Gods, I wish they would hurry. Sestius, where are they?"

"They were right behind me, Lady Servilia," he said.

And sure enough hooves clattered outside, and my mother turned towards the entrance.

"She isn't always like this," I whispered to Lucius Sestius. His face suddenly lit up in an enormous grin.

"I once had a centurion just as scary, in North Africa," he confided. And at last I laughed, for my mother was indeed scary.

"I have never met a centurion," I managed to get out, "but I can imagine my mother giving orders to a thousand Roman veterans and them all doing exactly what she told them, believe me." And we had time for a one good honest snigger, before the atrium filled with people and the polite scurry of greetings took over. Cassius took one long moment to scrutinise my face before he bent and gave me a light kiss. I waited for his comment, but all he said was, "I shall just go and change my tunic, Tertulla. Don't let them start without me." It sounded so ordinary, I was grateful.

As the atrium filled up, I realised that Marcus Cicero was present. My mother's lips pursed and I thought I heard somebody mutter, "Who invited him?" but I could not be sure. Maybe it was just an echo from my own thoughts. The question as to who had invited him was soon answered as Brutus walked over to him with every sign of enthusiasm, clapping him on the back and saying, "I am so glad that you could come." I did not dare look at my mother.

Most people were already seated on couch or chair or stool around the atrium and Lucius Sestius was ready to take notes, so Cicero assumed that he was chairing the meeting and waded right in with, "So Brutus so what is it that you propose to do?"

"I'd like to hear your views first," said my brother, much to my dismay. This meeting was going to be hard enough without listening to a professional windbag who had been given permission to orate. Sure enough, Cicero looked extremely pleased and launched straight in.

"There is just one thing left to do. You must take care for your safety - on this depends the safety of the republic itself -"

And to my relief Cassius re-entered at this point.

"Oh Cicero," he said, and it was clear that he was angry, "it's you of course. What is this? Are you telling us that we must be content to accept this pathetic grain commission I've heard about? Maybe I should write a thank-you letter as well?"

He strode up to Cicero, who looked uncomfortable. "Well, I for one do not accept insults even when they are presented as favours. I have no intention of going to Sicily." And he turned and walked over to me and sat next to me, his hand seeking mine.

"Well," said Cicero, recovering well and putting on an air of ever-so-slightly ironic reasonableness, "what do you intend to do instead, then?"

"I shall go to Greece," said Cassius shortly, and I thought that following in the footsteps of Pompey was not auspicious. Cicero cast his eyes heavenward and with a short dismissive splay of both hands, he turned to my brother.

"And you Brutus?" he asked. The figure hunched on a couch next to Porcia did not look like my brother. The face he raised to Cicero was full of uncertainty. He spoke like a schoolboy trying to please the teacher without understanding the question.

"To Rome?" he said and there was a question in his voice, "Is that what you think?" He sounded almost pleading.

"Good gods no, you wouldn't be safe there," Cicero sounded appalled that the idea had crossed Brutus' mind.

"Well let's say that I was safe, would you say that I should go?"

"If you were safe, yes of course and I wouldn't want you to leave for a province now, but I honestly cannot advise you to risk yourself by going to Rome," and Cicero carried on in this vein for some time, until my mother turned the conversation to the grain commissions being offered. This had the desired effect and several voices rose in indignation at once. Cassius witheringly asked Cicero why he had allowed this futile Senate meeting to take place.

The talk became more general. The sticking point was that Brutus genuinely did not know what he should do next. It was clear that he did not understand why people could not accept what he had done. He complained about Anthony, about Dolabella, even about Cicero himself though he stopped that at a signal from Porcia. Cassius said shortly that if they had taken his advice and killed Antonius too, they would not be in this position, but it was too late to worry about that now. I closed my eyes and rested my hand on my empty stomach and wondered if I would still have my baby if Marcus Antonius had died on the Ides of March. I doubted it.

Eventually as Cicero began another speech telling everybody that they should have summoned the Senate and spoken to the people and thus taken the leadership of the Republic, my mother stood up and said loudly, "I have never heard such nonsense." Considering that she was only saying what everyone was thinking, we should not have looked surprised, but as my own mouth fell open, I saw a flurry of movements around the atrium as eyes widened and hands flew to mouths. Cicero looked as though he had been slapped, as she stalked out of the atrium saying that she would arrange for food to be brought out since it was clear that hunger was driving the sense from us all. It was a simple thing, but I thought that she was right. Over a subdued meal Brutus acknowledged that he would have to give up any thought of returning to Rome and the games that he was organising would be held in his absence. And once more my mother clinched the deal by announcing that she would ensure that the proposal about the corn commissions would be altered. We all knew that she was more than capable of going around the entire Senate and persuading them to alter what they had decided on two days before. The conference broke up, with Cicero making the hastiest farewell that courtesy allowed.

I had a few brief words with Cassius before he left with my brother, not in private of course, but with the bustle of people getting ready around us. Slaves tidied the atrium, and Lucius Sestius sat at his desk still, scribbling away furiously.

"When will you go to Greece?" I asked.

"I don't know, Tertulla," he said, his eyes begging me not to scold or whine. "I need time and some space to build up my contacts, get some support lined up, turn the tables on Antonius if I can."

My mother joined in. "And Octavianus?"

He looked confused for a moment and then nodded in recognition. "Oh, the boy. What about him?"

"He is Caesar's heir," said my mother in a tone of withering patience.

"He is eighteen years old and is ill all the time," said Cassius dismissively. "And Antonius already has him squashed."

My mother shook her head.

"He canvasses support amongst Caesar's veterans all over Italy," she said. "That is the power base you needed to convince, not the feckless sons of Italian middle classes. You needed a platform with the soldiers, but you were too slow, and now he has blocked you. He is clever."

"I am a soldier myself," said Cassius beginning to look angry. My mother had not been given to criticising her sons-in-law, and certainly not in public. He took a breath and said more calmly, "I mean that I know how soldiers think and yes, they will at first be charmed by the idea of supporting Caesar's son."

"Adopted son," my mother cut in. Cassius held up a yielding hand.

"But soldiers also appreciate a leader, a general who looks after them without being soft, who promises victory and brings them wealth. Octavianus cannot be that leader. My concern is that Antonius will be my enemy, not Octavianus."

"If Antonius is your enemy, then stay and fight him here," I broke in. "Why run to Greece?"

"Tertulla, I have already explained that," said Cassius. "Look, I must go."

But I had one more thing to say.

"You were under the command of the last person who fled to Greece to make a stand," I said. "But Pompey put you in his fleet and so you missed Pharsalus. You don't have to mirror him now just to assuage some sense of guilt that you weren't there."

Cassius was already turning as I spoke, but he stopped and looked back at me, saying, "I am not going to Greece because I feel guilty. I'm going for the same reasons as Pompey, to call on a power base that my enemies do not have any link with - and I shall do it properly. I am not Pompey, and I shan't end up like Pompey. I promise you that. I'd rather fall on my own sword."

Something inside my head screamed, and he must have seen an echo of that scream flit across my face. He came back to me, took my hands, and kissed me, very gently. And then he left with my brother. My mother came to stand at my side and we watched the men getting their horses, giving orders. With an embarrassed apology, Sestius scrambled past us, bundling wax tablets into his bag, and before we had time to say any words of farewell, the group was off down the track.

My mother laid a hand on my arm, and said, "He really does care for you, Tertulla."

I said, "He didn't mention the baby at all."

She turned me towards her, so that I could put my head once more on her shoulder. I was too tired to cry, but I needed to feel someone holding me.

It was only when I returned to the atrium, that Felix handed me a pair of wax tablets, folded and sealed, and for one moment I thought that it was from Cassius: but it was from Cicero. Puzzled, I opened it and read:

My dear Tertulla - as I hope you do not mind me calling you. I am so close to your husband and brother that I am going to presume, and you must forgive an old man if I presume too far.

I was extremely sad when I heard the news about your miscarriage. We Romans are supposed to meet tragedy with lips pressed tight and eyes dry, but the loss of a child, whenever it happens, is a terrible thing for any parent.

When I lost my daughter just over a year ago, I thought nobody understood and that I would never recover. People told me to be brave and that I must think of the Republic, and I dismissed this advice as useless because they did not understand. Now what am I going to say to you? Why, to be brave and think of the Republic. Because though I miss my daughter as much as ever, I have learned to live with that loss and see that in serving the country I love I may regain some purpose.

Tertulla, I ask you to be strong enough to support your husband who is one of the finest men I have ever met. A man prepared to risk his life to follow his principles is worth supporting, and in you he has the wife who will enable him to keep do what still needs to be done. We ask a great deal of our womenfolk, and we have always been fortunate in how they meet every challenge. May you meet your sorrow and not be overcome by it.

Felix waited patiently as I read this and when I looked up, speechless, he held out a basket, saying, "Marcus Cicero left these for you, Mistress. He said they were picked fresh this morning from his garden at Astura."

Red strawberries filled the basket, and their tight skins, dimpled with golden seeds, blurred as the tears came to my eyes.

Chapter 25

It was to this that Nilla and Isauricus returned from his governorship of Asia. The news of Caesar's death had reached them at the end of March and Nilla had been all for setting off at once, but Antonius had told Isauricus to stay put for the time being, and wait for the next governor, Trebonius, to arrive. By the time May was advancing, Isauricus decided to wait no more. He had discovered that not only was Trebonius near, but the man had also been one of Caesar's killers, and what Isauricus thought about the Liberators was not to be put in a letter.

Nilla and Isauricus arrived at Antium in the middle of June, after a swift journey, using the official courier ships all the way. As soon as they arrived in Antium, they took up residence with Junia in Lepidus' house which was bigger than my Antium villa, and we gave them a day to rest from the journey before going over. I wondered briefly if they had decided to avoid me because of Cassius, then dismissed the thought. Even if it were true, there was no point in brooding.

"I really do not understand, to be honest with you all," said Isauricus. "Why is Trebonius still governor of Asia? Why has Decimus been allowed to go to govern Gaul? And all the way here, we kept hearing about Brutus and Cassius going around raising support in Italy. Support for what? They have been pardoned, haven't they? They are going to get commissions from the Senate. What more can they want?"

"They want people to understand," I said. "They want to be tyrannicides, not assassins. They want to be Harmodius and Aristogeiton."

Isauricus frowned. "Remind me."

"Harmodius and Aristogeiton killed the Athenian tyrant, Hippias, about five hundred years ago," I said.

My mother stirred. "They killed the tyrant's brother, Hipparchus. They were executed for it. The Athenians still honour their bravery though, and statues were put up to them as soon as the tyranny ended."

"What happened in Athens hundreds of years ago is of no relevance here, surely," said Isauricus.

"To Brutus it is," said my mother.

Isauricus shook his head. "And we are meant to just carry on? As if nothing happened? What of all Caesar's friends? How do they feel?"

"Caesar's friends mourn the man and keep quiet about Caesar the Dictator," said my mother quietly.

Junia carried on, "Antonius is trying to keep things running as normal, and many Senators are keeping well away from Rome. The people are very upset. Brutus is hoping that the Games he is putting on next month will help. He is thinking of putting on plays which all reflect the theme of tyrannicide."

Isauricus groaned. "Tell him not to, for all our sakes."

"He is leaving the organisation to others," said my mother. "No political messages will be delivered, I can assure you. These will just be very generous Games, put on at the expense of the Praetor, as is usual."

"Oh gods, I had forgotten he was Praetor," said Lepidus. "And Cassius as well, of course. Tertulla, how is Cassius?"

"I hardly know," I said. "Sometimes I think he regrets what he has done, other times he writes at length justifying his actions. I don't know why he feels he has to convince me. He did not consider me at all while he was planning this." I just managed to say this before my voice stopped. Isauricus patted my hand. He really was very sweet.

I was good at drying my tears quickly by now, and the conversation went on - my mother, dry-eyed, Junia looking pale and worried, and Nilla biting her bottom lip as she listened. Isauricus asked for a full description of the murder and the aftermath and what Brutus and Cassius had planned and done so far. But I don't think we told him much he did not know already. I found it interesting that Isauricus immediately assumed that Caesar's death was a tragedy for Rome.

"He was a great man, and an excellent soldier," he said. "His exploits in Gaul were staggering and his leadership - well, his men adored him. The army must be very troubled. I hope Antonius can handle that."

"Many of the soldiers have already started to follow the boy Octavius," said my mother. "And yes, I know he is now Caesar by adoption, but he is the son of a Senator who was the first in his family to reach Praetor, and that is all."

"His mother is Caesar's niece," I said. "His stepfather is very distinguished. And he is Caesar's nearest male relative. That, and the fact that Caesar adopted him, will be enough for the troops."

"He is only eighteen," said Junia. "And Antonius has already dismissed him. When he came to Rome and asked for his inheritance, Antonius just laughed."

Isauricus looked up at the ceiling.

"I am so tired of this," he announced.

There was a pause. We were all tired of it. But we had no escape either.

On the next morning Junia and Nilla arrived early to take me off for a walk along the cliffs of Antium, and we caught up properly. I told them about the lost baby, and they hugged me and cried with me a little, before we compared husbands. Nilla and Isauricus got along just as well as ever - "better if anything," said Nilla, smiling at some memory she was not about to share. Junia thought that Lepidus, away now in Spain, was missing her, and Nilla and I exclaimed, "At last!" together, which made us laugh more than was tactful. Junia didn't seem to mind, she smiled along with us and said, "He really isn't as bad as you two think, you know."

"Well thank Juno and Diana for that," said Nilla.

The sea stretched away before us with a line of dark dots on the horizon, ships making for Ostia, or south to the Bay of Neapolis, while others were peeling away to come into Antium's harbour. I wondered, as always, who was arriving, what goods were coming in, how many dangers the sailors had faced over the years.

"Do you ever wonder about the people on those boats?" said Junia as if she had heard my thoughts. And Nilla shrugged and said, "Not really."

"Tell us about Ephesus," I said, turning away from the hypnotic brightness of the waves, and turning to head back to the villa.

Nilla had enjoyed being the Governor's Wife.

"We had a lovely house and excellent staff," she said, "which of course was because we had so much entertaining to do. Local businessmen usually, but sometimes someone really interesting. I wanted to stay and meet Trebonius, but Lepidus said he could not face the man after what he had done. He really is upset over Caesar's death. I had not realised how much he genuinely admired Caesar."

"Our brother admired Caesar," said Junia bitterly. "I don't know whether he is a fool or wicked..." but Junia could never have finished a sentence like that.

"Brutus once told me that even at school Cassius could never bear anyone who made themselves out to be better than anyone else, bullies, boastful people," I said.

"Caesar was none of those things," said Nilla.

"He wasn't a bully," I agreed, "but towards the end, Nilla, the things he was doing, the honours he was accepting - it did look as though he was setting himself up to be king."

"And he celebrated triumphs for campaigns fought against other Romans - people did not like that," said Junia.

"But did he have to be assassinated?" asked Nilla.

"It is different for men, I suppose," said Junia. "We watch what is happening but cannot do anything about it, while men have to make a choice. Do you remember the meeting we all had here just before Caesar crossed the Rubicon? It's more than five years ago now. Then it did not seem so bad that Brutus and Cassius were on different side to Lepidus and Isauricus. They agreed to differ. This time, it all seems more complicated."

We walked on over the still green grass, the crumbling cliff-side to our left and the villa before us. Soon we would reach the boundary with the gardens behind the house, though "gardens" was a rather grand term for the little area of pebbled walks lined with herbs and bushes and pots of flowers.

219

Nilla stopped to look down at the beach. "I remember playing there when we were young," she said. "Junia collected shells, and you, Tertulla, were always falling over on the rocks."

"And you hated getting wet," I retorted.

"Hush, children," said Junia, and we returned to the villa in a good mood. When my mother suggested that we gather up the children and have a picnic on the beach once the sun was not too hot, it seemed a very good move. Junia's elder son, Marcus, was with his father in Spain, but her younger son Quintus was only slightly older than Publius and little Servilia, and none of them were too old for running on the hot sand and paddling and exploring the caves just in case someone had left treasure in any of them. It was a perfect afternoon. For a while I forgot about Cassius and Caesar and the baby, and dreamed of three little girls, with Nanny and Felix in tow, scampering across the little waves as they broke on the shore. My dream was broken as my niece Servilia, bounced up and exuberantly planted herself next to me, all elbows and sand, but still thinking she should fling her arms around me.

"This is the best place in the world, Auntie Tulla."

"It is," I agreed. "Have you tired of the boys?"

"They are teasing a crab," said Servilia. "It's very tedious of them."

For a moment she sounded just like Nilla and I smiled.

"That's a good word for boys when they are being silly," I said.

"I wish Marcus was here," said Servilia. "I love Marcus."

I doubted if Marcus now at the grand old age of fourteen, would find his nine-year-old cousin anything but a little tedious too, but did not say anything. Instead, I hugged my gritty, salty niece to me as we watched the late afternoon sun lay a path of shining silver across the sea, and we discussed which sea gods or nymphs would come walking or swimming along this path to greet us.

A couple of years ago, I thought of that afternoon. My great-niece Aemilia had got into trouble, to some extent of her own doing. But it was decided by somebody high up - our beloved

Emperor Tiberius, I suppose - that she was to be made an example, and she was tried by the Senate, in the Senate House if you can believe it. I had never heard of such a thing and found some grim amusement in the thought that my mother would have been angry. Before the trial started, I was visited by my great-nephew, Aemilia's brother Manius, who was defending her.

"We need your help, Aunt Tertulla," he said straight away.

"Oh, yes? You want the help of an old lady, do you?"

"Aunt Tertulla, you could be very influential," he said earnestly. "People see you as a living legend."

I had to laugh. "Fluff!"

"It is true, I assure you," he said, but his face was beginning to widen into a smile. "How old are you now?"

"Old enough, young Manius," I said, smiling back. The younger members of my family are always trying to find out my exact age and Manius is persistent. He nodded to show he knew I had fobbed him off again and continued.

"We plan a demonstration in the middle of the trial," he said. "There will be a break in proceedings while the Games take place, and one of the events is going to be a play at Pompey's Theatre, a production of the Helen by Euripides. It's ideal - it shows how a wife is charged with adultery and reviled by everyone but turns out to be perfectly innocent after all. We are getting all the distinguished women we know to accompany Aemilia to the performance and sit with her, in a show of support. If you came, it would really add some…" and he started to flounder while looking the right word.

"You mean I would bring the gravitas of extreme age? And I am too old for Tiberius to bother about?" I asked.

"You have lived through Caesar, the Triumvirate, the establishment of Augustus as Leading Citizen, and the transfer of power to Tiberius," he said.

"So has Livia," I pointed out.

"Believe me, if I thought Livia still had influence with Tiberius, I would ask her too," he said. "But the whispers are that the two of them are getting on very badly now. Tiberius can't wait for his beloved mother to die."

"So you want me to come along so that people can goggle at me and whisper?" I asked. "I cannot see that it will help Aemilia very much, but, yes, I shall be there. Make sure you get me a seat near the front. I can't do stairs nowadays."

He grinned. "Aunt Tertulla, my two strongest bodyguards will carry you to your seat, I promise," and skipped out of the way as I leaned forward to rap his knuckles.

The charges against Aemilia included adultery (of which she was certainly guilty), consulting an astrologer about when Tiberius was going to die (technically treason, though she denied it furiously), of pretending to have a child by her first husband Quirinius (nobody could work out what the crime was there, and she said she had no idea what was behind the charge) and trying to poison him (presumably after she had not had a child by him). She denied that as well. I could see no reason she should try to kill him. She and Quirinius had divorced years before, and she had remarried and had a family with a nice man called Scaurus.

"So why now?" mused Sulpicia, as I brought her up to date in the Painted Garden.

"I have no idea," I said. "But Tiberius is a very strange man."

The trial started. I, of course, was not allowed into the Senate, but I paid one of the clerks for a full account, and it was a shabby travesty, as has become usual. We have all had friends and relatives condemned and exiled for trivial or contrived wrongdoings.

Sulpicia devoured this account of course and was as outraged as I was.

"Poisoning?" she almost shouted. "Poisoning? Suddenly we Romans have become experts in exotic poisons, brought from all corners of the Empire, just so that wealthy and well-born men and women can poison random acquaintances. Whatever happened to our prowess with daggers? And why is it that poor people don't use poison?"

"Livia has made it fashionable, and this has put up the prices?" I said, and Sulpicia laughed until she had to be thumped on the back.

"Oh dear," she sighed. "Really we mustn't. I know your staff are all lovely and trustworthy, but they are slaves just like other slaves and can be corrupted or tortured."

"I really don't think I am worth bothering about," I said wearily. I had had this conversation many times over the years, and when I was young enough to want to avoid trouble, I did everything I was supposed to do. I lived quietly and unostentatiously, I did not parade my wealth, I kept few slaves, I visited family and a small number of friends only. I was old, I found it hard to care.

The day after the trial started the Games began, and Aemilia had a few days of respite, and time to put her affairs in order. None of us thought she would be found innocent. She sweetly visited me to bestow an appallingly hideous statue of a rampant satyr upon me.

"You don't actually need anything, Aunt Tertulla," she explained, "but I thought it would make you laugh."

I had prepared something for her as well. I reached for the small package of documents on my desk and held it out to her.

"I am assuming that you plan to go East for your exile," I said. "So here is a letter for a banker in Athens and one in Antioch. There should be enough to at least keep you in a few comforts."

She embraced me with genuine affection.

"Aunt Tertulla, you never cease to amaze me. Are you sure you can afford it? I always thought…you know after your husband died…"

"One of the most valuable lessons my mother taught me was to keep control of the money," I said. "Don't tell anyone about this though."

"Why help me though?" she asked. "I'm hardly the worthiest member of the family."

"There are no worthy members of our family left besides myself," I said. "But you, Aemilia, have always made me laugh. Be careful, my dear, and try not upset anyone before you leave Rome."

"If I leave Rome," she said, and her eyes filled with tears, which she did her best to blink away.

"I do hope you are not thinking of suicide, you silly girl," I said in my briskest manner. "Life is not to be wasted like that."

"You don't think I have disgraced my name and family and should do the proper thing?" she asked, sniffing a little as she collected herself.

"Certainly not. If everyone who slept with someone not their spouse committed suicide there would be nobody left in Rome," I said. "We all know that you have poisoned nobody, and you are not guilty of treason. We have no idea what Tiberius is doing, but I have no doubt you are just unfortunate."

"Aunt Tertulla, I shall miss you," she said. "Well, not for long, because I am attending the theatre with you tomorrow, and looking forward to it immensely," I said. "And now I need a nap, so be a good girl and go home. Have a lovely dinner and drink lots of wine."

She laughed, kissed me and left, unfortunately without the satyr, which looked lasciviously at me over his pipes. "You do not impress me at all," I told him. "Those pipes aren't even near your lips. You are a fraud." And I sat back, remembering Aemilia's father with his cousins, on the beach at Antium.

I hired a litter the next morning to take me and Sulpicia over to Aemilia's house. There we joined a crowd of the most respectable matrons Rome could offer and escorted Aemilia in a procession to the theatre. We made an impression. True to his word, Manius had provided bodyguards and two of them very kindly carried me up the steps of the seating to the block Manius had reserved for Aemilia and her female entourage. I don't know if you know Euripides' Helen, but it tells the tale of how Helen was kidnapped by Paris - kidnapped, as in she did not go voluntarily and therefore start the Trojan War all on her own for mere lust, as most of the poets tell. In this version, Paris' ship is blown off course to Egypt where Helen is hidden in a temple, and a sort of ghost-Helen goes to Troy in her place. When the Greeks win the war, Menelaus takes the ghost-Helen with him, but he too is blown off course to Egypt so that he can be reconciled with the real Helen and learn that he hasn't really been cuckolded for the last ten years. I expect this was a relief for him, though it does mean that all those men died for nothing.

Throughout this absurd piece there were many places where the lines resonated with Aemilia's situation. We thoroughly enjoyed ourselves weeping and moaning throughout the play, and by the end most of the audience were gazing at us rather than the stage. I noticed with satisfaction the number of Senators, who had been dragged along by their wives, looking more and more uncomfortable as they realized what was at the heart of this demonstration.

"And have we achieved anything, I wonder?" mused Sulpicia as we bumped out way back home in our litter.

"I don't think even Tiberius will dare to impose the death penalty now," I said.

"But was that ever likely?" asked Sulpicia.

"Tiberius is unpredictable," I said, and we fell silent.

In the end, Tiberius had to have Quirinius' slaves tortured to gain evidence of attempted poisoning, as none of Aemilia's would betray their mistress. Manius did his best to query this without pressing it too much, a delicate path to tread. Aemilia went into exile, of course.

Chapter 26

You will have guessed that I did not see my husband again. He and Brutus moved from house to house in central Italy, then down to the Bay of Neapolis, visiting people and asking for support. They were in close touch with several supporters in Rome, so they would know if Antonius made a mistake. Brutus clearly wanted to be available should any chance offer itself, but Cassius had given up hope of this, and planned to leave Italy. I do still have this letter, the last he wrote to me on Italian soil:

Cassius to his wife, from the island of Nisis

I'm staying at your brother's house on the island and am enjoying the best possible view across the Bay to Misenum. There, I can see the ships I have already gathered, which will follow me east, to Athens and later to Syria, where I shall meet with Trebonius. Do you remember the boy Lucius Sestius who took the notes at Antium for us? I was extremely touched when he appeared with five ships borrowed from his family's wine business, the biggest ships in their fleet. Given that his father was always a supporter of Caesar, I thought this was a very fine gesture. If we can persuade more families like the Sestii to show their support in material terms like this, I shall be happy.

I have decided to make for Syria as my final stop for two reasons, one, our friend Trebonius is there already and two, I still have friends and supporters there from my time fighting the Parthians. The troops there know me and I hope respect me - maybe even respect what I did.

Of course, the real question is whether you, my dearest wife, respect what I did, and my greatest fear is that you do not. In your mind, do you feel that I killed your father? All I can say is that I honestly believe that Caesar was not your father, and even if he was, I did not kill the man, I killed the tyrant. I had to. I have grieved for Caesar, believe me Tertulla, or rather I have grieved for his greatness. He was great, and I do not deny that. He was an outstanding soldier, and his measures while Dictator showed concern for all the citizens of Rome. But he aspired to become a king, and this could not happen.

I realise that you have been through loss and I grieve for you. At the moment we are apart and so we see different things, even though I imagine you looking out at the sea, just as I am doing now. We both are actors in a play, but our roles are different. A decent play demands many roles and together we contribute to the whole performance, Tertulla. I hope you will forgive all the metaphors.

I cannot see what will happen of course, but I truly hope that we shall be together again, in a Rome that is free from tyranny and discord. Being married to you is one of the things which keeps me sane and hopeful. Keep yourself safe, my lovely Tertulla.

I read this, as he said in the letter, sitting in the garden at Antium on a beautiful July evening, as the sun set over a golden sea. The summer had warmed me at last and while I still felt shaken, I could see my way ahead. I read his letter again and picked it apart. Did he really imagine that this was ever going to end in our joyful reunion? I was not in a play, but on a journey, and I did not think the rest of my journey would ever be with Cassius. He would never recover his position in Rome again and I knew his pride would not let him accept anything less.

My mother and sisters had attended Brutus' games in Rome, but I could not face it. The house on the Palatine was closed up now, with just a few slaves to keep watch over it, and I did not want to stay there. Even my Painted Garden could not tempt me back. I used the excuse of the heat, and Nanny and Felix stayed in Antium with me. Brutus did not attend the games of course. Just as Cicero had done in June, everyone advised him to stay away. My sisters were safe. Junia wrote that Antonius had even come over to where they were all sitting at the theatre and suggested that his daughter Antonia should become betrothed to her son Marcus. She and Lepidus were consulting each other by letter.

It suits everyone really - Lepidus and Antonius can cement their recent support for one another. The family is an old and noble one, so Mother is pleased. It is a pity that Antonius is not still married to the girl's mother, whom I far prefer to Fulvia, but I daresay we shall manage. But I have asked Lepidus put Antonius off for a while - I want to wait and see how things go. Anyway there are years to go before they can marry and who knows what will happen between now and then?

"What indeed," I thought, remembering the years of betrothal to Cassius, during which I only had to worry about whether he would return from the war in Syria.

In August, Cassius and Brutus were officially given the governorships of two small and unimportant provinces, Cyrene and Crete.

"It will do for now," said my mother, who had lobbied everyone she knew in the Senate for a month to achieve this and had no intention of stopping there. But it gave both my husband and my brother an official reason to be absent from Italy. Neither travelled to their official provinces of course. Brutus went to Athens and Cassius to Syria, and we waited for news, spending many a useless conversation wondering what they would do next.

The year wore on and for a long time, I thought that Cassius was right, and that Antonius was the enemy. He had used Caesar's funeral to turn the people of Rome against Caesar's assassins, and he clearly saw himself as the senior statesman in the aftermath. He was Consul and bribed the other Consul to let him manage things his way; he enacted decree after decree which he said came from Caesar's plans for the city and empire; he used treasury reserves to build up support; he swatted away the attempt of the young man Octavianus, the heir, to claim Caesar's wealth. But he was not Julius Caesar. He had little genuine experience in the military, and despite being a decent enough speaker, he had no political sense. He loathed the experienced politicians of the generation above him but did not try to reach out to Cassius or Brutus. To me it was clear that he was just waiting for the right time.

Letters from Cassius and Brutus were few and took a long time to arrive as the year turned into autumn and the sailing season ended. They also wrote to Cicero, and he made sure copies of these letters and his own replies were sent to my mother and me as a courtesy. I began to appreciate how slowly things had to move when they were so far away from us - and increasingly from each other. Cassius had headed straight for Syria, the scene of his courageous actions after the Battle of Carrhae, while Brutus of course had begun his journey in Athens so that he could meet philosophers.

"The plan is for Brutus to move to Macedonia from Greece," said my mother. "Once Cassius is firmly entrenched in Syria, then we shall petition the Senate to confirm them as governors. They will then control much of the East and many legions."

"Antonius won't be pleased with that idea," I said dubiously.

"Antonius is not as powerful as he supposes," said my mother. "And his Consulship ends in a couple of months. Hirtius and Pansa take over, and they are not going to carry out Antonius' wishes, just because he tells them."

"And the young Caesar is very popular with the army," I said. "He might decide to prosecute Antonius once Antonius isn't Consul."

"The young Caesar?" said my mother with a raised eyebrow.

"Cicero says that Octavianus is insisting on being called Caesar," I said. "After all he has the right, through adoption."

My mother ignored this and said, "We are past the days when officials were held accountable by the fear of being prosecuted after their term of office."

"Antonius would not give young Caesar his inheritance," I said. "How else is he going to get his hands on the money except by prosecuting him?"

"Antonius will have to leave for his province," said my mother. "He could try to get Decimus on his side, then gather legions from all over Gaul. Then he should go around the other governors, asking for support. Lepidus will back him. Between them, Lepidus and Antonius could then persuade your brother and husband. Once the Senate sees that Italy is surrounded by

Antonius' allies, and an army is threatening from Gaul, they will have to give up their hostility towards Antonius."

It was what she would do, she meant. It might have worked. Antonius of course did not go down this path. He decided to attack the city of Mutina, where Decimus had set up his seat as governor of Nearer Gaul. This was bad news for us, because now Antonius showed that he was willing to pursue Caesar's assassins - a strategy that cut right across the policy of amnesty which he had been so keen to promote in the aftermath of the Ides of March. But had to leave behind his enemies in the city and leave Brutus and Cassius in the East for the time being. It was a huge risk.

Antonius left Rome in November and young Caesar Octavianus and the Senate leapt to take advantage of his absence. There was not only condemnation of Antonius, led by Cicero, but the new year had barely begun before the Senate sent the two Consuls and Octavianus to rescue Decimus. Civil war loomed once more, as though we had learned nothing from the last ten years.

Early in the spring, Lepidus wrote to Junia from Spain, where he was carefully keeping the peace and observing what was going on in Italy and Gaul. He had decided to make an official alliance with Antonius by betrothing his son Marcus to Antonius' daughter. Junia was thrown into a panic.

"This means Lepidus is committed to Antonius just when the Senate have declared against him," said my mother. "It is a gamble, but if Antonius succeeds, then Lepidus will be very well placed. Don't worry, Junia, Lepidus has a knack of ending up on the winning side."

Junia nonetheless decided to move to Antium for the time being, while Nilla and Isauricus remained in Rome, keeping up a flow of almost daily letters.

The news throughout the spring was unremittingly grim, armies, sieges, who had declared for Antonius, who was remaining neutral, who had retreated. The fighting started in April, and Nilla wrote as soon as news reached Rome:

Mutina sounds like it was absolutely awful. The two consuls were leading different parts of the army, and apparently Pansa was still several days' march behind Hirtius - and Antonius managed to get to Pansa's army without anyone finding out, and smashed them - they were inexperienced troops, Isauricus says. Pansa was injured, so Antonius retreated back to Mutina, and there was a huge battle there, and Hirtius was killed. It seems extraordinary that the only person left to lead the Senate's army is young Caesar Octavianus, and he didn't even fight. I don't know why; everybody gossips about it, but nobody knows for certain. Antonius has retreated - I get hazy over who is where - I can't remember what has happened to Decimus. Maybe he is still at Mutina? Anyway, young Caesar is triumphant - sort of - and gods alone know where we are going next. I haven't heard anything about Lepidus, I'm sorry, Junia.

Her next letter came later the same day:

We have just heard that the Consul Pansa has died of his wounds. The rumours are terrible - some say he was poisoned. More when I know more.

"We must go back to Rome," said my mother. She spent a day furiously writing letters, then once more we set off on the journey I knew so well. It was already the beginning of July, and the sea was calm and blue, every wave glinting, and sometimes, when we were close to the shore, people saw us and waved. Children, I expect. Most people are too busy to wave at passing ships.

Once more my mother called a council, and this time Cicero was a welcome guest. He was leading the opposition to Antonius in Rome, the only person of his generation and seniority who was still alive and willing to enter the fray. In particular, he had embarked on a series of speeches and pamphlets that attacked Antonius ruthlessly, and even worse, poked fun at him. He made an enemy he did not understand, the worst mistake of his life.

Atticus was also present. My mother said that his long policy of never taking sides would come in useful.

"I still think we need Brutus and Cassius to return," said Cicero. He leaned forward, eager to convey his ideas. "Antonius has lost, and is on the run, politically and militarily. Young

Caesar has a name but no experience - did you hear that he took no part in the actual fighting at Mutina?"

"He is frequently ill, apparently," said my mother without any hint of censure on her tone.

"The soldiers will have noticed," said Cicero. "Add to that the successes your son and son-in-law have been having on the East and both Caesar Octavianus and Antonius are not looking good. Servilia, will you write and try to persuade Brutus to return?"

My mother thought about this.

"I agree with you," she said slowly. "Now is the time for him to return. But I do not think that he will, Cicero, not even if the whole Senate wrote to add their pleas to yours."

Brutus and Cassius had been busy collecting men and money, sorting out local disputes, making alliances, sometimes forcing alliances. Cassius had even said in his last letter that he was thinking of going to Egypt to recruit the soldiers left there by Caesar a mere five years ago. I hoped that he would not meet Cleopatra, charming as she had been when I met her. I did not know how she would react to encountering one of Caesar's killers, and she had a ruthless side as all the Ptolemies did. Cleopatra had not baulked at watching her own sister walk in a triumphal procession as a prisoner and would have endured Arsinoe's death with equanimity. I had no doubt that she was capable of dispatching any Roman who displeased her.

I came back to the discussion when Atticus said, "I wish you would listen to me."

I had learned from my mother to respect Atticus' opinion.

"Young Caesar is the danger," he protested. "That boy has an ambition I have never encountered, and, whatever you may think of his personal courage and fighting ability, he is the only leader we have in the field, in charge of thousands of men. He has a cold streak which I find frightening, and he does not admire you, my dear Cicero, as much as you think. You have made it too obvious that you don't rate him. He will hold that against you."

"He is nineteen years old," protested Cicero. "Nineteen! I am sixty-three and of consular rank, with a career behind me, which, I flatter myself, can be rivalled by very few. Why should I rate him?"

"Because he is another Sulla in the making," said Atticus. "He has Sulla's single-minded ambition, he has a clear grasp of what is going on in our pitiful Republic, and he has none of Caesar's charm - so he will have to dispose of people because he won't be able to persuade them. There are barely a dozen men of consular rank in Rome at the moment, so disposing of you all would be easy. All that boy has to do is send a squad or two of veterans and they would cut you all down in a day and meet no opposition."

There was a silence at this. Eventually my mother said, "What do you advise, Titus?"

"Get your money out of Rome," said Atticus, promptly. "I have already sold a lot of Brutus' assets, and I shall happily do the same for you, if you would like. If you are certain that your sons-in-law Lepidus and Isauricus are in a position to protect you, good. Otherwise, find and buy a house in a town where your family does not have connections. Make it as far from Rome as you can bear and keep a couple of absolutely trustworthy staff there. Then you have a bolthole. Make sure that you have copies of all vital papers sent there. Be prepared to leave Rome."

My mother nodded. "Thank you, Titus. At least we are already used to leaving Rome, and I do indeed have confidence in my sons-in-law. Nevertheless, I shall consider your advice carefully."

She turned to Cicero. "My dear Marcus, I am sorry to have to say this, but we are facing yet another crisis and I have no confidence that we shall come through this one. Do look after yourself. That boy is not to be trusted in any way; do you hear me? And stop going around telling people We shall extol him, lift him up - and let him down. He will hear that - someone will make sure of it."

Atticus tsked. "You really must resist the temptation to be clever, Marcus."

But Cicero laughed. "I'm too old to stop showing off now, Titus. My dear friends, I promise to take care and at least my passion for acquiring houses throughout Italy means that I have plenty of places to hide. But we are not so low yet that we need fear the boy Caesar."

I sat quietly through the discussion, listening and yet so far apart from the main players. I was only there because I was Cassius' wife, thought to have influence with him. I noticed that nobody asked me to write to Cassius and beg him to return, for which I was grateful. I did not know how I would write such a letter. Cassius was carving out his own path now and I was no longer part of his life, I was sure of that. What I did not know was whether Cassius himself knew that. He wrote to me of course, usually asking me to raise money. I passed all these requests on to Atticus, asked him to oversee the discreet sale of a piece of property, and took no more interest. The only thing that was sacrosanct was the estate at Lanuvium, where my stepson young Gaius lived. I was determined about two things, that he would not join his father and that he would not lose all his inheritance. Gaius' tutor kept a close eye on him and reported that the boy showed no sign of restlessness. Maybe the years of growing up without his father were going to benefit Gaius in this.

I also took the opportunity to safeguard my own wealth. I met with Atticus and my mother, and we drew up some careful plans.

"I suggest that you transfer the villa at Antium back to me," said my mother briskly. "I shall of course put a clause into my will to ensure that it is bequeathed to you."

The investments I had made using my dowry were also sold - to my sisters, ostensibly so that my niece and nephews should benefit if I died. I made a careful inventory of all the precious things Cassius, and I owned between us and many of them were sold by Atticus. Some of the money was sent to Cassius, and some I sent secretly to Barates in Antioch. I now owned a string of shops there, mostly concerned with the fabric business. I had never told anyone about Barates and the arrangement, not even Atticus, who now carried on,

"You must be prepared for the worst. If the young Caesar gets his way, Brutus and Cassius will be declared public enemies.

Their property will be seized for the state, which means for Caesar himself. He has an army to pay after all."

We did not sell everything, because if things went badly, I had to have something to show when the confiscators came. "I hope that he will not touch your own property," said Atticus. "But I think we had better prepare for the worst. I suggest that your other daughters and you, Servilia, transfer small properties to Tertulla, enough to look like the remains of her dowry. We can say that Cassius took the rest."

The young Caesar came back in August, and he was not in any mood for reconciliation. With the deaths of both Consuls at Mutina, he now led the army himself, and he marched right up to the walls of Rome, and camped there, receiving the adulation of the people who streamed out to greet him.

"There are booths set up and a little market and sideshows all over the Campus Martius," Kleia reported. She was always urging me to do things, go on little forays, treating myself. She was keeping a careful eye on me to make sure that I did not descend into the depression of last year, and I appreciated her kindness. It did sound fun and Rome had not had a lot of fun recently, so I decided I would go. I made the mistake of persuading my mother to come along with me and Kleia and a bodyguard and see what was happening. We got out the litters because it was August and made our way over to the Campus Martius.

It was a lovely day, hot of course, but there were soldiers offering water at regular intervals, and the whole area was decked with bunting and garlands of flowers. Everywhere there were little stalls selling food, wine, flowers, toys. People took their time, strolling and visiting the various sellers. We had not had anything like this in Rome for what seemed like years, and I could easily have enjoyed it, if my mother had not been at my side, frowning and tutting.

"Why did you come?" I eventually asked her, exasperated. "What did you expect?"

"I expected this," said my mother.

"And doesn't this feel good? It feels relaxed, happy," I said. "It is a relief to be out of doors and walking along a street and not worried about being attacked."

"I have never worried about that," said my mother.

"You are not -" and I stopped. I had of course been about to say, "You are not Cassius' wife" but even in this atmosphere I could not say his name aloud.

"You need a honey cake," said my mother and I heard Kleia smother a laugh behind us.

Caesar Octavianus announced that he wished to be elected Consul and to my mother's disgust, he succeeded. The Senate, terrified and uncertain, handed over power to him without question.

Now was the point where we wished that Cicero had become the second Consul, so that a team of military youth and political experience could give respectability to the spectacle of a nineteen-year-old as leader of Rome. Instead, the young Caesar discovered an obscure relative in Quintus Pedius.

"Who?" I asked.

My mother wrinkled her brow.

"Grandson of Caesar's sister, not Atia's mother of course, the other sister. He was Praetor a few years ago, I think."

"So now he finds himself Consul alongside a cousin he had not realised he had," I said sourly.

"Time to pack again," said my mother. "I don't trust that young man."

I packed.

We left Rome on the next morning, as Quintus Pedius obediently launched a law to prosecute the assassins of Julius Caesar. Young Caesar moved quickly.

In the autumn, we received a letter from Atticus:

My dear Servilia,

I need you to read this then go immediately to the house I bought for you. All the staff there know what to do, and I shall be joining you soon. News from the north is that not only has Lepidus met with Antonius and joined him, the two have persuaded young Caesar to attend a meeting with them - just the three of them on an island in the middle of the river, all very dramatic.

Seriously, this is what I have been dreading. They will no doubt come to an arrangement, and they first need money - all three have armies to be paid and plans to be funded. I do not trust any of them to raise this money legally or without violence. I have made my plans of course, long ago, and I know you have too, so our money is safely hidden, but I really think it wise to be lying low for the next few months. At the moment, the only thing protecting Brutus' mother and Cassius' wife is Lepidus - do you see what I mean? Yes, of course you do, Servilia. Hurry, and I shall see you soon. The bearer of this letter has instructions to offer his services as a guide. Please use those services.

My mother and I lost no time in doing as Atticus had asked and made a hurried journey to a house we had never been to before. Clever Atticus, how like him to have a bolthole. We left Felix in charge of Antium, and he sent messages to Junia and Nilla to reassure them that we were safe.

To avoid the constant hectoring and criticism that had followed The Three, this Triumvirate carried out the most feared of all measures - proscription. They would publish lists of men they disliked, or felt opposed them, and pin the list on noticeboards in the Forum - and that gave anyone the right to hunt the named men down and be rewarded for it. Top of the list were their own friends and families, and Cicero. It is hard to think of the old man as he now was as a threat to the Triumvirate, but apparently Marcus Antonius had found Cicero's cutting jibes and personal insults hard to laugh off. I cannot imagine how hard it was for Junia to watch her husband being a part of this, but she wrote to us from Rome with the news.

The troops sent by Antonius caught up with Cicero and killed him at once. The head that dreamed up those wonderful speeches and the hands that wrote them were cut off Cicero's warm corpse and nailed to the Speakers' platform in the Forum. In the grey light of a dismal December, when fear hung in the air, hundreds of people crept down to witness the appalling sight. My mother and I, never Cicero's greatest admirers, read with horror the account sent us by Junia. I thought of his strawberries and said, "He did not deserve this." Accounts of Cicero's death are well known and all I shall say is that I am glad he was brave, and it was quick. He died before his beloved Roman Republic was destroyed.

This was just a preliminary to the real work, and soon the Triumvirate was in pursuit of my husband and brother. In deference to his wife and mother-in-law, Lepidus made sure that he was the one left behind in Rome, while Antonius and Octavianus Caesar moved troops and provisions down Italy and across the sea. My mother and I felt able to move back to Antium safely.

The two sides - Cassius and Brutus against Antonius and Octavianus - met at a small town called Philippi.

Chapter 27

I was twenty-six years old when Cassius died, and I am now
ninety. You might think that the last sixty-two years has been a
blank, a waiting for death, and it certainly has not been lived at
the intensity which I see when looking back. But it has been full
of drama, and my family has survived, despite the deaths of the
most important men in my life. I have noticed this about men,
that they die off, but the women go on.

I have not married again of course. Marriage brings great
happiness for some, and I was as lucky as a woman can get with
Cassius. My decision meant that I did not have children, but I
do not regret that. I have always surrounded myself with young
people, nieces and nephews, friends and slaves. The young man
who is writing this down is my latest acquisition, and he is
proving satisfactory, but then he is on best behaviour. He thinks
that he will be freed in my will, and that he has not got long to
wait.

I have a pretty good knowledge of how Cassius died. We
heard the news quickly of course, as military messengers were
sent straight back to Rome. But for the details I was obliged to
Lucius Sestius, the young man who had acted as secretary at
that fateful meeting at Antium after Caesar's assassination.
Lucius Sestius had accompanied first my husband, then my
brother Brutus, through two years of travelling around Asia and
Macedonia and was one of the people with whom my husband
dined on the night before the first battle of Philippi. Sestius
survived both this and the second battle in which my brother
was defeated and died, and then fled to Sicily and waited, as so
many did, until he was pardoned by the young Caesar (by the
time he had disposed of Julius Caesar's killers, nobody called
young Caesar "the boy Octavianus"). It was four years after
Philippi that Sestius visited me to tell me about my husband's
last days.

"He was always very calm and optimistic," said Sestius. "But
without being false."

I had invited him to sit in my Painted Garden and he had talked and talked, telling me of the travels and the fighting in Asia, the squabbles with other people who were supposedly on their side, the tensions of never knowing where they stood with people back in Rome. But they had always known that it must come down to a battle.

"By the time the fighting started we were almost looking forward to it," said Sestius, "if only to get it out of the way. The weather was good, it was autumn and quite chilly, but it hadn't rained too much. We were in our camp - we were south of Brutus's camp; you know that don't you?"

I nodded. I knew about the camp lay-out, Brutus on the right wing opposite the young Caesar, and Antonius and Cassius facing each other to the south. Brutus had mountains behind him, Cassius had a marsh to the south. Antonius had forced the battle by making a route through the marshes allowing him to threaten the army on one flank, so Brutus had decided on a frontal attack. My husband, who had actual military experience, was reluctant. He was all for defending until the opposition's lack of supply lines forced them to retreat for the winter.

"The trouble was," said Sestius, "that the mist that began every day for an hour or so, decided on this day it would linger and we were hampered by that for the whole battle. We were never exactly sure what the other parts of the army were doing, which sounds ridiculous, but over an area that size and in mist - well…. We thought that Antonius would try and attack from the south using his marsh causeway so most of us had been sent to look out for him there. And, of course, he actually attacked the camp straight on and overran it easily."

His account was fluent and swift, one he had made many times before. And, of course, it was heavily edited for my benefit. There was no reference to the sights, sounds and smells of a battle, little reference to what Sestius himself had done or thought.

"Looking back on it I can't believe that we made such a basic mistake, but I suppose it's easy to be wise now. When Cassius heard the news, we also had no idea what was happening with the northern army and Brutus - the mist was in the way, and we heard reports that young Caesar had overrun Brutus' camp as well. It was only then that your husband despaired. It did not take him long to reach his decision, and he went into a nearby copse of trees on his own. After a few minutes a few of us followed and found him already dead."

There was a silence. Sestius was sitting on a stool in my beautiful Painted Garden and gazing at the wall above my head. Despite his attempt at distancing himself, he was for a few moments on a battlefield, mist and marshes around, wondering what to do with the body of the commander who had inspired him to spend years following him to this disaster. After a while Sestius carried on, "Later of course we discovered that Brutus was alive and had inflicted serious damage on Caesar's troops."

And of course, I knew about Caesar Octavianus. We all did. The official story was that his doctor had had a warning in a dream the night before the battle and had taken the ailing young man out of his tent first thing in the morning and hidden him in the marshes. He had played no part in the battle, but his officers had managed everything for him. He was fortunate that both sides had lost so many men that both decided to withdraw at the end of that day.

"Nobody knew who had won," said Sestius, "We had inflicted greater casualties, but we had lost one of our generals. There was no question of retreating to winter quarters and so we stayed."

"You don't have to tell me anymore," I said.

"I need to tell you one more thing," he said. "When we broke the news to Brutus, he called your husband "the last of the Romans", because Rome will never see men like him again. And I agree. Then Brutus gave me the task of escorting your husband's body to Thasos, where we buried him with all the proper observances."

"Thasos?" I asked. "But - Thasos is an island, isn't it? I had no idea it was near Philippi. Why bury him there?"

Sestius looked at the floor as he said, "Brutus - your brother - thought it would be better for morale if Cassius were not given a funeral on the battlefield."

"Better for morale? For his men not to be given the chance to mourn him? Sestius, how many people were in attendance at my husband's funeral?" A very nasty idea was beginning to form in my mind.

"All those of us in the escort were there, Lady Junia, and many people from Thasos itself came to pay their respects. Your brother sent money to the people of Thasos to build a tomb."

"How many people, Sestius? Or rather, how many Romans?"

Sestius was turning red with embarrassment - or was it shame? But he spoke clearly and did not avoid the question.

"Six officers and the escort of thirty legionaries," he said.

"He was Praetor," I whispered. "He saved hundreds of men after the battle of Carrhae. He defended Syria from the Parthians. There should have been more. His son should have been there. All Rome should have been there. Could my brother not have given him a decent funeral?"

Lucius Sestius said nothing. I stood and wished that there were no tears running down my face.

"I am grateful that you took the time to come and tell me."

"I could not have done otherwise, Junia Tertia," he said. "Your husband was my general and he was a man worth following."

Yes, he was, I thought. But my brother did not want to remind the army of my husband's valour, so he tidied the corpse out of sight as soon as he could.

"After the funeral," said Sestius, "I returned to your brother and was in time for the final defeat."

What could one say to someone who went through such a battle?

"I hope you will excuse me now, Lucius Sestius," I said keeping my voice firm and defying him to notice my tears. "I hope that I shall have the pleasure of your company at dinner in the near future but for now I must retire and think about what you have told me."

"Of course," he said and got up quickly, relieved to be going. I let him find his own way out of the house as I sank back onto the chair. What would have happened if Cassius had survived, I thought, if he could have helped Brutus lead that final fight…

but there was no use in wondering that now. I had not asked about my brother's suicide. I had no heart to hear of yet more ostentatious nobility. I had no doubt that Lucius Sestius was even now trudging over to my mother's house to do his duty. I knew of at least three other men who had visited her in the last couple of months, a pilgrimage stop on the way back to Rome and respectability.

I wondered where I could find out about Thasos, and to whom I could write about Cassius' tomb. Maybe I really would invite Lucius Sestius to dinner and find out. Someone should make sure that Cassius had a decent tomb, because I had no faith in my brother.

"What did you do?" asked Sulpicia.

"I sent money to Thasos," I said. "They assured me that in addition to the tomb they built at the time, they then raised a decent memorial. I don't think Cassius would expect anything more."

There was a pause.

"They told me that Sestius had paid for the original tomb himself, you know. Not Brutus."

Sulpicia put her hand on mine and said nothing. I added,

"Maybe he didn't have time to send any money?"

I think we both knew the answer to that.

"And your stepson?"

"Poor lamb. We had planned to visit Thasos together, when things were - quiet. But he died not long after at Lanuvium. One of the winter pestilences. He was learning how to run an estate. And so Caesar Octavianus -"

"The Divine Augustus," said Sulpicia.

"Indeed, as he became. Well, he decided not to penalise Gaius for being his father's son. Generous. He took the estate after Gaius died of course. Octavianus was always in need of land for his retired troops to settle."

"He left you with your property intact too, didn't he? This house as well." Sulpicia was not asking me to do anything but state facts. It still made me feel very tired.

"I know very well that at any time Octavianus, Augustus if you must, could have taken this away from me," I said. "I suppose our current Emperor could do it now, if he wished. I have never taken this house for granted. But I refuse to be grateful."

"I'm glad, Tertulla. I don't think you would be the same woman I love if you were ever grateful," And Sulpicia's eyes gleamed at me with a wicked challenge.

I pointed at her across my Painted Garden. "Don't!"

She picked up her wine-cup and toasted me, still smiling.

"To you and your ingratitude, my dearest Tertulla."

Chapter 28

The period of my life following the Battle of Philippi was grim. My sisters were married to men who supported the young Caesar and though they tried, I found it so hard to accept their help as I mourned Cassius. I did not mourn Brutus. The brother I had adored as a child did not exist, possibly had never really existed, and as I grew, everything I loved about him seemed to fall away.

The young man who took Caesar's name was generous to me. A letter arrived soon after Philippi, informing me that the Triumvirate had decided to let me keep property to the value of my dowry, to include any jewellery and clothing that could reasonably be accounted mine, even if they had been the present of Cassius. I kept the house on the Palatine, and Kleia. Young Gaius was granted his father's estate at Lanuvium, and along with his tutor Aristides, spent all his time there living a noticeably quiet life. We decided that it would be better if he and I did not meet though we sent each other letters to check on each other's health, and he was keen to travel to Philippi and Thasos to see his father's tomb one day. I had no need to see it but was touched when the boy asked me to go with him, and we planned the journey through letters, as we waited for the time to be right to ask permission. He died of an autumn fever two years after his father. Aristides subsequently committed suicide in a diplomatically unobtrusive manner, leaving me a courteous note saying that at his age he did not want to try and start any sort of a new life. I was amazed to discover that he was more than seventy and I respected his nobility. Felix went down to Lanuvium to oversee the double funeral, and the construction of a suitable memorial to them both.

At the age of twenty-eight, my last tie with Cassius had gently dissolved, and instead of turning to my sisters, I spent months with my mother at the villa in Antium, reading letters from Rome with interest but not feeling as though I were a part of it anymore. I discussed with her everything that was happening, and as usual admired her insight and knowledge of all the relationships, the informal agreements, the grand official treaties. I could not resist pushing her just a little every now and then. Take this typical conversation, from the year after Philippi:

"Your sister writes that the young man has agreed to become betrothed to her daughter Servilia," said my mother.

And, as always, I remarked, "And by "the young man" do you mean Caesar Octavianus, heir of Julius Caesar?"

"I shall never call that young man "Caesar", as you know well," and my mother smiled to herself as she read more from Nilla's letter. "Isauricus is beside himself with excitement at such a good match and feels that along with gaining the consulship for the second time this year, he has reached the dizzy heights."

"I wouldn't call it "gaining the consulship" exactly," I said. "He was given it for service rendered."

"Dear Isauricus," said my mother. "He was given his last consulship by a Caesar too." She was still smiling, and I could not help joining her. We both liked Isauricus, and he was good at picking sides, but he was never going to rule the world.

It wasn't long before Nilla's letters were announcing the end of that particular engagement.

"Isauricus is so disappointed, though he tries not to mind, of course, dear man. He is getting to look just a bit too old nowadays, if you know what I mean? He isn't really in the midst of the top people anymore, and I suppose is hurting a little."

"So, I wonder why, suddenly, Isauricus' daughter is not for young Caesar," I said. "What does Nilla say?"

"My little Servilia does not give a piece of fluff for her sudden demotion and declares she always intended to marry her cousin Marcus anyway. Sweet! And of course, I wouldn't mind at all, my gorgeous girl marrying one of Junia's boys."

"I am not sure I approve of cousins marrying," said my mother frowning. "I hope they nip that thought in the bud."

But to my amusement, little Servilia dug her heels in and got her way. I do not know how much of a say my nephew Marcus got.

We found out later that young Caesar had decided to enter a betrothal with Claudia, the stepdaughter of Marcus Antonius, which I suppose helped underline their alliance. I don't know why he bothered as that didn't last either. He seemed to get attached on a moment's whim, depending on who was his latest ally. Once he married, it did not last beyond a year or two, because he lost his head over a woman called Livia Drusilla, divorcing his own wife on the day the poor woman gave birth to his daughter Julia. He married Livia Drusilla while she was still pregnant by her first husband, having made sure that the priests gave their permission of course. It gave me something to laugh about.

Letters from my sisters of course also focussed on the political drama that unfolded over the ten years after Philippi - the downfall of the Triumvirate. There were marriages and quarrels and treaties to patch things up - and I was surprised that it took several years before Marcus Antonius and young Caesar tired of my brother-in-law Lepidus, just as we had all tired of him years before. Nilla's letter announced the news:

Isauricus can hardly believe that Lepidus has been so stupid and Junia is devastated. It seems that Lepidus genuinely thought he could use the bad feeling between Caesar and Antonius to carve out a slice more power for himself and of course it went wrong the moment he set a foot outside the lines. He has managed to bring the two closer together to condemn him and they have sent him into permanent exile in Circeii.

"Near us," I remarked. "Should we visit?"

My mother shot me a reproving look and said, "This must be dreadful for your sister."

"Lepidus has been dreadful for Junia for years," I replied. "He is stupid and uncaring and she should divorce him. I don't know why Caesar and Antonius have let him get away with his life."

My mother sniffed. "For once Tertulla, I agree with you, about the stupidity at least. However, even you must see that it would be unbelievably bad form to execute the Chief Priest."

"Oh yes," I said. "I had forgotten he was Chief Priest."

"Nearly everyone forgets that." said my mother.

Needless to say, Junia did not divorce Lepidus, but my mother bought a house in Circeii so that Junia could more easily visit her husband. Antonius broke the betrothal between his daughter and my nephew Marcus, but he and young Caesar graciously allowed Junia to keep the house near ours at Antium. Her sons Marcus and Quintus bore their father's disgrace by never mentioning him again, and never visiting, though Marcus as we later discovered brooded over the whole unhappy affair. He had been with Lepidus for all the years of the Triumvirate, with him when he made his foolish bid for power, with him when he walked over to young Caesar's army to surrender himself.

"I did not take to Caesar," was all he said about that particular episode. He and Quintus decided to spend some time on their education and visited Athens and the famous school of rhetoric in Rhodes, staying away from Italy for several years. I approved of their good sense.

Those years were not happy, but we survived. We had to conceal our losses while watching a series of ridiculous manoeuvres by young Caesar and Marcus Antonius, as they circled each other, and idly my mother and I wondered who would be first to declare war on the other. I was fascinated by the role their womenfolk played in all these negotiations. Caesar persuaded Marcus Antonius to marry Octavia, his older sister, held up to us all as a paragon. She dutifully had children by Antonius while looking after the children they both brought from former marriages, until she ended up with an enormous brood. And of course, once this wonderful woman was completely his, Marcus Antonius left her to go to Egypt and start a devastating affair with Cleopatra. Do you remember that I told you that Cleopatra only had two lovers? Well, Marcus Antonius was the second and she was by all accounts besotted with him. He certainly could not stop himself running off to her whenever the opportunity arose.

"I cannot see what any intelligent woman sees in Marcus Antonius," said my mother. "Cleopatra could be Queen of Egypt and Friend of the Roman People still, and she throws away that potential to be his lover. Do you see it, Tertulla?"

I thought back to the one occasion I had seen Marcus Antonius in an intimate setting, the dinner two days after Julius Caesar's assassination, and all I remembered was someone who was clearly very annoyed, though not annoyed enough to refuse to take advantage of the situation if he could.

"He is not particularly attractive," I said. "He was completely under Fulvia's thumb at the time I met him, and I did not think him clever enough to get Rome out of the mess after Caesar…." I did not need to finish that sentence and my mother nodded.

"And now he has messed up his alliance with that young man" - "At least call him Young Caesar," I muttered - "and is hopelessly embroiled with Egypt. What is Cleopatra thinking?"

I am weary of this litany of stupidity so I shall just tell you that it all ended up with Antonius and Cleopatra losing the Battle of Actium and committing suicide. Young Caesar, now middle-aged, was lone survivor of all those years of fighting and ruled of Rome by military power, and authority. And by dint of there being nobody else left.

"And that was not the end, was it?" said Sulpicia, thoughtfully. "We all had to get used to living with a new set of rules, unwritten, unspoken rules."

I looked at her surprised.

"Were you aware of such things at such a tender age?"

"I listened to the adults talking, just like you, Tertulla," she said. "I knew perfectly well that not everyone appreciated our new Caesar. The gods know there have been enough attempts to get rid of him over the years."

I looked over my little courtyard garden and said, "My nephew was the first, you know."

Sulpicia looked surprised, then stricken. "Tertulla, I am so sorry – what a tactless thing to say. Marcus Aemilius Lepidus the younger, the year after Actium – he was your nephew, wasn't he?"

"He was executed, and his wife did the decent thing and committed suicide. She was my sister Nilla's daughter, Servilia. I remember her about nine years old, sitting on the beach at

Antium with me and telling me that she loved her cousin Marcus. I really think that she did love him."

"I am so sorry," said Sulpicia. She took my hand and said, "I don't know how you cope with something like that after everything else."

"It killed my brother-in-law," I said. "He died a few months later. It meant that we all had to walk a careful line until we had shown how harmless we were. We held a double funeral for them, under the cover of night and in silence. Nilla collapsed before we reached the pyre, and Junia took her back to my mother's house. My mother and Isauricus and I stood and watched the flames until dawn, and I swear his hair turned a shade greyer overnight."

Chapter 29

Once he had returned from Actium, and Egypt, Caesar Octavianus felt that he had to emulate his adopted father by celebrating multiple triumphs to mark the end of the struggle with Antonius. He made a point of inviting us, mother and sisters and I, giving us official seats at all three processions. Many people said we were lucky to have been forgiven after my nephew's disgrace of the year before, but the events of the fifteen years since Caesar's death had been so tumultuous and strange that this seemed almost normal.

So once more I sat and watched a triumphal procession, every day for three days, the victorious general in his chariot, the troops, the prisoners, the displays of the defeated. And of course, I remembered that first procession I had watched with my father, the one where Pompey had worn the cloak of Alexander the Great. Now, more than thirty years later, the general was younger than me, and some of the enemies defeated were Roman, but of course we could not point that out. We took our seats in the back row of the stand built on the steps of the Temple of Castor. Ahead and slightly to the left, was a new temple, this one to be dedicated to Julius Caesar by his devoted son. Adopted son, as I quickly said to myself. At boring parts during the long procession, I could turn and admire the clean new lines of each corner or column and find my mind struggling to comprehend the strange truth that Julius Caesar was now officially and by Senatorial decree - a god. I still wondered about being Caesar's daughter, thought I might well be – but it mattered less. The desire I felt earlier in my life was now buried so deep within me that I had to work hard to dig it up. I gazed at his temple and did not know what to feel.

On the third day I paid attention to the triumph itself for it celebrated the defeat of Egypt. Carts trundled past, laden with exotic furniture, and gold, all displayed to display the alien nature of the country. There was a huge picture depicting a typical Nile scene, with strange birds and the inevitable

251

hippopotamus in the middle. At one point a tall square pointed pillar came past on three carts - an obelisk, all corners and spike, so unlike out own soft rounded columns, I thought sardonically. The highlight, just before Caesar Octavianus in his chariot, was a scene set on a long, wheeled stage. Two children sat at the front with their attendants, looking so small and terrified that the crowd stopped cheering and whispered as they came past. Behind them was a huge and beautiful couch, furnished with red cushions, every edge decked out with a gold fringe. On this couch was a life-size image of Cleopatra reclining as though she were about to start her dinner. Here there was no simple dress and hairstyle, no, this image was of the Queen of Egypt, Goddess on earth to her people, the woman who once had been the Friend and Ally of the Roman People. She had sat in practically this seat I now sat in. The statue wore the black wig with a gold headdress that framed the face, and a white sheath dress. Gold bracelets, a gold collar and long earrings decorated the Queen's image, and the odd vibrant make-up on the wooden face emphasised only that this was a statue, and a crude one at that.

"She doesn't look like a real person at all," murmured a woman near us.

"She is a legend now," said my mother. "And to some a goddess. What that stupid young man is parading is a piece of wood."

People around us clearly heard her, because there was that sudden hush as everybody stopped talking and strained their ears in the hope she would say more. I had long ago stopped trying to make her discreet when it came to voicing her opinion of those who ruled us, but I wished she would give in and just call "that young man" by the name he demanded - Caesar. She said it confused her, but apart from the fact that my mother was never confused, nobody ever mistook the great-nephew of Julius Caesar for the man - god - himself.

"What will happen to the children?" I wondered aloud, knowing as we all did that Cleopatra's children by Marcus Antonius would always be a threat. The child Caesarion, borne to Julius Caesar all those years ago, was dead. My half-brother the little boy I had never met, was dead at barely seventeen years old. The story went that our troops caught up with him and his tutor as they were trying to escape to safety after his mother killed herself. I hoped the soldiers were swift and did not torment him.

"They are not as much a threat as Caesarion was," said my mother in her decided voice. "They may be allowed to live. Besides, they live with his sister" – "Caesarion's sister?" I asked bewildered, but she carried on, ignoring my stupidity - "and reports are that she is fond of them. He won't kill them if she pleads for them."

"Could you at least name him in contexts where not naming him causes confusion?" I asked, and behind us someone sniggered, then hurriedly coughed.

My mother did not answer of course, but she gazed after the procession as Cleopatra's image rolled on through a silent Forum. Nobody shouted insults at the sobbing children or the wooden Queen.

All this took place in the middle of August, so we sweltered, though young Caesar thoughtfully decked the Forum with awnings and slaves sprinkled us with water at intervals. Cleopatra's memorial marked the end of the triumphal processions, and as we slowly took the ramp behind the temple back up to the Palatine, my mother said, "I am going to Antium tomorrow, Tertulla."

I felt relief, but thought I had better check.

"Are you sure you want to miss tomorrow? The dedication of the Temple of the God Julius? We are invited."

"I am sure," said my mother.

"I will go with you," I said.

"Do you believe your father is a god, Tertulla?" Sulpicia's question was so softly spoken, I could have imagined it. She was echoing my own heart.

"Men are not gods," I said. "After they die, though, they cease to be men. Maybe someone like Julius Caesar has that inside him which lives on and - that part of him is divine. Yes, it must be that."

"I walk past his temple almost every day," said Sulpicia. "Every time I come to visit you here."

"I have been inside and left an offering to him," I said. "I didn't know what I was asking him though."

"To be your father," said Sulpicia.

I shook my head.

"The man was my father, not the god."

Sulpicia looked thoughtful but when she spoke it was not of Caesar.

"The statue in the Temple of Venus, Tertulla, the one that is supposed to be of Isis - it is Cleopatra really, isn't it?"

"To her people, she was Isis," I said. "I don't think the sculptor was aware of how the Romans would see it."

"Not many of us are willing to credit Cleopatra with divine essence," said Sulpicia drily. "The establishment would not be pleased with that. But it is so ironic. Julius Caesar puts a statue of Cleopatra in his temple to the goddess of love - and his heir defeats Cleopatra and drives her to suicide."

"Augustus destroyed what he was unable to understand. And he certainly had no respect for his so-called father," I said, knowing that she would not be easy with such blasphemy.

"And now Augustus himself is a god," she said clearly and carefully.

"Death turns everybody into a god," I said, and she half gasped and half laughed, covering her mouth and automatically looking round my empty Painted Garden, checking for spies amid the painted flowers and fruit.

Chapter 30

My mother fell ill during the year that young Caesar took the name and persona Augustus - and that was a truly astounding transformation. My mother always maintained that names were important, and this proved her right, as the man who was born Octavius and fought under the name of Caesar, finally settled into middle age as Augustus - the Revered One. But I must finish my story. Augustus will find plenty of willing biographers to concoct his.

At the start of that year, there was a period of about three weeks when my mother could not leave her bed, finding it difficult to breathe. There was a gentle spring and she recovered well, regaining all her usual strength by the summer. When autumn brought the usual round of disease however, she weakened and soon we knew that this would be the end. Every day I visited, and we sat and talked about everything except that one subject, Caesar. I still could not ask her directly. After each visit, I would walk back to my house - the one Augustus had so graciously allowed me to keep - and sit looking at the wall-paintings in my study, naming all my birds, imagining the smell of the green leaves and grass. And wondering if I could ever ask her.

On the day I decided, I did not know that I would ask that question until I walked into her room and saw her lying asleep on her bed. Her face was relaxed, and I remembered her beauty which had so fascinated me as a child. Her maid was there, and I waved the woman away, whispering that I would call for her if needed. And I took her place on the stool next to the bed and very gently held my mother's hand, so soft, even with the wrinkles and age spots. I resisted stroking it, thinking of what I would say if she woke up to find me doing something so strange. I did not think that approaching death would soften my mother. And as I thought that her eyes opened and she said, "Tertulla." I asked her. I made it as casual as I could.

"I have always wondered - was Caesar my father?"

255

There was a pause then she smiled and said, "Hello Tertulla. What time is it?"

For a moment, I thought I must have imagined myself speaking the question aloud - then I just waited. I could not say anything more.

"Caesar," she said. "He gave me that pearl. I have left it to you in my will. Nothing else. You don't need anything else."

And she shut her eyes again. For one terrible moment I thought she had died but then heard the whisper of her breath. Gently, I squeezed her hand, willing her open her eyes again but she just said, "I'm tired. Fetch Aretus for me."

And I walked home thinking about the pearl which I would never own because she had thrown it into Caesar's funeral pyre more than seventeen years previously - hadn't she?

She died during that night. A messenger found me at breakfast the next morning and broke the unsurprising news. When I arrived at her house, she was already washed and laid out in the atrium and looked so beautiful. Junia stood by her and came over to me to hold me as we both cried. When we broke apart, Junia said, "I've sent a messenger to Nilla," and stepped back to give me a moment on my own. I pretended to brush a stray hair from her cool forehead and stood there with the tears slowly falling down my face, until the steward Aretus came up to me and led me into a corner of the atrium, where he had set out a chair and table with some wine. He made me sip a cup of sweet, spiced wine, warm and soothing.

Aretus had already put on an old grey tunic in respect of his mourning and he too looked old and grey. He was, I thought, not much younger than my mother. He made sure that I had drunk some wine before he continued with what he had to tell me.

"The lady Servilia has left all her affairs in perfect order as you might have guessed," he said. "If you would come to her room, there is a message for you."

We left Junia standing over my mother, and Aretus let me into my mother's room, and the familiarity of the sights and smells almost overpowered me. It wasn't only that I thought that a faint scent of my mother's perfume hung in the air. What completely took me by surprise was the strangeness of the room. There were the familiar objects, desk, couch, the painted trees, and I could still smell ink, papyrus, and wood, but my mother was gone and so everything was now different. As I stood and tried to make sense of this, the room itself decided to help me, and it gathered together everything that I could still remember about her, until I could see her, sitting on her chair at the desk. Ghosts of all the people of my family seemed to gather in the air, and there I saw three little girls lined up in height order, myself at the far end, while my mother bent over a scroll on her desk. Brutus lounged on the couch, and in the corner stood the ghost of my father and as I caught sight of him, he smiled and whispered, "Tertulla". All of this took no more than a few moments but for those few moments I felt crushed by my memories - and then Aretus was standing next to the desk holding out a small scroll, and a cotton bag, tied with a thread of green silk. As I moved over, I saw that the desk was filled with neat piles of scrolls and wax tablets. No doubt my mother had ordered that her will and funeral arrangements, her last wishes and messages should be ready to be distributed when she had died.

I took the scroll but could not read it then and there, so tucked it into the folds of my shawl and thanked Aretus. We went back into the atrium where I clipped a little lock of my hair and laid it in the bowl at my mother's feet. Junia still stood there, lost in her own thoughts, and I did not say goodbye.

I walked back to my own house in a daze, unsure as to how life went on in Rome without Servilia. All around me were preparations for the Saturnalia festival in the midst of Augustus's brand-new rebuilt Rome, a Rome whose warm and crumbling brick was being closed off by sheets of marble. There were plans afoot for new temples, a library, and festivals, games, theatrical performances. At home and abroad, Rome was at peace. I had never known a time when Rome was at peace. And yet I found this new regime hard to accept. To go on living through it without my mother's presence - impossible! How could she be alive no longer, when the little grey shadow that was me still breathed? When I got home, I went straight to my Painted Garden where there were no ghosts, not even of Cassius, just a pair of painted finches forever singing to me. I sat at my desk and took out the scroll.

My dear Tertulla,

I know that for most of your life you have wondered about my love for Caesar and whether you are the product of that love.

I do not know why you want Caesar to be your father, but the present I have left you will tell you all you need to know. I will not discuss why I began an affair with him when Decimus Junius Silanus was such a good man, and a loving husband to me. I have been married twice and while I have never understood why one marriage works and another doesn't, my marriage to your father worked. He never regretted not having a son. He loved your brother, he loved me, and he loved his three little girls. Please, Tertulla, believe this. You were loved by your him, and by me. I know that I do not show love easily, I never have, it is not my way.

I hope that you are content to be who you are - the third daughter of a distinguished family. My daughter, beautiful, intelligent and much loved.

Written on the ides of October in the year in which Gaius Julius Caesar Octavianus took the name Augustus.

This day had proved too much for me, and I bowed my head over my desk and wept. And the little bag? I knew before I opened it, for the hard, round shape that I prised from a nest of wool was, of course, Caesar's pearl.

As you will have realised, my relationship with my mother improved a great deal from my marriage to her death. The grown-up me realised a lot more about her and her character, and I appreciated her strength as I had not when I was a child. In particular, she helped me through those years of Philippi as we went through a similar loss and a similar grief. Brutus was the child into which she poured her ambition and brilliance, and poor Brutus let her down so terribly by being philosophical. Similarly, Cassius gave me so much to look forward to and then let me down.

Now, I completely understand my mother's words. And the pearl. This is what I think: my mother did not want me to long for the unattainable. She was telling me that my dream was to be put away. Silanus was the man who loved me as a daughter, and being Caesar's child could not be acknowledged, it could not be useful. Caesar had indeed been my father, but what good had that been to me? Cleopatra claimed the same for her son and look what happened to him. A dream would have to do for me.

This is what it is to be the third daughter, to never quite be enough. This is the secret that I have never told anyone.

Epilogue – 22CE

Junia Tertia lies in the atrium of her house on the Palatine Hill in Rome. She is dead.

The people crowding the room can hardly believe it, for here lies a woman who is the stuff of history. She is rumoured to be the daughter of Julius Caesar himself. She has lived through Caesar's wars, the fight against Caesar's killers and the struggle to power of Caesar's heir. She has outlived every member of her generation and has been a widow since before the birth of the current emperor. None of the people gazing at her can remember a time when she was not there. Nobody is as old as Junia Tertia.

"She says she was born before her father became consul…"

"- well, that was the year of the Battle of Pistoria, which was the year after the Emperor Augustus was born…."

"And Augustus has been dead for eight years."

"So, she is - was - at least eighty-five, maybe ninety…."

The whispers run around the atrium as they stand before the couch that is raised up on a couple of tables, the whole draped in lengths of white woollen cloth. Junia Tertia herself is robed in her finest with bracelets, necklace and earrings clearly visible. There is a garland around her hair - still her own hair, they whisper - and more garlands are pinned all around the couch. Little lamps burn at each corner, and the room smells hot, damp, and flowery.

"She could be over ninety," they say and each Roman leaves a carefully trimmed wisp of hair in honour of the spirit of Junia Tertia.

A quotation from the historian Tacitus:

"In the sixty-fourth year after Philippi died Junia, niece of Cato, wife of Cassius, sister of Brutus. Her will was the subject of popular gossip because although she was rich and made bequests to many, she left nothing to the Emperor. He graciously made no matter of this and allowed all the usual rites to be held, along with a speech from the Speakers' Platform. The funeral images of twenty illustrious families were in the processions, and Brutus and Cassius, because their images were not present, outshone them."

Author's Note

Many of the people in this novel "really" existed, and the sources have supplied a lot of the material.

Cicero's letters are a mine of fascinating insights, and when he writes to Atticus, his closest friend, he is delightfully open about the people he encounters. It is in Cicero that I found the reference to Junia Tertia's miscarriage in May 44.

When I needed some good gossipy information about Julius Caesar and Augustus, I went with Suetonius, the biographer writing under Hadrian, who tells us that Servilia was Caesar's favourite mistress.

If you are looking for a modern description of the downfall of the Roman Republic, you can do no better than Rubicon, by Tom Holland.

Susan Treggiari's Servilia and her family is a scholarly and readable account of a Roman noblewoman's life, which I found invaluable, as is her work on the lives of Cicero's womenfolk, Terentia, Tullia and Publilia.

I am very happy to talk about the last years of the Roman Republic, and can be contacted through my website https://fionaforsythauthor.co.uk ,Twitter (@for_fi) or Instagram (www.instagram.com/fionaforsythauthor)

Printed in Great Britain
by Amazon